PENGUI

The Great Wall of China
and Other Short Works

Franz Kafka was born of Jewish parents in Prague in 1883. The family spoke both Czech and German; Franz was sent to German-language schools and to the German University, from which he received his doctorate in law in 1906. He then worked for most of his life as a respected official of a state insurance company (first under the Austro-Hungarian Empire, then under the new Republic of Czechoslovakia). Literature, of which he said that he 'consisted', had to be pursued on the side. His emotional life was dominated by his relationships with his father, a man of overbearing character, and with a series of women: Felice Bauer from Berlin, to whom he was twice engaged; his Czech translator, Milena Jesenská-Pollak, to whom he became attached in 1920; and Dora Diamant, a young Jewish woman from Poland in whom he found a devoted companion during the last year of his life. Meanwhile, his writing had taken a new turn in 1917 with the outbreak of the tubercular illness from which he was to die in 1924. Only a small number of Kafka's stories were published during his lifetime, and these are published in Penguin as *Metamorphosis and Other Stories*. He asked his friend, Max Brod, to see that all the writings he left should be destroyed. Brod felt unable to comply and undertook their publication instead, beginning with the three unfinished novels, *The Trial* (1925), *The Castle* (1926) and *Amerika* (1927). Other shorter works appeared posthumously in a more sporadic fashion, and a representative selection of them is collected in this volume.

Malcolm Pasley was born in 1926 and was educated at Sherborne School and Trinity College, Oxford. He is an Emeritus Fellow of Magdalen College, Oxford, a Fellow of the British Academy and a member of the German Academy for Language and Literature. As one of the editors of the Critical Kafka Edition, he was responsible for *The Castle* (1982), *The Trial* (1990) and *Posthumous Writings and Fragments: Volume I* (1993). His recent publications on Kafka include a collection of essays, *'The script is unalterable ...'* (1995).

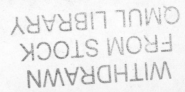

PENGUIN BOOKS

The Great Wall of China
and Other Short Works

Franz Kafka was born of Jewish parents in Prague in 1883. The family spoke both Czech and German; Franz was sent to German-language schools and to the German University, from which he received his doctorate in law in 1906. He then worked for most of his life as a respected official of a state insurance company (first under the Austro-Hungarian Empire, then under the new Republic of Czechoslovakia). Literature, of which he said that he 'consisted', had to be pursued on the side. His emotional life was dominated by his relationships with his father, a man of overbearing character, and with a series of women: Felice Bauer from Berlin, to whom he was twice engaged; his Czech translator, Milena Jesenská-Pollak, to whom he became attached in 1920 and Dora Diamant, a young Jewish woman from Poland in whom he found a devoted companion during the last year of his life. Meanwhile, his writing had taken a new turn in 1912 with the outbreak of the tubercular illness from which he was to die in 1924. Only a small number of Kafka's stories were published during his lifetime, and these are published in Penguin as Metamorphosis and Other Stories. He asked his friend, Max Brod, to see that all the writings he left should be destroyed. Brod felt unable to comply and undertook their publication instead, beginning with the three unfinished novels, The Trial (1925), The Castle (1926) and America (1927). Other shorter works appeared posthumously, in a more sporadic fashion, and a representative selection of them is collected in this volume.

Malcolm Pasley was born in 1926 and was educated at Sherborne School and Trinity College, Oxford. He is an Emeritus Fellow of Magdalen College, Oxford, a Fellow of the British Academy and a member of the German Academy for Language and Literature. As one of the editors of the Critical Kafka Edition, he was responsible for The Castle (1982), The Trial (1990) and Posthumous Writings and Fragments, Volume I (1992). His recent publications on Kafka include a collection of essays, The Writer in ... (1995).

FRANZ KAFKA

THE GREAT WALL
OF CHINA

AND OTHER SHORT WORKS

**TRANSLATED FROM THE GERMAN
AND EDITED BY
MALCOLM PASLEY**

PENGUIN BOOKS

PENGUIN BOOKS

Published by the Penguin Group
Penguin Books Ltd, 80 Strand, London WC2R 0RL, England
Penguin Putnam Inc., 375 Hudson Street, New York, New York 10014, USA
Penguin Books Australia Ltd, 250 Camberwell Road, Camberwell, Victoria 3124, Australia
Penguin Books Canada Ltd, 10 Alcorn Avenue, Toronto, Ontario, Canada M4V 3B2
Penguin Books India (P) Ltd, 11 Community Centre, Panchsheel Park, New Delhi – 110 017, India
Penguin Books (NZ) Ltd, Cnr Rosedale and Airborne Roads, Albany, Auckland, New Zealand
Penguin Books (South Africa) (Pty) Ltd, 24 Sturdee Avenue, Rosebank 2196, South Africa

Penguin Books Ltd, Registered Offices: 80 Strand, London WC2R 0RL, England

www.penguin.com

This translation first published under the title
Shorter Works, Volume 1, by Martin Secker & Warburg 1973

Published in Penguin Books 1991
Reprinted in Penguin Classics 2002

10

Translation copyright © Malcolm Pasley, 1973
All rights reserved

Filmset in Lasercomp Ehrhardt

Printed in England by Clays Ltd, St Ives plc

ISBN-13: 978–0–141–18646–7

www.greenpenguin.co.uk

CONTENTS

EDITOR'S PREFACE

THE present volume contains the major short works left by Kafka, and it presents them for the first time in the order of their composition. The sequence and dating of the works is particularly important, because of the very close links between his life and his writing. So it may be useful to mention here some of the relevant biographical facts, although of course these cannot by themselves supply an interpretation of the stories. Kafka's work is full of autobiographical material, but equally it is more than just a kind of veiled autobiography. He did indeed say that some of his pieces were 'really no more than jottings or doodlings of an entirely private nature', but his chief aim in turning his life into literature was to go beyond the merely personal, to bring out the fundamental – mythical – patterns of human existence, and so to 'raise the world into the pure, the true, the immutable' (diary of 25 September 1917).

Franz Kafka was born in 1883 of Bohemian-Jewish parents, and spent most of his life in Prague, that city of mixed tongues and national conflict, dominated by a magnificent castle that no longer contained a king. His experience of Prague always enters into the depiction of cities in his works, whether it is the accursed city of Babylon – to which he lends the Prague coat of arms with its clenched fist ('The City Coat of Arms') – or the Imperial City of Peking ('The Great Wall of China'). In Prague he was well acquainted with the business world – his father ran a wholesale firm dealing in fashion accessories in the Old Town Square – and with the administrative and legal world also: after studying law at the Charles University he served from 1908 to 1922 in the 'Workers' Accident Insurance Office for the Kingdom of Bohemia', as a conscientious and respected official of what he privately called 'a dark nest of

bureaucrats'. The operations of commerce, law, and public administration find their way into many of his stories, either as real background ('My Neighbour', 'The Married Couple') or as a kind of
metaphorical framework ('The Refusal', 'The Problem of Our Laws',
'Advocates'), and the semi-ironical use of legal and official jargon
becomes an integral part of his literary style. Most important of all,
Prague was the city where Western European Jewish intellectuals,
like Kafka and almost all his friends, had become most painfully
aware of their own rootlessness. Largely emancipated from the faith
of their fathers, they were for the most part incompletely and unhap-
pily assimilated to the German culture which held sway over a Slav
population. In these circumstances many of them, such as Kafka's
friend and literary champion Max Brod, become ardent Zionists.
The idea of a return home to Palestine came to attract Kafka as well
in his later years, but this solution always seemed to him rather too
particular, and in any case a little too good to be true, like a fairy
tale. He first became really aware of his own Jewishness when he got
to know a group of Yiddish actors from Poland who were visiting
Prague in 1911 (this decisive experience is echoed in the episode of
the seven 'dog musicians' in 'Investigations of a Dog', which of all the
stories in this volume comes closest to autobiography); he became
conscious of the mysterious power that still seemed to reside in the
genuine Jewish communities of Eastern Europe. It appears from his
diaries and letters that he found relatively primitive and superstitious
communities at once sympathetic, comic, and strangely awe-
inspiring, as if for all their limitations they were in possession of a
secret from which he was excluded; this applied also to the village
communities of the Czech provinces, whose contrast to the intellectual Babel of Prague struck him so forcibly on his journeys
from the city (cf. 'The Village Schoolmaster').

Kafka's father, Hermann, was a powerful and self-assertive man
who filled him with a strong sense of inadequacy and guilt. Franz
felt that marriage and family life had been somehow annexed by his
father, and that he could not compete in this sphere. Thus he
remained a bachelor, and this was one of the ways in which he knew
the deep sense of isolation and estrangement to which his early
works testify ('Blumfeld, an Elderly Bachelor'). The guilt-feelings

associated with his failure to marry reached their peak in 1914, at the time of his first and more short-lived engagement to Felice Bauer, a thoroughly sensible middle-class girl from Berlin whose very self-possession attracted him: this was the period of *The Trial* and 'In the Penal Colony'. More obviously than in the present volume, Kafka's unhappy relationship with his father is reflected in earlier stories such as 'The Judgement' and 'The Transformation', which belong – like 'In the Penal Colony' – to that small corpus of work which he regarded as successful and published in his own lifetime. By the end of 1916, when he took a little house of his own – almost a monastic cell – in the Alchimistengasse on the slopes of the castle hill, he had succeeded in putting these oppressive private difficulties to some extent in perspective, and had begun to acquire a certain precarious confidence in his lonely mission as a writer. He regarded this mission, however uncertain it still remained, increasingly in spiritual and indeed in religious terms (cf. 'The Collected Aphorisms'). The outbreak of his turberculosis in 1917 allowed him to concentrate on his meditations and his writing more fully; it actually afforded him a welcome release from the long and painful relationship with Felice, and he was also granted generous periods of sick-leave by his insurance office until he was finally pensioned off five years later.

It may seem strange to suggest that Kafka achieved even a precarious confidence in his mission as a writer, in view of the post-1916 stories in this volume which dwell so much on ludicrous inadequacy and seemingly inevitable failure. But this is just where the documents of his life allow us to recognize that his fatally incompetent heroes are not so much self-portraits as self-caricatures. In 'The Bridge', for example, the man who fails so abjectly in his attempt to perform a bridging function is not quite identical with his author, who found at least sufficient confidence to assert in his diary: 'I am an end or a beginning'. Equally in 'The Hunter Gracchus': while Kafka had several times arrived – like Gracchus – at Riva on Lake Garda, feeling like a visitor from another planet on his rare foreign holidays from Prague, he nevertheless viewed his own real case somewhat less despondently, declaring in his diary that a man who is 'dead in his own lifetime' may in fact 'see more than others' and be 'the real survivor'.

Despite the fact that during the very productive year of 1917 he withdrew so deeply into himself and his writing, the tension between isolation and human contact soon reasserted itself. In 1919 he met the lively Julie Wohryzek, who came from a Jewish family of humble circumstances, and again tried to persuade himself into marriage. And in 1920 his attachment to Milena Jesenská, the translator of some of his stories into Czech, threw him back once more into the turmoil of combined longing and anxiety (see the *Letters to Milena*). There then followed, at the end of 1920, a spell of intense literary activity: in the short pieces and sketches of this time many of the themes of *The Castle* are announced ('The Refusal', The Problem of Our Laws', 'The Conscription of Troops').

Most of 1921 was spent in a sanatorium at Matliary in the High Tatra mountains of Slovakia. The evidence suggests that these were relatively happy months, comparable to those spent in the Bohemian village of Zürau from September 1917 to June 1918, after the first appearance of his illness. He was free from Prague and from any intensely emotional relationships; the friendships he formed were easier, calmer; he enjoyed the company of young people, such as the medical student Robert Klopstock, whose vitality and idealism fascinated him and who in turn looked to him for his infinitely scrupulous guidance. In these circumstances he rediscovered – too late – his own will to live (cf. the episode in 'Investigations of a Dog', in which the dog who denies himself nourishment so as to 'pass over into the truth, out of this world of falsehood' is reclaimed to life by the youthful vigour of the hunting-hound).

Nineteen twenty-two was the year of his most ambitious and all-embracing work, *The Castle*; such is the coherence and self-consistency of his imaginative world that almost all the works in this volume bear some relation to it. In 1923, while visiting a holiday camp for refugee Jewish children on the Baltic coast, he met Dora Diamant, the young girl who cared for him with such devotion during the final months of his life. It was in their little flat in Berlin that Kafka wrote 'The Burrow', fully aware of the nearness of that last enemy whose approach could be heard threateningly in the passages of his throat and lungs. His advanced tubercular condition worsened, and he died in June 1924 in a sanatorium near Vienna.

*

Since the works that Kafka left, as opposed to the small number that he saw fit to publish, have yet to appear in a sound text in the original German, this edition has been prepared directly from the author's manuscripts. These English translations therefore represent, for the first time, the authentic text of the works concerned, however surprising this may seem more than fifty years after Kafka's death.

The result differs, often quite markedly, from what has been presented before. It now emerges, for instance, that 'The Hunter Gracchus' consists of four separate attempts on Kafka's part to treat this suggestive myth of total estrangement. In the case of the aphoristic diary entries known as 'He', considerable changes were required to restore the original order and content. Restoration on a smaller scale was necessary for some of the very short pieces of a parable or fable type, so characteristic of the post-1916 work: thus for example 'The Departure' and 'A Crossbreed' now appear in an extended and a truncated form respectively.

One of the most disturbing features of the existing published texts is that they contain a good deal that was plainly deleted in the manuscript, and which it is therefore quite wrong to present as Kafka's work (except as variants within the framework of the text-critical edition which is still in progress). All such deleted material is omitted here, save for one short passage in 'The Great Wall of China' (which is printed in brackets and referred to in the notes below). The more extensive of the deleted passages now omitted are also indicated in the notes. Here again the accepted picture is often considerably altered: for instance, a lengthy scene which has previously appeared as part of 'The Warden of the Tomb' was clearly rejected by the author.

It is of course true that Kafka was not satisfied with any of the work he left – this applies equally to the three unfinished novels *America*, *The Trial* and *The Castle* – and that in an access of self-condemnation he even gave instructions for it all to be destroyed (Max Brod gives his reasons for disobeying these instructions in his postscript to *The Trial*). But Kafka's very perfectionism in literary matters is an added reason for treating his posthumous work, now that it has become public, with respect; as least we ought to pay it the normal respect of distinguishing between what he deleted in his manuscript and what he allowed to stand, even if the result may sometimes appear less coherent and less well-rounded than before.

The published German texts – on which of course all previous translations have been based – contain furthermore frequent errors of detail. One example will suffice. The published text of 'An Everyday Occurrence', which is a very short piece, omits thirteen words from the MS and shows fifteen faulty readings in addition. One of these misreadings – *'Verwirrung'* ('confusion') for *'Heroismus'* ('heroism') in the opening sentence – has even provided the piece with an erroneous title. The effect of such errors is cumulative, and it therefore seemed advisable in most cases to re-translate from the manuscript, rather than to amend the existing renderings – based unwittingly on an unsound text – by Willa and Edwin Muir, Tania and James Stern, and Ernst Kaiser and Eithne Wilkins. It has proved possible to follow them in some cases, however, where only minor amendments were needed; the details are given in the notes. Needless to say these earlier translations have been carefully consulted throughout, and grateful use has been made of them even where they have not been adhered to exactly. What has been done by these translators, and in particular by the Muirs, to make Kafka's work available to the English-speaking world is well-known, but it would be an act of false piety to accord greater respect to their rendering than to the original.

Something should be said finally about the contents of this volume, described above as containing 'the major short works left by Kafka'. When Max Brod set about publishing Kafka's literary remains, he began in the twenties with the three novels. He then singled out from the great mass of material those shorter works that seemed to him either formally complete or else sufficiently coherent and substantial to stand on their own as independent pieces. The result of this was the volume *Beim Bau der chinesischen Mauer* (1931), which was translated by the Muirs and published by Martin Secker as *The Great Wall of China* (1933). This was expanded in 1936, under the new title *Beschreibung eines Kampfes*, and again in 1946: it is on this latter selection, which appeared in English as *Description of a Struggle and The Great Wall of China* (Secker & Warburg, 1960), that the present one is based.

The title story, 'Description of a Struggle', a very early work of Kafka's (it has much in common with the little opening labyrinth described in 'The Burrow'), is not included here. It exists in two separate manuscript versions, which Max Brod conflated in an attempt to produce a coherent and readable text. It would run contrary to the principles of this edition to reprint the English rendering of Brod's conflation; on the other hand, the only satisfactory alternative would have been to offer translations of both versions, and this would have meant giving excessive prominence to what is undeniably an immature work. 'The Bucket Rider' is also excluded, since it is now known to have appeared during Kafka's lifetime, and so it belongs henceforth among the published works. Against this, certain posthumous pieces have been added which are clearly capable of standing on their own, and which Brod himself presented elsewhere as independent works: 'The Proclamation', 'New Lamps', 'The Collected Aphorisms', 'An Everyday Occurrence', 'The Truth about Sancho Panza', 'The Silence of the Sirens', and 'Prometheus'.

The principles governing Brod's original selection of the shorter posthumous works were not entirely clear or consistent, but the basic decisions he took in 1931 have now become so well established that it seems right to adhere to them. At the same time it is worth remembering that there are some pieces, published either in *The Diaries* or in the collection *Wedding Preparations in the Country and Other Posthumous Prose Writings* (Secker & Warburg, 1954), which may have no less claim to be considered among the 'major short works' left by Kafka at his death.

Essentially, therefore, this volume is traditional in its list of contents; but within these traditional limits it can claim a quite new fidelity to the author's text.

Oxford   MALCOLM PASLEY
May 1991

NOTES

The Village Schoolmaster (December 1914). This story has previously been published as 'The Giant Mole'. Kafka always referred to it as *'Dorfschullehrer'* ('Village Schoolmaster').

p. 13: After '... about something quite different' a passage of twenty-five lines, deleted in the MS, has been omitted.

Blumfeld, an Elderly Bachelor (probably February 1915). No author's title. This translation, with very minor amendments, is that of Tania and James Stern.

p. 19: After '... his French magazine' a passage of thirty lines, deleted in the MS, has been omitted.

The Warden of the Tomb (December 1916). No author's title. There is a fair copy of this work, in the author's typescript, as far as p. 42 'on the other hand he is the only one ...' This typescript shows little change from the MS version, on which our text has to be based from that point. After the stage direction on p. 44 'Goes to the window, looks out', there follows a long deleted scene which is now omitted. It was replaced by the concluding passage translated here. Apart from this final section the translation, with minor amendments, is that of Willa and Edwin Muir.

The Bridge (December 1916). No author's title.

The Hunter Gracchus. No author's title. This story exists in four separate fragmentary versions. The first two were written in December 1916. Although conflated in previous editions they are textually distinct: the first consists of narrative and dialogue, the second takes the form of a written account by Gracchus. The third fragment was written in the author's diary of 6 April 1917, and is reproduced here for the sake of completeness. The fourth fragment, the conversation between Gracchus and the visitor to his boat, was written at about the same time.

p. 48: *Riva.* A town on the shores of Lake Garda, often visited by Kafka.

The Proclamation (December 1916). No author's title.

The Great Wall of China (Early 1917). Author's title: '*Beim Bau der chinesischen Mauer*'.

p. 66: 'The emperor, so it is told . . .': the remainder of this paragraph was published by the author, with minor alterations, as '*Eine kaiserliche Botschaft*' ('A Message from the Emperor').

p. 68: After '. . . lord of the village' a passage of twenty-eight lines, deleted in the MS, has been omitted.

p. 69: 'among our people . . .': at this point in the MS there follow some deleted attempts to find a transition to the next section beginning 'Such was the world . . .' One of them runs as follows: 'The above indications may perhaps suffice for it to be understood what the decision to build the wall signified in a world of this kind.'

p. 70: The final passage, printed in brackets, is deleted in the MS; it is reproduced here, exceptionally, to show how this last completed part of the story was linked to the earlier parts in the author's mind.

The Knock at the Manor Gate (early 1917). No author's title.

My Neighbour (April 1917). No author's title.

A Crossbreed (April 1917). Author's title. Several passages previously included in this story were deleted in the MS and are omitted here.

New Lamps (August/September 1917). No author's title.

The Collected Aphorisms (October 1917 to February 1918). No author's title. Previously published under the title 'Reflections on Sin, Suffering, Hope, and the True Way'. Late in 1920 Kafka copied out these aphorisms on separate numbered sheets; he then made a further fair copy, in typescript, on which this text is based. It seems likely that he considered publication.

An Everyday Occurrence (October 1917). No author's title. The previous titles ('A Common Confusion', 'An Everyday Confusion') rest on a faulty reading of the manuscript.

The Truth about Sancho Panza (October 1917). No author's title.

The Silence of the Sirens (October 1917). No author's title.

Prometheus (January 1918). No author's title. The translation is based on that of Willa and Edwin Muir.

He: Aphorisms from the 1920 Diary, untitled. These aphoristic notes were entered in Kafka's diary between 6 January and 29 February 1920. All the sheets on which they were written, except the first, were then torn from the book – presumably when he sent his diaries to Milena Jesenská. The whole sequence is restored here for the first time.

p. 107: *a picture*. Probably 'Boulter's Lock, Sunday Afternoon', oil painting by Edward John Gregory (as reproduced in *The Studio*, 15 November 1909).
p. 109: *the Laurenziberg*. A hill on the outskirts of Prague.
p. 110: *Casinelli's*. A Prague bookshop.

The City Coat of Arms
Poseidon
Fellowship
At Night
The Refusal
The Problem of Our Laws

The Conscription of Troops
The Test
The Vulture
The Helmsman
The Top
A Little Fable
Homecoming

All the above stories were written in late 1920. Only 'The Problem of Our Laws' is an original title ('*Zur Frage der Gesetze*'). The translations of 'Poseidon', 'Fellowship', 'The Refusal', 'The Test', 'The Vulture', 'The Helmsman', and 'The Top' are by Tania and James Stern, slightly amended where necessary.

The Departure (early 1922). No author's title.

Advocates (early 1922). No author's title. The translation is based on that of Tania and James Stern.

Investigations of a Dog (autumn 1922). No author's title.

p. 154: After '. . . that I truly expect no longer' a passage of twenty-five lines, deleted in the MS, is omitted.

The Married Couple (late 1922). Author's title: '*Das Ehepaar*'. This story exists in two MS versions. The later one, which is followed here, is a very careful fair copy and suggests that Kafka considered publication.

A Comment (December 1922). Previously published as 'Give it up!' The present title is the author's ('*Ein Kommentar*').

On Parables (probably 1922 or 1923). No author's title.

The Burrow (winter 1923–4). No author's title. In the case of this story a revised German text has already been published (*Der Heizer, In der Strafkolonie, Der Bau*, Cambridge University Press, 1966).

THE GREAT WALL OF CHINA AND OTHER WORKS

THE VILLAGE SCHOOLMASTER

THOSE, and I am one of them, who find even a little ordinary-sized mole disgusting, would probably have died of disgust if they had seen the giant mole that was observed a few years ago, not far from a small village which gained a certain passing notoriety on that account. Today, of course, that village has long since sunk back into obscurity, and thus merely shares the ingloriousness of the whole incident, which has remained wholly unexplained and which indeed no one has taken much trouble to explain; and so, as the result of an incomprehensible apathy in those very circles which should have concerned themselves with it, and which do in fact concern them- selves energetically with far more trifling matters, the affair has been forgotten without ever having been closely examined. This can cer- tainly not be excused by the fact that the village lies a long way off from the railway; many people came great distances out of curiosity, even from abroad; it was only those who should have shown some- thing more than curiosity that failed to come. In fact, if it had not been for a few quite simple people, people whose ordinary daily work hardly permits them a moment's peaceful relaxation, if these people had not selflessly taken the matter up, the rumour of this particular phenomenon would probably never have spread beyond the immediate locality. It must be admitted that even rumour, which is after all usually impossible to restrain, was in this case positively sluggish; unless it had been literally pushed it would never have spread. But that was certainly no reason for refusing to take an interest in the matter; on the contrary, here was another phenomenon which ought to have been investigated.

Instead of that the writing-up of the case was left exclusively to the old schoolmaster, and he, though an excellent man in his own profession, was equipped neither by his abilities nor his training to produce a thorough and generally serviceable description, let alone an explanation. His little treatise was printed, and had a good sale among the visitors to the village in those days; it even received some measure of recognition, but the teacher was wise enough to realize that these fragmentary efforts of his, in which no one supported him, were basically worthless. The fact that he continued with them none the less, and made this question, which by its very nature became more hopeless from year to year, into his life's work, proves on the one hand the extremely powerful effect that the appearance of the mole was capable of producing, and on the other how much tenacity and firmness of conviction may be found in an old and obscure village schoolmaster. But that he suffered deeply from the cool attitude of the recognized authorities is proved by a small supplement with which he followed his treatise up; though that was not until some years later, in other words at a time when there was hardly anyone left who could remember what it was all about. In this supplement he complains – and his argument carries conviction by its honesty if not by its skill – of the lack of understanding he had met with among people where it was least to be expected. Of such people he remarks appositely: 'It is not I, it is they who talk like old village schoolmasters.' And among other things he quotes the pronouncement of a scholar whom he had gone to see expressly about his affair. The name of this scholar is not mentioned, but from a number of attendant circumstances it is possible to deduce who it was. It was only after great difficulty that the teacher even succeeded in gaining access to this authority, despite the fact that he had announced his visit weeks in advance, and then he at once perceived from the manner of his reception that the scholar was in the grip of an immovable prejudice in respect of his affair. The absence of mind with which he listened to the long account that the teacher gave him, on the basis of his monograph, can be gauged from the comment that he made, after a pause for ostensible reflection: 'The soil in your neighbourhood is known to be particularly black and rich. Well, so it also provides moles with particularly rich nourishment, and they become exceptionally large.' 'But not as large as all that!' cried the teacher, and exaggerating a little in his fury he measured off a couple of yards against the wall. 'Oh certainly,' replied the scholar, who evidently regarded the whole thing as highly amusing. With that verdict the teacher returned home. He recounts how his wife and six children were waiting for him that evening by the side of the main road in a snowstorm, and how he had to confess to them the final collapse of his hopes.

At the time that I read of the scholar's behaviour towards the teacher I was not even acquainted with the teacher's main treatise. But I immediately decided to collect and collate on my own account everything that I could discover about the case. Since I could hardly attack the scholar with my bare fists, I would at least use my pen to defend the teacher, or more exactly, not so much defend the teacher as defend the good intentions of an honest but uninfluential man. I must admit that I regretted this resolve later, for I soon became aware that in carrying it out I should place myself in a curious position. On the one hand even my own influence was nothing like sufficient to change the scholar's mind in the teacher's favour, let alone change public opinion, while on the other the teacher was bound to notice that I was less concerned with his own main objective, which was to prove the fact of the great mole's appearance, than with the defence of his honesty, which of course seemed to him self-evident and to require no defence. So what was bound to happen was that I, while wishing to ally myself with the teacher, would meet with no understanding on his part, and probably that instead of helping I would need a new helper myself, who was most unlikely to be forthcoming. Besides, I had saddled myself with a great deal of work by taking this decision. If I wanted to convince, I could not afford to invoke the teacher, for of course he had been unable to carry conviction. A knowledge of his treatise would only have confused me, and I therefore refrained from reading it before my own work was completed. In fact, I did not even make contact with the teacher. It is true that he learned indirectly of my inquiries, but he did not know whether I was working for him or against him. Indeed he probably even suspected the latter, although he later denied it, for I have evidence to show that he placed a number of obstacles in my path. This was quite easy for him, since I was naturally compelled to undertake afresh all the investigations which he had already carried out, and so he was always in a position to forestall me. But that was the sole objection that could justifiably be made to my mode of procedure, moreover it was an unavoidable objection, and was deprived of much of its force by the caution, indeed the self-denial, with which I came to my conclusions. But in all other respects my own treatise was quite free from the teacher's influence, and perhaps I was even excessively scrupulous on this point; it was just as if no one had investigated the matter before, as if I had been the first to interrogate the eye-witnesses and the ear-witnesses, the first to put the evidence together, the first to draw conclusions.

Later, when I read the teacher's monograph – it had a very circumstantial title: 'A mole, of a size greater than ever previously observed' – I did in fact find that we were at variance on a number of major points, though we both believed we had proved our principal point, namely, the existence of the mole. However, these individual points of disagreement prevented the friendly relations growing up between us that I had still hoped for despite everything. On his side there developed something like hostility. True, he always remained modest and humble in his behaviour towards me, but that only made his real feelings the more obvious. The truth was that in his opinion I had done both him and his cause nothing but harm, and my own belief that I had been, or could have been, of any help to him was at best foolishness, and more probably arrogance or trickery. He was particularly fond of pointing out that all his previous opponents had displayed their opposition, if at all, only in confidential discussion, or anyway only by word of mouth, while I had considered it necessary to rush straight into print with all my objections. Moreover, the few opponents of his who had really occupied themselves with the matter, if but superficially, had at least listened to his, the teacher's, opinion, that is to say the authoritative opinion, before they expressed their own; while I, on the strength of evidence that had been un-systematically collected and partially misunderstood, had published conclusions which, even if correct on the principal matter at issue, could not fail to appear implausible, as much to the general public as to educated people. But the faintest hint of implausibility was the worst thing that could happen in this case. To these reproaches which he brought forward, albeit in a veiled manner, I could easily have found an answer – for instance his treatise itself represented just about the height of implausibility – but it was less easy to contend with his further suspicions, and that was why I was always extremely guarded in my dealings with him. For what he secretly believed was that I had tried to deprive him of the fame that belonged to him as the first public champion of the mole.

Now of course there was no fame attaching to him whatsoever, merely a little ridicule, and even that was restricted to a progressively diminishing circle and I certainly had no wish to compete for it. Besides, in the foreword to my treatise I had expressly declared that the teacher must be regarded for all time as the discoverer of the mole – not that he was its discoverer in any case – and that it was solely my personal sympathy with the teacher's fate that had moved me to compose the treatise. 'It is the aim of this work' – so I ended up in rather too resounding a manner, but it matched the strength of my feelings at the time – 'to help the teacher's monograph gain the publicity it deserves. Should this aim be achieved, then it is right that my own name, which has become temporarily and only indirectly associated with this affair, should be expunged from it forthwith.' Thus I disclaimed positively any major part in the affair; it was almost as if I had somehow anticipated the teacher's unbelievable accusation. Nevertheless it was precisely in that passage that he found a handle against me, and I cannot deny that what he said – or rather indicated – did contain some apparent trace of justification; indeed it sometimes struck me that he showed almost more penetration where I was concerned than he had done in his treatise. What he asserted was that my foreword was disingenuous. If my sole purpose had really been to publicize his treatise, why had I not dealt with him and his treatise exclusively, why had I not demonstrated its virtues, its irrefutability, why had I not restricted myself to emphasizing and making clear the significance of the discovery, why had I intruded myself instead into the actual making of the discovery, while passing over his treatise in utter silence? Did I perhaps imagine that the discovery had not already been made? Did I suppose that anything further remained to be done in that respect? But if I really thought it was necessary for me to make the discovery all over again, why was it that I solemnly renounced all claim to the discovery in my foreword? That could have been false modesty, but it was really something worse. I was belittling the discovery, I was only drawing attention to it in order to belittle it, I had investigated it only to lay it aside; by that time the matter had perhaps quietened down a little, then along I had come and stirred it up again, but in doing so I had made the teacher's position more difficult than ever. What did the teacher care about the defence of his honesty? His concern was for the matter at issue, and for that alone. And that was what I had betrayed, because I failed to understand it, because I could not appreciate it properly, because I lacked all feeling for it. It was worlds beyond the grasp of my intellect. He sat there opposite me, looking at me calmly with his old, wrinkled face and yet that was precisely what he thought of me.

In fact, it was not true that his sole concern was for the matter at issue; he was actually quite ambitious, and wanted financial profit as well, which in view of his large family was entirely understandable; but all the same my own concern for the matter seemed to him so trivial by comparison that he felt able to represent himself as wholly disinterested without departing too far from the truth. And indeed I could not even get private satisfaction by telling myself that the root cause of the man's reproaches was the fact that he clung on to his mole with both hands, so to speak, and called anyone who wished to lay as much as a finger on it a traitor. For that was not the case; his attitude was not to be explained by possessiveness, or at least not by possessiveness alone, but rather by the touchiness that his great labours and their total lack of success had engendered in him. Yet even this touchiness did not explain everything. Perhaps my interest in the matter really was too trivial; as far as strangers were concerned, the teacher had grown accustomed to lack of interest, and while it distressed him in general, it no longer distressed him in particular cases; but now at last someone had come along and taken the matter up with exceptional vigour, and even he failed to understand it. Once the charge against me was pressed along those lines I had no wish to deny it. I am no zoologist; perhaps if I had discovered this case myself I might have espoused it with heart and soul, but I had not discovered it. A mole of such size is certainly a curiosity, but one cannot expect the entire world to accord it permanent attention, especially if the existence of the mole has not been established wholly beyond doubt and at all events it cannot be produced. And I had to admit also that even if I had been the discoverer of the mole, I should probably never have taken up the cudgels on its behalf in the way that I took them up, gladly and of my own free will, on behalf of the teacher.

Now the misunderstanding between me and the teacher would probably have been soon resolved if my treatise had met with success. But that was just what failed to happen. Perhaps it was not written well enough, not convincingly enough; I am a business man, perhaps the powers needed to compose such a treatise lie even further outside my sphere of competence than was the case with the teacher, although in the kind of knowledge required I was certainly far superior to him. But it was also possible to interpret my lack of success in another way: perhaps my treatise had appeared at an unfavourable time. On the one hand the discovery of the mole, which had failed to gain acceptance, did not lie far enough in the past for people to have forgotten about it altogether, so that my treatise could have come as a surprise to them; on the other hand, however, sufficient time had elapsed to ensure that such limited interest as had existed originally was now totally exhausted. Those who gave any thought at all to my treatise told themselves, with the hopeless gloom that had character- ized the debate from the outset, that no doubt the futile exertions in support of this dreary matter were about to begin again, and some of them even confused my treatise with that of the teacher. In a leading agricultural journal there appeared the following notice, fortunately only at the end and in small print: 'The treatise on the giant mole has been submitted to us again. We remember having laughed heartily over it once before some years ago. Since then it has grown no wiser and we no more stupid. We merely find it impossible to laugh the second time. Instead we would ask our teaching associations whether more useful work cannot be found for our village school- masters than chasing after giant moles.' An unforgivable confusion! They had read neither the first treatise nor the second, and the two wretched terms 'giant mole' and 'village schoolmaster', picked up in haste, were sufficient for these gentlemen to show off as the representatives of established interests. Certainly, various means would have been open to me to counter this effectively, but I was deterred from trying them by the lack of understanding between myself and the teacher. Instead, I tried to conceal the journal from him for as long as I possibly could. But he very soon discovered it, as I recognized from a remark in one of his letters, in which he announced his intention of visiting me during the Christmas holidays. He wrote: 'It is a wicked world, and people make things easy for it', by which he intended to convey that I belonged to the wicked world, but instead of resting content with my own private store of wickedness I was making things easy for the world, that is, I was actively engaged in enticing the general wickedness out into the open and helping it to victory.

Well, I had made all the necessary decisions in advance; I could calmly await him and calmly observe him when he came, as he greeted me even less politely than usual, sat himself down opposite me in silence, carefully drew out the journal from the breast-pocket of his curiously padded overcoat, opened it and pushed it across to me. 'I've seen it,' I said, and pushed the journal back unread. 'You've seen it,' he said with a sigh; he had the old schoolmasterish habit of repeating other people's answers. 'Of course I won't take this lying down,' he went on, tapping the journal excitedly with his finger and looking at me sharply as he did so, as if I was of the contrary opinion; very likely he had some inkling of what I was going to say; indeed this was not the first time that I seemed to detect, not so much from his words as from other signs, that he could often sense my intentions with great accuracy, but then resisted his intuition and allowed himself to be distracted. What I said to him on that occasion I can reproduce almost word for word, for I made a note of it shortly after our discussion. 'Do what you will,' I said, 'from this day on our ways divide. I imagine that that is neither unexpected nor unwelcome news to you. This notice in the journal here is not the reason for my decision, it has merely finally confirmed it; the real reason is that while I originally believed I could assist you by my intervention, I am now forced to recognize that I have damaged you on every side. Why things should have taken this course I do not know, the causes of success and failure are always open to a variety of interpretations, do not seek out only the ones that are unfavourable to me. Reflect on your own case: you also had the best intentions, and yet, when one considers the whole thing in perspective, you have failed. I do not mean it as a joke, for the joke would be at my own expense, when I say that your association with me must unfortunately be counted among your failures as well. My withdrawal from the affair at this point is neither cowardice nor treachery. Indeed it is not without a struggle that I can bring myself to do so; my treatise is sufficient evidence of the high regard in which I hold you personally, in a certain sense you have become a teacher to me, and I have even almost become attached to the mole. Nevertheless, I now step aside; you are the discoverer, and despite all my efforts I constantly obstruct the possible fame that might come your way, while at the same time I attract failure and transmit it to you. At least that is your own opinion. Enough of that. The sole expiation that I can make is to beg your forgiveness, and – should you require it – to repeat publicly, for instance in this journal, the confession that I have made to you here.'

These were my words; they were not entirely sincere, but the sincerity in them was easy to see. My decision had roughly the effect on him that I had anticipated. Most old people have something deceptive, something mendacious about them in their dealings with those younger than themselves; one lives beside them peacefully, imagines the relationship to be secure, knows their prevailing opinions, receives unremitting confirmations of harmony, regards everything as a matter of course, and then suddenly, when something decisive does happen and the time comes for the long-cultivated state of calm to prove effective, these old people rise up like strangers, they possess deeper and stronger convictions, they positively unfurl their banner for the first time and with terror one reads upon it the new device. The reason for this terror lies chiefly in the fact that what the old say now is really far more just, more sensible, and – as if there were degrees of self-evidence – even more self-evident than before. But the supremely deceitful thing about it is that they have basically always been saying what they now come out with, and that even so it is generally quite impossible to see it coming. I must indeed have probed deep into this village schoolmaster, seeing that what he now said failed to take me wholly by surprise.

'My child,' he said, laying his hand on mine and rubbing it amicably, 'how did you ever take it into your head to get involved in this affair? The very first time I heard about it I discussed the matter with my wife.' He pushed his chair back from the table, spread out his arms, and stared at the floor as if his miniature wife was standing down there and he was conversing with her. '"For so many years," I said to her, "we have been fighting alone, but now it seems that a noble benefactor in the city has taken up our cause, a city business man, a Mr So-and-so. Now that should make us very pleased, shouldn't it? A business man in the city is a person of some importance; if some ragged peasant believes us and says so, that's of no use to us, for what a peasant does is always improper, and whether he says 'The old schoolmaster is right' or whether he perhaps spits in an unseemly manner, the effect is the same in both cases. And if instead of one peasant, ten thousand peasants should stand up for us, the effect would be if possible even worse. A business man in the city, on the other hand, is quite a different thing; a man like that has connections, even his casual remarks become known to a wide circle of people, new patrons will interest themselves in our case; one of them may perhaps say 'There is something to be learnt even from village schoolmasters', and the very next day a whole crowd of people are whispering it to one another, people from whom one would never expect it, to judge by their appearances. And now funds for the cause begin to roll in, one gentleman starts collecting and the others press their money into his hand; they decide that the village schoolmaster must be hauled out of his village; they come, they pay no heed to his appearance, they gather him up, and since his wife and children cling to him they take them along as well. Have you ever observed people from the city? They twitter unceasingly. When there's a whole row of them together the twittering goes from right to left and then back again, to and fro. And so, twittering, they hoist us into the carriage, there's hardly time to nod to everybody. The gentleman on the coach-box adjusts his pince-nez, flourishes his whip, and away we go. They all wave farewell to the village, as if we were still there and not sitting in their midst. Some carriages with particularly impatient people come out from the city to meet us. As we approach they stand up from their seats and crane their necks to see us. The gentleman who collected the money directs every-thing and makes an appeal for calm. By the time we drive into the city we form a long procession of carriages. We suppose the reception is now concluded, but no, it is only just beginning outside the hotel. After all, in the city a single announcement is enough to bring a great crowd together in a flash. One man's concern becomes instantly the concern of the next. As they take each other's breath away they take each other's views away too and adopt them. Not all the townsfolk could afford a carriage, so these are waiting in front of the hotel; others could well have driven out to meet us but were too self-important to do so. They are waiting too. It is astonishing how the gentleman who collected the money manages to keep an eye on everything."'

I had listened to him calmly; indeed I had grown ever calmer as his speech went on. On the table I had piled up all the copies of my treatise that were still in my possession. Only a very few were missing, for I had recently issued a circular demanding the return of all the copies I had sent out, and most of them had come in. I had in addition been informed very politely by a number of correspondents that they had no recollection of ever having received such a treatise, and if it should be that it had reached them after all, then it must regrettably have been lost. Well, that solution was quite satisfactory too; basically that was all I wanted. Only one reader asked to be allowed to keep the treatise as a curiosity, and he pledged himself in the spirit of my circular to show it to no one for the next twenty years. The village schoolmaster had not yet seen this circular; I was glad that his words made it so easy for me to show it to him. I had no qualms about doing this in any case, for I had been most circum-spect in drawing it up and had kept the interests of the schoolmaster and of his cause in mind throughout. The crucial passage in this document ran as follows: 'I do not ask for the return of the treatise because I retract in any way the opinions advanced there or because there are any particular sections which I now regard as erroneous or even as undemonstrable. My request is made for purely personal reasons, which are, however, most compelling; but it permits no conclusions whatsoever to be drawn as regards my attitude to the actual matter of the treatise; I beg to draw your special attention to this, and would also be glad if you would kindly pass the information on.'

For the moment I covered this circular with my hands and said: 'Do you want to reproach me because things did not turn out as you describe? Why do you want to do that? Let us not embitter our parting. And do try at last to see that though you've made a discovery, this discovery doesn't necessarily surpass everything else, and therefore the injustice you suffer doesn't surpass everything either. I'm not acquainted with the statutes of our learned societies, but I don't believe that in the most favourable circumstances you would have been given a reception even remotely resembling the one you seem to have described to your wife. If I myself had any hopes that my treatise might achieve something, I suppose that the attention of a professor might perhaps be drawn to our case, that he might set some young student the task of looking into the matter, that his student might come to see you and check your inquiries and mine once again on the spot in his own way, and that finally, if his results seemed to him worth mentioning – one must bear in mind here that all young students are full of doubts – he might publish a treatise of his own in which your account would be put on a scientific basis. But even supposing this hope had been fulfilled, still not much would have been achieved. The student's treatise, in defence of such a curious case, might well have been held up to ridicule. You can see from the example of this agricultural journal how easily that can be done, and academic journals are even more ruthless in this respect. And that's understandable, too; professors bear a great responsibility towards themselves, towards scientific knowledge, towards posterity, they can't fling themselves straight into the arms of each new discovery. We others have the advantage of them there. But I'll leave that aside and assume that the student's treatise had found acceptance. What would have happened next? Your name would no doubt have received honourable mention a few times, you would probably have done some service to your profession as well, people would have said: "Our village schoolmasters keep their eyes open", and this journal here would have had to offer you a public apology, if for the sake of argument journals had a memory and a conscience; some sympathetic professor would then have been found to secure you a scholarship, and it really is possible that an attempt might have been made to get you to the city, to provide you with a post in a municipal primary school, and so give you the opportunity to make use of the scientific resources offered by the city in order to improve yourself. But if I am to be frank I must say I doubt whether it would ever have got further than the attempt. You would have been summoned here, and you would have come, but it would have been as an ordinary petitioner like hundreds of others, without any question of a festive reception; they would have talked to you, would have acknowledged the honest worth of your efforts, but at the same time they would have recognized that you were an old man, that at your age it was hopeless to embark on academic study, and above all that you had arrived at your discovery more by chance than by design, and that you did not even intend to carry your researches beyond this one particular case. For these reasons they would probably have left you in your village. Your discovery would no doubt have been taken further, for it is not so trifling that it could ever be forgotten again once it had achieved recognition. But you would not have heard much more about it, and what you did hear you would barely have understood. Every discovery is at once absorbed into the great universe of scientific knowledge, and with that it ceases in a sense to be a discovery; it dissolves into the whole and disappears; if one is still to recognize it then, one needs a trained scientific eye. It becomes immediately attached to principles of whose existence we have never heard, and caught up in scientific controversy it is hoisted by those principles into the clouds. How can we expect to understand that? If we listen to a debate of that kind we may for instance imagine that it is about your discovery, while all the time it is about something quite different.'

'Very well,' said the village schoolmaster, taking out his pipe and starting to fill it with the tobacco that he carried about loose in all his pockets. 'You took up this thankless business of your own free will, and now of your own free will you withdraw from it. That is all perfectly in order.'

'I am not an obstinate man,' I said. 'Perhaps you have some criticism to make of my proposal?'

'No, none at all,' said the schoolmaster, and his pipe was already going nicely. I could not stand the smell of his tobacco and so I stood up and walked about the room. I knew well enough from our previous interviews that the schoolmaster was very taciturn in my company, and that despite this, once he had come to my room, he showed no inclination to budge. I had often found this most disturbing; there must be something else he wants from me, I always thought at such times, and I would offer him money, which he regularly accepted. But as for going away, that he never did until it suited him. Usually by then he had finished his pipe, he would whip round to the back of his chair, push it carefully and respectfully in to the table, seize his walking-stick from the corner, shake me vigorously by the hand, and go. But today I found it positively irksome that he should go on sitting there in silence. When one has proposed a final parting to someone, as I had done, and this person has said that he finds that perfectly in order, then surely one gets through what little common business remains with all possible speed and does not pointlessly burden the other man with one's silent presence. Looking at the stubborn little old fellow from behind, as he sat at my table, one might almost have despaired of ever being able to shift him from the room. His long stiff overcoat, which he never took off, was rucked up all round him and stood well out from his body, making him into a broad and massive hulk.

coughs, chokes from some pain; one wraps it in a rug, whistles a

BLUMFELD, AN ELDERLY
BACHELOR

ONE evening Blumfeld, an elderly bachelor, was climbing up to his
apartment – a laborious undertaking, for he lived on the sixth floor.
While climbing up he thought, as he had so often recently, how
unpleasant this utterly lonely life was: to reach his empty room he
had to climb these six floors almost in secret, there put his dressing-
gown on, again almost in secret, light his pipe, read a little of the
French magazine to which he had been subscribing for years, at the
same time sip at a home-made kirsch, and finally, after half an hour,
go to bed, but not before having completely rearranged his bedclothes
which the unteachable charwoman would insist on arranging in her
own way. Some companion, someone to witness these activities,
would have been very welcome to Blumfeld. He had already been
wondering whether he shouldn't acquire a little dog. These animals
are gay and above all grateful and loyal; one of Blumfeld's colleagues
has a dog of this kind; it follows no one but its master and when it
hasn't seen him for a few moments it greets him at once with loud
barkings, by which it is evidently trying to express its joy at once
more finding that extraordinary benefactor, its master. True, a dog
also has its drawbacks. However well kept it may be, it is bound to
dirty the room. This just cannot be avoided; one cannot give it a hot
bath each time before letting it into the room; besides, its health
couldn't stand that. Blumfeld, on the other hand, can't stand dirt in
his room. To him cleanliness is essential, and several times a week he
is obliged to have words with his charwoman, who is unfortunately
not very painstaking in this respect. Since she is hard of hearing she
usually drags her by the arm to those spots in the room which he
finds lacking in cleanliness. By this strict discipline he has achieved
in his room a neatness more or less commensurate with his wishes.

By acquiring a dog, however, he would be almost deliberately introducing into his room the dirt which hitherto he had been so careful to avoid. Fleas, the dog's constant companions, would appear. And once fleas were there, it would not be long before Blumfeld would be abandoning his comfortable room to the dog and looking for another one. Uncleanliness, however, is but one of the drawbacks of dogs. Dogs also fall ill and no one really understands dogs' diseases. Then the animal sits in a corner or limps about, whimpers, coughs, chokes from some pain; one wraps it in a rug, whistles a little melody, offers it milk – in short, one nurses it in the hope that this, as indeed is possible, is a passing sickness while it may be a serious, disgusting, and contagious disease. And even if the dog remains healthy, one day it will grow old, one won't have the heart to get rid of the faithful animal in time, and then comes the moment when one's own age peers out at one from the dog's oozing eyes. Then one has to cope with the half-blind, weak-lunged animal, all but immobile with fat, and in this way pay dearly for the pleasures the dog had once given. Much as Blumfeld would like to have a dog at this moment, he would rather go on climbing the stairs alone for another thirty years than be burdened later on by such an old dog which, sighing louder than he, would drag itself up, step by step.

So Blumfeld will remain alone, after all; he really feels none of the old maid's longings to have around her some submissive, living creature that she can protect, lavish her affection upon, and continue to serve – for which purpose a cat, a canary, even a goldfish would suffice – or, if this cannot be, rest content with flowers on the windowsill. Blumfeld only wants a companion, an animal to which he doesn't have to pay much attention, which doesn't mind an occasional kick, which even, in an emergency, can spend the night in the street, but which nevertheless, when Blumfeld feels like it, is promptly at his disposal with its barking, jumping, and licking of hands. This is what Blumfeld wants, but since, as he realizes, it cannot be had without serious drawbacks, he renounces it, and yet – in accordance with his thoroughgoing disposition – the idea from time to time, this evening for instance, occurs to him again.

While taking the key from his pocket outside his room, he is startled by a sound coming from within. A peculiar rattling sound, very lively but very regular. Since Blumfeld has just been thinking of dogs, it reminds him of the sounds produced by paws pattering one after the other over a floor. But paws don't rattle, so it can't be paws. He quickly unlocks the door and switches on the light. He is not prepared for what he sees. For this is magic – two small white celluloid balls with blue stripes jumping up and down side by side on the parquet; when one of them touches the floor the other is in the air, a game they continue ceaselessly to play. At school one day Blumfeld had seen some little pellets jumping about like this during a well-known electrical experiment, but these are comparatively large balls jumping freely about in the room and no electrical experiment is being made. Blumfeld bends down to get a good look at them. They are undoubtedly ordinary balls, they probably contain several smaller balls, and it is these which produce the rattling sound. Blumfeld gropes in the air to find out whether they are hanging from some threads – no, they are moving entirely on their own. A pity Blumfeld isn't a small child, two balls like these would have been a happy surprise for him, whereas now the whole thing gives him rather an unpleasant feeling. It's not quite pointless after all to live in secret as an unnoticed bachelor, now someone, no matter who, has penetrated this secret and sent him these two strange balls.

He tries to catch one but they retreat before him, thus luring him on to follow them through the room. It's really too silly, he thinks, running after balls like this; he stands still and realizes that the moment he abandons the pursuit, they too remain on the same spot. I will try to catch them all the same, he thinks again, and hurries towards them. They immediately run away, but Blumfeld, his legs apart, forces them into a corner of the room, and there, in front of a trunk, he manages to catch one ball. It's a small cool ball, and it turns in his hand, clearly anxious to slip away. And the other ball, too, as though aware of its comrade's distress, jumps higher than before, extending the leaps until it touches Blumfeld's hand. It beats against this hand, beats in ever faster leaps, alters its angle of attack, then, powerless against the hand which encloses the ball so completely, springs even higher and is probably trying to reach Blumfeld's face. Blumfeld could catch this ball too, and lock them both up somewhere, but at the moment it strikes him as too humiliating to take such measures against two little balls. Besides, it's fun owning these balls, and soon enough they'll grow tired, roll under the cupboard, and be quiet. Despite this deliberation, Blumfeld, near to anger, flings the ball to the ground, and it is a miracle that in doing so the delicate, all but transparent celluloid cover doesn't break. Without hesitation the two balls resume their former low, well-coordinated jumps.

Blumfeld undresses calmly, arranges his clothes in the wardrobe which he always inspects carefully to make sure the charwoman has left everything in order. Once or twice he glances over his shoulder at the balls which, unpursued, seem to be pursuing him; they have followed him and are now jumping close behind him. Blumfeld puts on his dressing-gown and sets out for the opposite wall to fetch one of the pipes which are hanging in a rack. Before turning round he instinctively kicks his foot out backwards, but the balls know how to get out of its way and remain untouched. As Blumfeld goes off to fetch the pipe the balls at once follow close behind him; he shuffles along in his slippers, taking irregular steps, yet each step is followed almost without pause by the sound of the balls; they are keeping pace with him. To see how the balls manage to do this, Blumfeld turns suddenly round. But hardly has he turned when the balls describe a semicircle and are already behind him again, and this they repeat every time he turns. Like submissive companions, they try to avoid appearing in front of Blumfeld. Up to the present they have evidently dared to do so only in order to introduce themselves; now, however, it seems they have actually entered into his service.

Hitherto, when faced with situations he couldn't master, Blumfeld had always chosen to behave as though he hadn't noticed anything. It had often helped and usually improved the situation. This, then, is what he does now; he takes up a position in front of the pipe rack and, puffing out his lips, chooses a pipe, fills it with particular care from the tobacco pouch close at hand, and allows the balls to continue their jumping behind him. But he hesitates to approach the table, for to hear the sound of the jumps coinciding with that of his own steps almost hurts him. So there he stands, and while taking an unnecessarily long time to fill his pipe he measures the distance separating him from the table. At last, however, he overcomes his faintheartedness and covers the distance with such stamping of feet that he cannot hear the balls. But the moment he is seated he can hear them jumping up and down behind his chair as distinctly as ever.

Above the table, within reach, a shelf is nailed to the wall on which stands the bottle of kirsch surrounded by little glasses. Beside it, in a pile, lie several copies of his French magazine. But instead of reaching down everything he needs, Blumfeld sits there tense, staring at the bowl of his still unlit pipe. He is lying in wait. Suddenly, quite unexpectedly, his numbness leaves him and with a jerk he turns round in his chair. But the balls, equally alert, or perhaps automatically following the law governing them, also change their position the moment Blumfeld turns, and hide behind his back. Blumfeld now sits with his back to the table, the cold pipe in his hand. And now the balls jump under the table and, since there's a rug there, they are less audible. This is a great advantage: only faint, hollow noises can be heard, one has to pay great attention to catch their sound. Blumfeld, however, does pay great attention, and hears them distinctly. But this is so only for the moment, in a little while he probably won't hear them any more. The fact that they cannot make themselves more audible on the rug strikes Blumfeld as a great weakness on the part of the balls. What one has to do is lay one or even better two rugs under them and they are all but powerless. Admittedly only for a limited time, and besides, their very existence wields a certain power.

Just now Blumfeld could have made good use of a dog, a wild young animal would soon have dealt with these balls; he imagines this dog trying to catch them with its paws, chasing them from their positions, hunting them all over the room, and finally getting hold of them between its teeth. It's quite possible that before long Blumfeld will acquire a dog.

For the moment, however, the balls have no one to fear but Blumfeld, and he has no desire to destroy them just now, perhaps he lacks the necessary determination. He comes home in the evening tired from work and just when he is in need of some rest he is faced with this surprise. Only now does he realize how tired he really is. No doubt he will destroy the balls, and that in the near future, but not just yet, probably not until tomorrow. If one looks at the whole thing with an unprejudiced eye, the balls behave modestly enough. From time to time, for instance, they could jump into the foreground, show themselves, and then return again to their positions, or they could jump higher so as to beat against the table top in order to compensate themselves for the muffling effect of the rug. But this they don't do, they don't want to irritate Blumfeld unduly, they are evidently confining themselves to what is absolutely necessary.

Even this measured necessity, however, is quite sufficient to spoil Blumfeld's rest at the table. He has been sitting there only a few minutes and is already contemplating going to bed. One of his motives for this is that he can't smoke here, for he has left the matches on his bedside table. Thus he would have to fetch these matches, but once having reached the bedside table he might as well stay there and lie down. For this he has an ulterior motive: he thinks that the balls, with their mania for keeping behind him, will jump on to the bed and that there, in lying down, on purpose or not, he will squash them. The objection, that what would then remain of the balls could still go on jumping, he dismisses. Even the unusual must have its limits. Complete balls jump anyway, even if not incessantly, but fragments of balls never jump, and consequently will not jump in this case, either. 'Up!' he shouts, having grown almost reckless from this reflection and, the balls still behind him, he stamps off to bed. His hope seems to be confirmed, for when he purposely takes up a position quite near the bed, one ball promptly springs on to it. Then, however, the unexpected occurs: the other ball disappears under the bed. The possibility that the balls could jump under the bed as well had not occurred to Blumfeld. He is outraged about the one ball, although he is aware how unjust this is, for by jumping under the bed the ball fulfils its duty perhaps better than the ball on the bed. Now everything depends on which place the balls decide to choose, for Blumfeld does not believe that they can work separately for any length of time. And sure enough a moment later the ball on the floor also jumps on to the bed. Now I've got them, thinks Blumfeld, hot with joy, and tears his dressing-gown from his body to throw himself into bed. At that moment, however, the very same ball jumps back under the bed. Overwhelmed with disappointment,

Blumfeld almost collapses. Very likely the ball just took a good look round up there and decided it didn't like it. And now the other one has followed, too, and of course remains, for it's better down there. 'Now I'll have these drummers with me all night,' thinks Blumfeld, biting his lips and nodding his head.

He feels gloomy, without actually knowing what harm the balls could do him in the night. He is a good sleeper, he will easily be able to ignore so slight a noise. To make quite sure of this and mindful of his past experience, he lays two rugs on the floor. It's as if he owned a little dog for which he wants to make a soft bed. And as though the balls had also grown tired and sleepy, their jumping has become lower and slower than before. As Blumfeld kneels beside the bed, lamp in hand, he thinks for a moment that the balls might come to rest on the rug – they fall so weakly, roll so slowly along. Then, however, they dutifully rise again. Yet it is quite possible that in the morning when Blumfeld looks under the bed he'll find there two quiet, harmless children's balls.

But it seems that they may not even be able to keep up their jumping until the morning, for as soon as Blumfeld is in bed he doesn't hear them any more. He strains his ears, leans out of bed to listen – not a sound. The effect of the rugs can't be as strong as that; the only explanation is that the balls are no longer jumping, either because they aren't able to bounce themselves off the rug and have therefore abandoned jumping for the time being or, which is more likely, they will never jump again. Blumfeld could get up and see exactly what's going on, but in his relief at finding peace at last he prefers to remain where he is. He would rather not risk disturbing the pacified balls even with his eyes. Even smoking he happily renounces, turns over on his side, and promptly goes to sleep.

But he does not remain undisturbed; as usual he sleeps without dreaming, but very restlessly. Innumerable times during the night he is startled by the delusion that someone is knocking at his door. He knows quite well that no one is knocking; who would knock at night and at his lonely bachelor's door? Yet although he knows this for certain, he is startled again and again and each time glances in suspense at the door, his mouth open, eyes wide, a strand of hair trembling over his damp forehead. He tries to count how many times he has been woken but, dizzy from the huge numbers he arrives at, he falls back to sleep again. He thinks he knows where the knocking comes from; not from the door, but somewhere quite different; being heavy with sleep, however, he cannot quite remember on what his suspicions are based. All he knows is that innumerable tiny unpleasant sounds accumulate before producing the great strong knocking. He would happily suffer all the unpleasantness of the small sounds if he could be spared the actual knocking, but for some reason it's too late; he cannot interfere, the moment has passed, he can't even speak, his mouth opens but all that comes out is a silent yawn, and furious at this he thrusts his face into the pillows. Thus the night passes.

In the morning he is awakened by the charwoman's knocking; with a sigh of relief he welcomes the gentle tap on the door, whose inaudibility has in the past always been one of his sources of complaint, and is about to shout 'Come in!' when he hears another lively, faint, yet all but belligerent knocking. It's the balls under the bed. Have they woken up? Have they, unlike him, gathered new strength overnight? 'Just a moment,' shouts Blumfeld to the charwoman, jumps out of bed and, taking great care to keep the balls behind him, throws himself on the floor, his back still towards them; then, twisting his head over his shoulder, he glances at the balls and – nearly lets out a curse. Like children pushing away blankets that annoy them at night, the balls have apparently spent all night pushing the rugs, with tiny twitching movements, so far away from under the bed that they are now once more on the parquet, where they can continue making their noise. 'Back on to the rugs!' says Blumfeld with an angry face, and only when the balls, thanks to the rugs, have become quiet again does he call in the charwoman. While she – a fat, dull-witted, stiff-backed woman – is laying the breakfast on the table and doing the few necessary chores, Blumfeld stands motionless in his dressing-gown by his bed so as to keep the balls in their place. With his eyes he follows the charwoman to see whether she notices anything. This, since she is hard of hearing, is very unlikely, and the fact that Blumfeld thinks he sees the charwoman stopping here and there, holding on to some furniture and listening with raised eyebrows, he puts down to his overwrought condition caused by a bad night's sleep. It would relieve him if he could persuade the char-woman to speed up her work, but if anything she is slower than usual. She loads herself laboriously with Blumfeld's clothes and shuffles out with them into the corridor, stays away a long time, and the din she makes beating the clothes echoes in his ears with slow, monoto-nous thuds. And during all this time Blumfeld has to remain on the bed, cannot move for fear of drawing the balls behind him, has to let the coffee – which he likes to drink as hot as possible – get cold, and can do nothing but stare at the drawn blinds beyond which the day is dimly dawning. At last the charwoman has finished, bids him good-morning, and is about to leave; but before she actually goes she hesitates by the door, moves her lips a little, and takes a long look at Blumfeld. Blumfeld is about to remonstrate when she at last departs. Blumfeld longs to fling the door open and shout after her that she is a stupid, idiotic old woman. However, when he reflects on what he actually has against her, he can only think of the paradox of her having clearly noticed nothing and yet trying to give the impression that she has. How confused his thoughts have become! And all on account of a bad night. Some explanation for his poor sleep he finds in the fact that last night he deviated from his usual habits by not smoking or drinking any kirsch. When for once I don't smoke or drink kirsch – and this is the result of his reflections – I sleep badly.

From now on he is going to take better care of his health, and he begins by fetching some cotton wool from his medicine chest which hangs over his bedside table and putting two little wads of it into his ears. Then he stands up and takes a trial step. Although the balls do follow he can hardly hear them; the addition of another wad makes them quite inaudible. Blumfeld takes a few more steps; nothing particularly unpleasant happens. Everyone for himself, Blumfeld as well as the balls, and although they are bound to one another they don't disturb each other. Only once, when Blumfeld turns round rather suddenly and one ball fails to make the counter-movement fast enough, does he touch it with his knee. But this is the only incident. Otherwise Blumfeld calmly drinks his coffee; he is as hungry as though, instead of sleeping last night, he had gone for a long walk; he washes in cold, exceptionally refreshing water, and puts on his clothes. He still hasn't pulled up the blinds; rather, as a precaution, he has preferred to remain in semi-darkness; he has no wish for the balls to be seen by other eyes. But now that he is ready to go he has somehow to provide for the balls in case they should dare – not that he thinks they will – to follow him into the street. He thinks of a good solution, opens the large wardrobe, and places himself with his back to it. As though divining his intentions, the balls steer clear of the wardrobe's interior, taking advantage of every inch of space between Blumfeld and the wardrobe; when there's no other alternative they jump into the wardrobe for a moment, but when faced by the dark, out they promptly jump again. Rather than be lured over the edge further into the wardrobe, they neglect their duty and stay by Blumfeld's side. But their little ruses avail them nothing, for now Blumfeld himself climbs backwards into the wardrobe and they have to follow him. And with this their fate has been sealed, for on the floor of the wardrobe lie various smallish objects such as boots, boxes, small trunks which, although carefully arranged – Blumfeld now regrets this – nevertheless considerably hamper the balls. And when Blumfeld, having now pulled the door almost to, jumps out of it with an enormous leap such as he has not made for years, slams the door and turns the key, the balls are imprisoned. 'Well, that worked,' thinks Blumfeld, wiping the sweat from his face. What a din the balls are making in the wardrobe! It sounds as though they are desperate. Blumfeld, on the other hand, is very contented. He leaves the room and already the deserted corridor has a soothing effect on him. He takes the wool out of his ears and is enchanted by the countless sounds of the waking house. Few people are to be seen, it's still very early.

Downstairs in the hall in front of the low door leading to the charwoman's basement apartment stands that woman's ten-year-old son. The image of his mother, not one feature of the woman has been omitted in this child's face. Bandy-legged, hands in his trouser pockets, he stands there wheezing, for he already has a goitre and can breathe only with difficulty. But whereas Blumfeld, whenever the boy crosses his path, usually quickens his step to spare himself the spectacle, today he almost feels like pausing for a moment. Even if the boy has been brought into the world by this woman and shows

every sign of his origin, he is nevertheless a child, the thoughts of a
child still dwell in this shapeless head, and if one were to speak to
him sensibly and ask him something, he would very likely answer in
a bright voice, innocent and reverential, and after some inner struggle
one could bring oneself to pat these cheeks. Although this is what
Blumfeld thinks, he nevertheless passes him by. In the street he
realizes that the weather is pleasanter than he had suspected from his
room. The morning mist has dispersed and patches of blue sky have
appeared, brushed by a strong wind. Blumfeld has the balls to thank
for his having left his room much earlier than usual; even the paper
he has left unread on the table; in any case he has saved a great deal
of time and can now afford to walk slowly. It is remarkable how little
he worries about the balls now that he is separated from them. So
long as they were following him they could have been considered as
something belonging to him, something which, in passing judgement
on his person, had somehow to be taken into consideration. Now,
however, they were mere toys in his wardrobe at home. And it
occurs to Blumfeld that the best way of rendering the balls harmless
would be to put them to their original use. There in the hall stands
the boy; Blumfeld will give him the balls, not lend them, but actually
present them to him, which is surely tantamount to ordering their
destruction. And even if they were to remain intact they would mean
even less in the boy's hands than in the wardrobe, the whole house
would watch the boy playing with them, other children would join
in, and the general opinion that the balls are things to play with and
in no way life companions of Blumfeld would be firmly and ir-
refutably established. Blumfeld runs back into the house. The boy
has just gone down the basement stairs and is about to open the
door. So Blumfeld has to call the boy and pronounce his name, a
name that to him seems as ludicrous as everything else connected
with the child. He does so. 'Alfred! Alfred!' he shouts. The boy
hesitates for a long time. 'Come here!' shouts Blumfeld. 'I've got
something for you.' The janitor's two little girls appear from the
door opposite and, full of curiosity, take up positions on either side
of Blumfeld. They grasp the situation much more quickly than the
boy and cannot understand why he doesn't come at once. Without
taking their eyes off Blumfeld they beckon to the boy, but cannot

fathom what kind of present is awaiting Alfred. Tortured with curios-ity, they hop from one foot to the other. Blumfeld laughs at them as well as at the boy. The latter seems to have figured it all out and climbs stiffly, clumsily up the steps. Not even in his gait can he manage to belie his mother, who, incidentally, has appeared in the basement doorway. To make sure that the charwoman also under-stands and in the hope that she will supervise the carrying out of his instructions, should it be necessary, Blumfeld shouts excessively loud. 'Up in my room,' says Blumfeld, 'I have two lovely balls. Would you like to have them?' Not knowing how to behave, the boy simply screws up his mouth, turns round and looks inquiringly down at his mother. The girls, however, promptly begin to jump around Blumfeld and ask him for the balls. 'You will be allowed to play with them too,' Blumfeld tells them, but waits for the boy's answer. He could of course give the balls to the girls, but they strike him as too unreliable and for the moment he has more confidence in the boy. Meanwhile the latter, without having exchanged a word, has taken counsel with his mother and nods his assent to Blumfeld's repeated question. 'Then listen,' says Blumfeld, who is quite prepared to receive no thanks for his gift. 'Your mother has the key of my door, you must borrow it from her. But here is the key to my wardrobe, and in the wardrobe you will find the balls. Take good care to lock the wardrobe and the room again. But with the balls you can do what you like and you don't have to bring them back. Have you understood me?' Unfortunately, the boy has not understood. Blumfeld has tried to make everything particularly clear to this hopelessly dense creature, but for this very reason has repeated everything too often, has in turn too often mentioned keys, room, and wardrobe, and as a result the boy stares at him as though he were rather a seducer than his benefactor. The girls, on the other hand, have understood everything immediately, press against Blum-feld, and stretch out their hands for the key. 'Wait a moment,' says Blumfeld, by now annoyed with them all. Time, moreover, is passing, he can't stand about much longer. If only the mother would say that she has understood him and take matters in hand for the boy! Instead of which she still stands down by the door, smiles with the affection of the bashful deaf, and is probably under the impression that Blumfeld up there has suddenly fallen for the boy and is hearing him his lessons. Blumfeld on the other hand can't very well climb down the basement stairs and shout into the charwoman's ear to make her son for God's sake relieve him of the balls! It had required enough of his self-control as it was to entrust the key of his wardrobe for a whole day to this family. It is certainly not in order to save himself trouble that he is handing the key to the boy rather than himself leading the boy up and there giving him the balls. But he can't very well first give the balls away and then immediately deprive the boy of them by – as would be bound to happen – drawing them after him as his followers. 'Don't you understand me then?' asks Blumfeld almost wistfully after having started a fresh explanation which, however, he immediately interrupts at sight of the boy's vacant stare. So vacant a stare renders one helpless. It could tempt one into saying more than one intends, if only to fill the vacancy with sense.

Whereupon 'We'll fetch the balls for him!' shout the girls. They are shrewd and have realized that they can obtain the balls only through using the boy as an intermediary, but that they themselves have to bring about this mediation. From the janitor's room a clock strikes, warning Blumfeld to hurry. 'Well, then, take the key,' says Blumfeld, and the key is more snatched from his hand than given by him. He would have handed it to the boy with infinitely more confidence. 'The key to the room you'll have to get from the woman,' Blumfeld adds. 'And when you return with the balls you must hand both keys to her.' 'Yes, yes!' shout the girls and run down the steps. They know everything, absolutely everything; and as though Blumfeld were infected by the boy's denseness, he is unable to understand how they could have grasped everything so quickly from his explanations.

Now they are already tugging at the charwoman's skirt but, tempting as it would be, Blumfeld cannot afford to watch them carrying out their task, not only because it's already late, but also because he has no desire to be present at the liberation of the balls. He would in fact prefer to be several streets away when the girls first open the door of his room. After all, how does he know what else he might have to expect from the balls! And so for the second time this morning he leaves the house. He has one last glimpse of the char-woman defending herself against the girls, and of the boy stirring his bandy legs to come to his mother's assistance. It's beyond Blumfeld's comprehension why a creature like this servant should prosper and propagate in this world.

While on his way to the linen factory, where Blumfeld is employed, thoughts about his work gradually get the upper hand. He quickens his step and, despite the delay caused by the boy, he is the first to arrive in his office. The office is a glass-enclosed room containing a writing-desk for Blumfeld and two standing desks for the two assistants subordinate to him. Although these standing desks are so small and narrow as to suggest they are meant for schoolchildren, this office is very crowded and the assistants cannot sit down, for then there would be no place for Blumfeld's chair. As a result they stand all day, pressed against their desks. For them of course this is very uncomfortable, but it also makes it very difficult for Blumfeld to keep an eye on them. They often press eagerly against their desks not so much in order to work as to whisper to one another or even to take forty winks. They give Blumfeld a great deal of trouble; they don't help him sufficiently with the enormous amount of work that is imposed on him. This work involves supervising the whole distribu-tion of fabrics and cash among the women home-workers who are employed by the factory for the manufacture of certain fancy com-modities. To appreciate the magnitude of this task an intimate know-ledge of the general conditions is necessary. But since Blumfeld's immediate superior has died some years ago, no one any longer possesses this knowledge, which is also why Blumfeld cannot grant anyone the right to pronounce an opinion on his work. The manufac-turer, Herr Ottomar, for instance, clearly underestimates Blumfeld's work; no doubt he recognizes that in the course of twenty years Blumfeld has deserved well of the factory, and this he acknowledges not only because he is obliged to, but also because he respects Blumfeld as a loyal, trustworthy person – he underestimates his work, nevertheless, for he believes it could be conducted by methods more simple and therefore in every respect more profitable than those employed by Blumfeld. It is said, and it is probably not incorrect, that Ottomar shows himself so rarely in Blumfeld's depart-

ment simply to spare himself the annoyance which the sight of
Blumfeld's working methods causes him. To be so unappreciated is
undoubtedly sad for Blumfeld, but there is no remedy, for he cannot
very well compel Ottomar to spend let us say a whole month on end
in Blumfeld's department in order to study the great variety of work
being accomplished there, to apply his own allegedly better methods,
and to let himself be convinced of Blumfeld's soundness by the
collapse of the department – which would be the inevitable result.
And so Blumfeld carries on his work undeterred as before, gives a
little start whenever Ottomar appears after a long absence, then with
the subordinate's sense of duty makes a feeble effort to explain to
Ottomar this or that arrangement, whereupon the latter, his eyes
lowered and giving a silent nod, passes on. But what worries Blumfeld
more than this lack of appreciation is the thought that one day he
will be compelled to leave his job, the immediate consequence of
which will be pandemonium, a confusion no one will be able to
straighten out because so far as he knows there isn't a single soul in
the factory capable of replacing him and of carrying on his job in a
manner that could be relied upon to prevent months of the most
serious interruptions. Needless to say, if the boss underestimates an
employee the latter's colleagues try their best to surpass him in this
respect. In consequence everyone underestimates Blumfeld's work;
no one considers it necessary to spend any time training in Blumfeld's
department, and when new employees are hired not one of them is
ever assigned to Blumfeld. As a result Blumfeld's department lacks a
younger generation to carry on. When Blumfeld, who up to then had
been managing the entire department with the help of only one
servant, demanded an assistant, weeks of bitter fighting ensued.
Almost every day Blumfeld appeared in Ottomar's office and explained to him calmly and in minute detail why an assistant was
needed in his department. He was needed not by any means because
Blumfeld wished to spare himself, Blumfeld had no intention of
sparing himself, he was doing more than his share of work and this
he had no desire to change, but would Herr Ottomar please consider
how in the course of time the business had grown, how every department had been correspondingly enlarged, with the exception of Blumfeld's department, which was invariably forgotten! And would he

consider too how the work had increased just there! When Blumfeld
had entered the firm, a time Herr Ottomar could probably not
remember, they had employed some ten seamstresses, today the
number varied between fifty and sixty. Such a job requires great
energy; Blumfeld could guarantee that he was completely wearing
himself out in this work, but that he will continue to master it
completely he can henceforth no longer guarantee. True, Herr Ottomar had never flatly refused Blumfeld's requests, this was something he could not do to an old employee, but the manner in which
he hardly listened, in which he talked to others over Blumfeld's
head, made half-hearted promises and had forgotten everything in a
few days – this behaviour was insulting to say the least. Not actually
to Blumfeld. Blumfeld is no romantic; pleasant as honour and recognition may be, Blumfeld can do without them; in spite of everything
he will stick to his desk as long as it is at all possible, in any case he
is in the right, and right, even though on occasion it may take a long
time, must prevail in the end. True, Blumfeld has at last been given
two assistants, but what assistants! One might have thought Ottomar
had realized he could express his contempt for the department even
better by granting rather than by refusing it these assistants. It was
even possible that Ottomar had kept Blumfeld waiting so long because he was looking for two assistants just like these, and – as may
be imagined – took a long time to find them. And now of course
Blumfeld could no longer complain; if he did, the answer could
easily be foreseen: after all, he had asked for one assistant and had
been given two, that's how cleverly Ottomar had arranged things.
Needless to say, Blumfeld complained just the same, but only because
his predicament all but forced him to do so, not because he still
hoped for any redress. Nor did he complain emphatically, but only
by the way, whenever the occasion arose. Nevertheless, among his
spiteful colleagues the rumour soon spread that someone had asked
Ottomar if it were really possible that Blumfeld, who after all had
been given such unusual aid, was still complaining. To which Ottomar answered that this was correct. Blumfeld was still complaining,
and rightly so. He, Ottomar, had at last realized this and he intended
gradually to assign to Blumfeld one assistant for each seamstress, in
other words some sixty in all. In case this number should prove

insufficient, however, he would let him have even more and would not cease until the bedlam, which had been developing for years in Blumfeld's department, was complete. Now it cannot be denied that in this remark Ottomar's manner of speech had been cleverly imitated, but Blumfeld had no doubts whatever that Ottomar would not dream of speaking about him in such a way. The whole thing was a fabrication of the loafers in the offices on the first floor. Blumfeld ignored it – if only he could as calmly have ignored the presence of the assistants! But there they stood, and could not be spirited away. Pale, weak children. According to their credentials they had already passed school age, but in reality this was difficult to believe. In fact their rightful place was so clearly at their mother's knee that one would hardly have dared to entrust them to a teacher. They still couldn't even move properly; standing up for any length of time tired them inordinately, especially when they first arrived. When left to themselves they promptly doubled up in their weakness, standing hunched and crooked in their corner. Blumfeld tried to point out to them that if they went on giving in to their indolence they would become cripples for life. To ask the assistants to make the slightest move was to take a risk; once when one of them had been ordered to carry something a short distance, he had run so eagerly that he had banged his knee against a desk. The room had been full of seamstresses, the desks covered in merchandise, but Blumfeld had been obliged to neglect everything and take the sobbing assistant into the office and there bandage his wound. Yet even this zeal on the part of the assistant was superficial; like actual children they tried once in a while to excel, but far more often – indeed almost always – they tried to divert their superior's attention and to cheat him. Once, at a time of the most intensive work, Blumfeld had rushed past them, dripping with sweat, and had observed them secretly swapping stamps among the bales of merchandise. He had felt like banging them on the head with his fists, it would have been the only possible punishment for such behaviour, but they were after all only children and Blumfeld could not very well knock children down. And so he continued to put up with them. Originally he had imagined that the assistants would help him with the essential chores which at the moment of the distribution of goods required so much effort and vigilance. He had imagined himself standing in the centre behind his desk, keeping an eye on everything and making the entries in the books while the assistants ran to and fro, distributing everything according to his orders. He had imagined that his supervision which, sharp as it was, could not cope with such a crowd, would be complemented by the assistants' attention; he had hoped that these assistants would gradually acquire experience, cease depending entirely on his orders, and finally learn to discriminate on their own between the seamstresses as to their trustworthiness and requirements. Blumfeld soon realized that all these hopes had been in vain and that he could not afford to let them even talk to the seamstresses. From the beginning they had ignored some of the seamstresses, either from fear or dislike; others to whom they felt partial they would sometimes run to meet at the door. To them the assistants would bring whatever the women wanted, pressing it almost secretly into their hands, although the seamstresses were perfectly entitled to receive it, would collect on a bare shelf for these favourites various cuttings, worthless remnants, but also a few still useful odds and ends, waving them blissfully at the women behind Blumfeld's back and in return having sweets popped into their mouths. Blumfeld of course soon put an end to this mischief and the moment the seamstresses arrived he ordered the assistants back into their glass-enclosed cubicles. But for a long time they considered this to be a grave injustice, they sulked, wilfully broke their nibs, and sometimes, although not daring to raise their heads, even knocked loudly against the glass panes in order to attract the seamstresses' attention to the bad treatment which in their opinion they were suffering at Blumfeld's hands.

But the wrong they do themselves the assistants cannot see. For instance, they almost always arrive late at the office. Blumfeld, their superior, who from his earliest youth has considered it natural to arrive half an hour before the office opens – not from ambition or an exaggerated sense of duty but simply from a certain feeling of decency – often has to wait more than an hour for his assistants. Chewing his breakfast roll he stands behind his desk, looking through the accounts in the seamstresses' little books. Soon he is immersed in his work and thinking of nothing else when suddenly he receives such a shock

that his pen continues to tremble in his hand for some while afterwards. One of the assistants has dashed in, looking as though he is
about to collapse; he is holding on to something with one hand while
the other is pressed against his heaving chest. All this, however,
simply means that he is making excuses for being late, excuses so
absurd that Blumfeld purposely ignores them, for if he didn't he
would have to give the young man a well-deserved thrashing. As it
is, he just glances at him for a moment, points with outstretched
hand at the cubicle, and turns back to his work. Now one really
might expect the assistant to appreciate his superior's kindness and
hurry to his place. No, he doesn't hurry, he dawdles about, he walks
on tiptoe, slowly placing one foot in front of the other. Is he trying
to ridicule his superior? No. Again it's just that mixture of fear and
self-complacency against which one is powerless. How else explain
the fact that even today Blumfeld, who has himself arrived unusually
late in the office and now after a long wait – he doesn't feel like
checking the books – sees, through the clouds of dust raised by the
stupid servant with his broom, the two assistants sauntering peacefully along the street? Arm in arm, they appear to be telling one
another important things which, however, are sure to have only the
remotest and very likely irrelevant connections with the office. The
nearer they approach the glass door, the slower they walk. One of
them seizes the door handle but fails to turn it; they just go on
talking, listening, laughing. 'Hurry out and open the door for our
gentlemen!' shouts Blumfeld at the servant, throwing up his hands.
But when the assistants come in, Blumfeld no longer feels like
quarrelling, ignores their greetings, and goes to his desk. He starts
doing his accounts, but now and again glances up to see what his
assistants are up to. One of them seems very tired, yawns and rubs
his eyes. When hanging up his overcoat he takes the opportunity to
lean against the wall. In the street he seemed lively enough, but the
proximity of work tires him. The other assistant, however, is eager
to work, but only work of a certain kind. For a long time it has been
his wish to be allowed to sweep. But this is work to which he is not
entitled; sweeping is exclusively the servant's job; in itself Blumfeld
would have nothing against the assistant sweeping, let the assistant
sweep, he can't make a worse job of it than the servant, but if the

assistant wants to sweep then he must come earlier, before the servant begins to sweep, and not spend on it time that is reserved exclusively for office work. But since the young man is totally deaf to any argument, at least the servant – that half-blind old buffer whom the boss would certainly not tolerate in any department but Blumfeld's and who is still alive only by the grace of the boss and God – at least the servant might be sensible and hand the broom for a moment to the young man who, being clumsy, would soon lose his interest and run after the servant with the broom in order to persuade him to go on sweeping. It appears, however, that the servant feels especially responsible for the sweeping; one can see how he, the moment the young man approaches him, tries to grasp the broom more firmly with his trembling hands; he even stands still and stops sweeping so as to direct his full attention to the ownership of the broom. The assistant doesn't actually plead in words, for he is afraid of Blumfeld, who is ostensibly doing his accounts; moreover, ordinary speech is useless, since the servant can be made to hear only by excessive shouting. So at first the assistant tugs the servant by the sleeve. The servant knows, of course, what it is about, glowers at the assistant, shakes his head and pulls the broom nearer, up to his chest. Whereupon the assistant folds his hands and pleads. Actually, he has no hope of achieving anything by pleading, but the pleading amuses him and so he pleads. The other assistant follows the goings-on with low laughter and seems to think, heaven knows why, that Blumfeld can't hear him. The pleading makes not the slightest impression on the servant, who turns round and thinks he can safely use the broom again. The assistant, however, has skipped after him on tiptoe and, rubbing his hands together imploringly, now pleads from another side. This turning of the one and skipping of the other is repeated several times. Finally the servant feels cut off from all sides and realizes – something which, had he been slightly less stupid, he might have realized from the beginning – that he will be tired out long before the assistant. So, looking for help elsewhere, he wags his finger at the assistant and points at Blumfeld, suggesting that he will lodge a complaint if the assistant refuses to desist. The assistant realizes that if he is to get the broom at all he'll have to hurry. So he impudently makes a grab for it. An involuntary scream from the other assistant heralds the imminent decision. The servant saves the broom once more by taking a step back and dragging it after him. But now the assistant is up in arms: with open mouth and flashing eyes he leaps forward, the servant tries to escape, but his old legs wobble rather than run, the assistant tugs at the broom and though he doesn't succeed in getting it he nevertheless causes it to drop and in this way it is lost to the servant. Also apparently to the assistant for, the moment the broom falls, all three, the two assistants and the servant, are paralysed, for now Blumfeld is bound to discover everything. And sure enough Blumfeld at his peephole glances up as though taking in the situation only now. He stares at each one with a stern and searching eye, even the broom on the floor does not escape his notice. Perhaps the silence has lasted too long or perhaps the assistant can no longer suppress his desire to sweep, in any case he bends down – albeit very carefully, as though about to grab an animal rather than a broom – seizes it, passes it over the floor, but, when Blumfeld jumps up and steps out of his cubicle, promptly casts it aside in alarm. 'Both of you back to work! And not another sound out of you!' shouts Blumfeld, and with an outstretched hand he directs the two assistants back to their desks. They obey at once, but not shamefaced or with lowered heads, rather they squeeze themselves stiffly past Blumfeld, staring him straight in the eye as though trying in this way to stop him from beating them. Yet they might have learned from experience that Blumfeld on principle never beats anyone. But they are over-apprehensive, and without any tact keep trying to protest their real or imaginary rights.

THE WARDEN OF THE TOMB

Small workroom, high window, beyond it a bare treetop. PRINCE *at writing table, leaning back in chair, looking out of window.* CHAMBERLAIN, *white beard, youthfully squeezed into tight jacket, standing against wall near centre door.*
Pause.

PRINCE [*turning from window*]: Well?

CHAMBERLAIN: I cannot recommend it, your Highness.

PRINCE: Why?

CHAMBERLAIN: I can't quite formulate my objections at the moment. I'm expressing only a fraction of what's on my mind when I quote the universal saying: 'Let the dead rest in peace.'

PRINCE: That's my opinion, too.

CHAMBERLAIN: In that case I haven't properly understood.

PRINCE: So it seems. [*Pause.*] Perhaps the only thing that disconcerts you is that instead of going ahead with the arrangement, I announced it to you first.

CHAMBERLAIN: The announcement certainly burdens me with great responsibility which I must endeavour to live up to.

PRINCE: Don't speak of responsibility! [*Pause.*] Let's see. Hitherto the tomb in the Friedrichspark has been guarded by a warden who lives in a lodge at the park's entrance. Was there anything wrong with this?

CHAMBERLAIN: Certainly not. The tomb is more than four hundred years old and has always been guarded in this way.

PRINCE: It could be an abuse. But it isn't an abuse, is it?

CHAMBERLAIN: It is a necessary arrangement.

PRINCE: All right then, a necessary arrangement. I've been here in the castle quite some time now, have gained some insight into details which hitherto have been entrusted to strangers – they manage fairly well – and I've come to this conclusion: the Warden up there in the park is not enough. There must also be a guard down in the tomb. It probably won't be a pleasant job. But experience has proved that willing and suitable people can be found for any job.

CHAMBERLAIN: Needless to say, any orders issued by your Highness will be carried out, even if the necessity of the order is not fully understood.

PRINCE [*starting up*]: Necessity! Do you mean to say that a guard at the park gate is necessary? The Friedrichspark belongs to the castle park, is entirely surrounded by it. The castle park itself is amply guarded – by the army, what's more. So why a special guard for the Friedrichspark? Isn't this a mere formality? A pleasant deathbed for the wretched old man who is keeping watch there?

CHAMBERLAIN: Formality it is, but a necessary one. A demonstration of reverence for the illustrious dead.

PRINCE: And what about the guard in the tomb itself?

CHAMBERLAIN: In my opinion this would have a police connotation. It would mean a real guarding of unreal things beyond the human sphere.

PRINCE: For my family this tomb represents the frontier of humanity, and it's on this frontier that I wish to post a guard. As for the police connotation, as you call it, we can question the Warden himself. I've sent for him. [*Rings a bell.*]

CHAMBERLAIN: He's a confused old man, if I may say so, already quite out of hand.

PRINCE: If that's so, all the more reason for strengthening the guard in the way I've suggested.

[*Enter servant.*]

PRINCE: The Warden of the tomb!

[*Servant leads in Warden, holding him tight round the waist to prevent him from collapsing. Ancient red livery hanging loosely about Warden, brightly polished silver buttons, several decorations. Cap in hand, he trembles under the gentlemen's gaze.*]

PRINCE: Put him on the divan!

[*Servant lays him down and goes off. Pause. A faint rattling in Warden's throat.*]

PRINCE [*again in armchair*]: Can you hear?

[WARDEN *tries to answer but fails, is too exhausted, sinks back again.*]

PRINCE: Try to pull yourself together. We're waiting.

CHAMBERLAIN [*leaning over Prince*]: What could this man give information about? And credible and important information at that? He ought to be taken straight to bed.

WARDEN: Not to bed – still strong – fairly – can still hold my end up.

PRINCE: So you should. You've only just turned sixty. Granted, you look very weak.

WARDEN: I'll pick up in no time – feel better in a minute.

PRINCE: It wasn't meant as a reproach. I'm only sorry you aren't feeling well. Have you anything to complain about?

WARDEN: Hard work – hard work – not complaining – but very weak – wrestling bouts every night.

PRINCE: What d'you say?

WARDEN: Hard work.

PRINCE: You said something else.

WARDEN: Wrestling bouts.

PRINCE: Wrestling bouts? What kind of wrestling bouts?

WARDEN: With the blessed ancestors.

PRINCE: I don't understand. D'you have bad dreams?

WARDEN: No dreams – don't sleep.

PRINCE: Then let's hear about these – these wrestling bouts.

[WARDEN *remains silent.*]

PRINCE [*to Chamberlain*]: Why doesn't he speak?

CHAMBERLAIN [*hurrying to Warden*]: He may die any minute.

[PRINCE *stands up.*]

WARDEN [*as Chamberlain touches him*]: Don't, don't, don't! [*Fights off Chamberlain's hands, then collapses in tears.*]

PRINCE: We're tormenting him.

CHAMBERLAIN: How?

PRINCE: I don't know.

CHAMBERLAIN: Coming to the castle, having to present himself

here, the sight of your Highness, this questioning – he no longer
has the wits to face all this.

PRINCE [*still staring at the Warden*]: That's not it. [*Goes to divan,
bends over Warden, takes his little skull in his hands.*] Mustn't cry.
What are you crying for? We wish you well. I realize your job
isn't easy. You've certainly deserved well of my family. So stop
crying and tell us all about it.

WARDEN: But I'm so afraid of that gentleman there – [*Looks at
Chamberlain, more threateningly than afraid.*]

PRINCE [*to Chamberlain*]: If we want him to talk I'm afraid you'll
have to leave.

CHAMBERLAIN: But look, your Highness, he's foaming at the mouth.
He's seriously ill.

PRINCE [*absent-mindedly*]: Please go, it won't take long.

[*Exit CHAMBERLAIN. PRINCE sits on edge of divan. Pause.*]

PRINCE: Why were you afraid of him?

WARDEN [*surprisingly composed*]: I wasn't afraid. Me afraid of a servant?

PRINCE: He's not a servant. He's a Count, free and rich.

WARDEN: A servant all the same, you are the master.

PRINCE: If you like it that way. But you said yourself that you were
afraid.

WARDEN: Afraid of saying things in front of him which are meant
only for you. Haven't I already said too much in front of him?

PRINCE: So we're on terms of intimacy, and yet today is the first
time I've seen you.

WARDEN: Seen for the first time, but you've always known that I
[*raising his forefinger*] hold the most important position at Court.
You even acknowledged it publicly by awarding me the medal
'Red-as-Fire'. Here! [*Holds up the medal on his coat.*]

PRINCE: No, that's the medal for twenty-five years' service at Court.
My grandfather gave you that. But I'll decorate you, too.

WARDEN: Do as you please and grant me whatever you think I
deserve. I've acted as your tomb Warden for thirty years.

PRINCE: Not mine. My reign has lasted hardly a year.

WARDEN [*lost in thought*]: Thirty years.

[*Pause.*]

WARDEN [*remembering only half of the Prince's remark*]: Nights last years there.

PRINCE: I haven't yet had a report from your office. What's your work like?

WARDEN: Every night the same. Every night till the heart beats as if it were about to burst.

PRINCE: Is it only night duty, then? Night duty for an old man like you?

WARDEN: That's just it, your Highness. It's day duty. A loafer's job. There one sits, at the front door, with one's mouth open in the sunshine. Sometimes the watchdog pats one on the knee with its paws, and then lies down again. That's all that ever happens.

PRINCE: Well?

WARDEN [*nodding*]: But it has been changed to night duty.

PRINCE: By whom?

WARDEN: By the lords of the tomb.

PRINCE: You know them?

WARDEN: Yes.

PRINCE: They come to see you?

WARDEN: Yes.

PRINCE: Last night, too?

WARDEN: Last night, too.

PRINCE: What was it like?

WARDEN [*sitting up straight*]: Same as usual.

[PRINCE *stands up.*]

WARDEN: Same as usual. Quiet till midnight. I'm lying in bed – excuse me – smoking my pipe. My granddaughter is asleep in the next bed. At midnight comes the first knock at the window. I look at the clock. Always to the minute. Two more knocks, they mingle with the striking of the tower clock, but I can still hear them. These are no human knuckles. But I know all that and don't budge. Then it clears its throat outside, it's surprised that in spite of all that knocking I haven't opened the window. Let his princely Highness be surprised! The old Warden is still there! [*Shows his fist.*]

PRINCE: You're threatening me?

WARDEN [*doesn't immediately understand*]: Not you. The one at the window!

PRINCE: Who is it?

WARDEN: He shows himself at once. All of a sudden window and
shutters are opened. I just have time to throw the blanket over my
grandchild's face. The storm blows in, promptly puts the light
out. Duke Friedrich! His face with beard and hair completely fills
my poor window. How he has grown throughout the centuries!
When he opens his mouth to speak the wind blows his old beard
between his teeth and he bites on it.

PRINCE: Just a moment. You say Duke Friedrich? Which Friedrich?

WARDEN: Duke Friedrich, just Duke Friedrich.

PRINCE: Is that the name he gives?

WARDEN [*anxiously*]: No, he doesn't give it.

PRINCE: And yet you know – [*breaking off*] – Go on!

WARDEN: Shall I go on?

PRINCE: Of course. All this very much concerns me. There must be
an error in the distribution of labour. You're overworked.

WARDEN [*kneeling*]: Don't take my job away, your Highness. Having
lived for you all these years, let me also die for you! Don't wall up
the grave I'm struggling towards. I serve willingly and am still
strong enough to serve. To be granted an audience like today's, to
take a rest with my master – this gives me strength for ten years.

PRINCE [*putting Warden back on divan*]: No one's going to take your
job from you. How could I get along without your experience?
But I'll appoint another Warden, then you'll become Head
Warden.

WARDEN: Am I not good enough? Have I ever let anyone pass?

PRINCE: Into the Friedrichspark?

WARDEN: No, out of the park. Who'd want to come in? If ever anyone
stops at the railing I beckon to him from the window and he runs
away. But out! Everyone wants to get out. After midnight you can
see all the voices from the grave assembled round my house. I think
it's only because they are so closely packed together that the whole
lot of them don't burst through my narrow window. If it gets too
bad, however, I grab the lantern from under my bed, swing it high,
and with laughter and moaning these incredible creatures scatter in
all directions. Then I can hear them rustling even in the furthest
bush at the end of the park. But they soon gather together again.

PRINCE: And do they tell you what they want?

WARDEN: First they give orders. Especially Duke Friedrich. No living being could be so confident. Every night for thirty years he has been expecting me to give in.

PRINCE: If he has been coming for thirty years it can't be Duke Friedrich, for he has been dead only fifteen years. On the other hand, he is the only one of that name in the tomb.

WARDEN [*too carried away by his story*]: That I don't know, your Highness, I never went to school. I only know how he begins. 'Old dog,' he begins at the window, 'the gentlemen are knocking and you just stay in your filthy bed.' They have a particular grudge against beds, by the way. And now every night we have the same conversation, he outside, I opposite him, my back against the door. I say: 'I'm only on day duty.' The Duke turns and shouts into the park: 'He's only on day duty.' Whereupon all the assembled aristocracy burst out laughing. Then the Duke says to me again: 'But it is day.' I say curtly: 'You're wrong.' The Duke: 'Night or day, open the door.' I: 'That's against my orders.' And with my pipe I point at a notice on the door. The Duke: 'But you're our Warden.' I: 'Your Warden, but employed by the reigning Prince.' He: 'Our Warden, that's the main thing. So open up, and be quick about it.' I: 'No.' He: 'Idiot, you'll lose your job. Prince Leo has invited us for today.'

PRINCE [*quickly*]: I?

WARDEN: You. [*Pause.*] When I hear your name I lose my firmness. That's why I took the precaution of leaning against the door in the first place. Outside, everyone's singing your name. 'Where's the invitation?' I ask weakly. 'Bedbug!' he shouts, and really wakes me up without meaning to, 'you doubt my ducal word?' I say: 'I have no orders, so I won't open, I won't open, I won't open!' – 'He won't open!' shouts the Duke outside. 'So come on, all of you, the whole dynasty! At the door! We'll open it ourselves.' And a moment later there's nothing under my window.

[*Pause.*]

PRINCE: Is that all?

WARDEN: All? My real service begins only now. I rush out of the door, round the house, and promptly run into the Duke and there we are, locked in combat. He so big, I so small, he so broad, I so thin, I can fight only with his feet, but now and again he lifts me up in the air and then I fight up there, too. All his comrades stand round in a circle and make fun of me. One, for instance, cuts open my trousers behind and they all play with the tail of my shirt while I'm fighting. Can't understand why they laugh, as until now I've always won.

PRINCE: How is it possible for you to win? Have you any weapons?

WARDEN: I carried weapons only during the first years. What good could they be against him? They only hampered me. We just fight with our fists, or rather with the strength of our breath. And you're in my thoughts all the time. [*Pause.*] But I never doubt my victory. Only sometimes I'm afraid the Duke will let me slip through his fingers and forget that he's fighting.

PRINCE: And when do you win?

WARDEN: At dawn. Then he throws me down and spits at me. That's his confession of defeat. But I have to go on lying there for an hour before I can get my breath back properly.

[*Pause.*]

PRINCE [*standing up*]: But tell me, don't you know what they really want?

WARDEN: To get out of the park.

PRINCE: But why?

WARDEN: That I don't know.

PRINCE: Haven't you asked?

WARDEN: No.

PRINCE: Why not?

WARDEN: It would embarrass me. But if you wish, I'll ask them today.

PRINCE [*shocked, loud*]: Today!

WARDEN [*authoritatively*]: Yes, today.

PRINCE: And you can't even guess what they want?

WARDEN [*thoughtfully*]: No. [*Pause.*] Perhaps I ought to add that sometimes in the early mornings while I'm lying there trying to get my breath and even too weak to open my eyes, there comes a delicate moist creature, rather hairy to the touch, a latecomer, the Countess Isabella. She runs her hand all over me, catches hold of my beard, her whole body glides along my neck, under my chin, and she's in the habit of saying: 'Not the others, but me – let me out.' I shake my head as much as I can. 'I want to go to Prince Leo, to offer him my hand.' I keep on shaking my head. 'But me, me!' I can still hear her crying, then she's gone. And my grand-daughter appears with blankets, wraps me up in them, and waits with me till I can walk on my own. An exceptionally good girl.

PRINCE: Isabella? The name's unknown to me. [*Pause.*] To offer me her hand! [*Goes to window, looks out. Back to table, rings.*]

[*Enter servant.*]

PRINCE: The Chamberlain.

[CHAMBERLAIN *enters, at same time* WARDEN *falls off divan with a little cry.*]

PRINCE [*leaps to his side*]: Eternal improvidence! I ought to have foreseen this! The doctor! The servants!

[*Exit* CHAMBERLAIN, *returns at once with servants, remains by open door.*]

PRINCE [*kneeling by Warden*]: Water! Prepare a bed for him! Wher-ever you like. Next to my bedroom. Bring a stretcher! Is the doctor coming? What a time he takes! The pulse is so weak. I can't feel his heart! These pathetic ribs! How worn out everything is. But wait, now he's breathing better. Healthy stock, still keeps going even in the last extremity. But the doctor! Will he never come? [*Looks towards door.*]

[WARDEN *raises his hand.* LORD HIGH STEWARD *enters slowly, remains by door.*]

LORD HIGH STEWARD [*youngish man, officer's uniform, coolly observ-ant gaze, loudly*]: The doctor can't be here for a quarter of an hour. He's gone out. A rider has been sent after him.

PRINCE [*more controlled, with a glance at Warden*]: We can wait. He's more peaceful.

[*Enter servant with stretcher.*]

PRINCE [*stands up; to* LORD HIGH STEWARD]: So you've come along too.

LORD HIGH STEWARD: I saw all the excitement in the corridors. I was forced to conclude that there had been an accident.

PRINCE [*without replying, by the stretcher-bearers, helps with loading*]:

Handle him gently. Go gently with your great paws! Lift his head a little. Nearer the stretcher. The pillow further down the back. His arm! His arm! You're wretched, wretched orderlies. Will you ever be so exhausted as this man on the stretcher? – There. – And now the very, very slowest step. And above all steadily. I'm keeping behind you.

THE BRIDGE

I WAS stiff and cold, I was a bridge, I lay over an abyss; my toes buried deep on one side, my hands on the other, I had fastened my teeth in crumbling clay. The tails of my coat fluttered at my sides. Far below brawled the icy trout stream. No tourist strayed to this impassable height, the bridge was not yet marked on the maps. Thus I lay and waited; I had to wait; without falling no bridge, once erected, can cease to be a bridge. One day towards evening, whether it was the first, whether it was the thousandth, I cannot tell – my thoughts were always in confusion, and always, always moving in a circle – towards evening in summer, the roar of the stream grown deeper, I heard the footstep of a man! Towards me, towards me. Stretch yourself, bridge, make yourself ready, beam without rail, hold up the one who is entrusted to you. If his steps are uncertain steady them unobtrusively, but if he staggers then make yourself known and like a mountain god hurl him to the bank. He came, he tapped me with the iron spike of his stick, then with it he lifted my coat-tails and folded them upon me; he plunged his spike into my bushy hair, and for a good while he let it rest there, no doubt as he gazed far round him into the distance. But then – I was just following him in thought over mountain and valley – he leapt with both feet on to the middle of my body. I shuddered with wild pain, quite uncomprehending. Who was it? A child? A gymnast? A dare-devil? A suicide? A tempter? A destroyer? And I turned over to look at him. A bridge turns over! And before I had fully turned I was already falling, I fell, and in a moment I was ripped apart and impaled on the sharp stones that had always gazed up at me so peacefully out of the rushing waters.

THE HUNTER GRACCHUS

I

TWO boys were sitting on the harbour wall playing dice. On the steps of a monument a man was reading a newspaper, in the shadow of the sword-wielding hero. A girl was filling her tub at the fountain. A fruit-seller was lying beside his wares, looking out across the lake. Through the empty window and door openings of a tavern two men could be seen drinking their wine in the depths. Out in front the proprietor was sitting at a table dozing. A bark glided silently into the little harbour, as if borne over the water. A man in a blue overall climbed ashore and drew the ropes through the rings. Two other men, wearing dark coats with silver buttons, carried out past the boatman a bier draped with a great tasselled cloth of flower-patterned silk, beneath which there evidently lay a man. Nobody on the quay troubled about the newcomers; even when they lowered the bier to wait for the boatman, who was still busy with the ropes, nobody approached, nobody asked them a question, nobody gave them a closer look.

The boatman was delayed a little longer by a woman who now appeared on deck with a child at her breast and her hair falling loose. Then he came up and indicated a yellowish two-storeyed house that rose abruptly on the left close to the water; the bearers took up their burden and carried it through the low but gracefully pillared door-way. A little boy opened the window just in time to see the party vanishing into the house, then hastily shut the window again. Now the door was shut too; it was of black oak, carefully joined. A flock of doves which had been flying round the bell-tower alighted in front of the house. As if their food were stored within, the doves gathered before the door. One of them flew up to the first floor and pecked at the window-pane. They were bright-hued, well cared-for, lively birds. The woman on the boat flung grain across to them in a great arc; they pecked it up and flew over to the woman.

An old man in a top-hat with a mourning-band came down one of the narrow, steep little alleyways that led to the harbour. He looked round attentively, everything disturbed him; the sight of some rubbish in a corner made him grimace, fruit skins were lying on the steps of the monument and he swept them off in passing with a stick. He rapped at the pillared door, at the same time taking his top-hat in his black-gloved right hand. The door was opened at once; some fifty little boys formed a lane in the long entrance-hall and bowed.

The boatman came down the stairs, greeted the gentleman in black and led him up; on the first floor he escorted him round the delicate loggia that framed the courtyard, and while the boys crowded after them at a respectful distance they both entered a cool, spacious room at the rear side of the building, from which no other house, but only a bare grey-black wall of rock was to be seen. The bearers were busy setting up and lighting several long candles at the head of the bier; but these gave no light to the room, it was just as if the shadows had been merely startled from their rest and sent flickering over the walls. The cloth covering the bier had been thrown back. Lying there was a man with wildly matted hair and beard, his skin sunburned, rather like a hunter in appearance. He lay there with his eyes closed, motionless and apparently without breathing, yet only the surroundings indicated that perhaps this man was dead.

The gentleman stepped up to the bier, laid his hand on the brow of the recumbent figure, then knelt down and prayed. The boatman made a sign to the bearers to leave the room; they went out, drove away the boys who had gathered outside, and shut the door. But even that did not seem to make it quiet enough for the gentleman; he looked at the boatman, who understood and went out through a side door into the next room. At once the man on the bier opened his eyes, turned his face towards the gentleman with a painful smile and said: 'Who are you?' Without visible surprise the gentleman rose from his kneeling position and replied: 'The burgomaster of Riva.'

The man on the bier nodded, feebly stretched out his arms to indicate a chair, and said, after the burgomaster had accepted the invitation: 'I knew that of course, Mr Burgomaster, but for the first few moments I always find that I have forgotten everything, everything is in a whirl, and it is better for me to ask even if I do know the answers. Probably you also know that I am the hunter Gracchus.'

'Certainly,' said the burgomaster. 'Your arrival was announced to me during the night. We had been asleep for some time. Then towards midnight my wife cried: "Salvatore" – that's my name – "look at that dove on the window-ledge!" It really was a dove, but as big as a cock. It flew over to my ear and said: "Tomorrow the dead hunter Gracchus is coming, receive him in the name of the town."'

The hunter nodded and passed the tip of his tongue between his lips: 'Yes, the doves fly on ahead of me. But do you think, Mr Burgomaster, that I should remain in Riva?'

'That I cannot yet say,' replied the burgomaster. 'Are you dead?'

'Yes,' said the hunter, 'as you see. Many years ago, indeed it must be an uncommonly long time ago, I fell from a rock in the Black Forest – that is in Germany – when I was hunting a chamois. Since then I have been dead.'

'But you are alive too,' said the burgomaster.

'To some extent,' said the hunter, 'to some extent I am alive too. My death boat went off course; a wrong turn of the wheel, a moment's absence of mind on the part of the helmsman, the distraction of my lovely native country, I cannot tell what it was; I only know this, that I remained on earth and that ever since my boat has been sailing earthly waters. So I, who asked for nothing better than to live among my mountains, travel after my death through all the lands of the earth.'

'And you have no part in the other world?' asked the burgomaster, knitting his brow.

'I am for ever,' replied the hunter, 'on the great stairway that leads up to it. On that infinitely wide and open stairway I clamber about, sometimes up, sometimes down, sometimes on the right, sometimes on the left, always in motion. But when I soar up with a supreme effort and can already see the gate shining above me, I wake up on my old boat, still forlornly stranded in some earthly sea. The fundamental error of my one-time death grins at me in my cabin; Julia, the boatman's wife, knocks at the door and brings to my bier the morning drink of the land whose coasts we happen to be passing.'

'A terrible fate,' said the burgomaster, raising his hand defensively. 'And you bear no blame for it?'

'None,' said the hunter, 'I was a hunter; am I to be blamed for that? I was assigned my place as a hunter in the Black Forest, where there were still wolves in those days; I used to lie in ambush, shoot, hit my mark, flay the skins from my victims: am I to be blamed for that? My labours were blessed. I was known as the great hunter of the Black Forest. Am I to be blamed for that?'

'I am not called upon to decide the matter,' said the burgomaster, 'but it seems to me too that all is blameless enough. But who, then, is to blame?'

'The boatman,' said the hunter.

'And now you have a mind to stay here in Riva with us?'

'I have no mind,' said the hunter with a smile, and to excuse the jest he laid his hand on the burgomaster's knee. 'I am here, more than that I do not know, more than that I cannot do. My boat has no rudder, it is driven by the wind that blows in the nethermost regions of death.'

2

Nobody will read what I write here, nobody will come to help me; even if there were a commandment to help me, all the doors of all the houses would stay closed, all the windows would stay closed, all the people would lie in their beds with the blankets drawn over their heads, the whole earth one great nocturnal lodging. And there is sense in that, for nobody knows of me, and if anyone knew of me he would not know where I could be found, and if anyone knew where I could be found he would not know how to help me. The idea of wanting to help me is a sickness, and it has to be cured in bed.

All this I know, and so I am not writing to summon help, even though in my lack of self-control I have moments, such as this one for instance, when I seriously consider it. But it will probably suffice to drive out such thoughts if I look round me and call to mind where I am, and where – as I may well be permitted to assert – I have been living for centuries.

As I write this I am lying on a wooden board; I wear – it is no pleasure to look at me – a filthy winding-sheet; my hair and beard, grey and black, are inextricably entangled; my legs are covered by a large woman's shawl of flower-patterned silk with long fringes. At my head stands a sacramental candle and gives me light. On the wall opposite me is a little picture, obviously of a bushman, who is aiming his spear at me and taking cover as best he can behind a magnificently painted shield. On ships one comes across many stupid depictions, but this is one of the stupidest. Otherwise my wooden cage is quite empty. Through the hole in the side come the warm airs of the southern night, and I can hear the water slapping against the old bark.

I have been lying here ever since the time when I, still the live hunter Gracchus at home in the Black Forest, was hunting a chamois and fell. Everything happened in good order. I gave chase, I fell, I bled to death in a ravine, I was dead, and this bark was supposed to convey me to the next world. I can still remember how cheerfully I stretched myself out on this board for the first time; never had the mountains heard such song from me as was heard then by these four still shadowy walls. I had been glad to live and was glad to die; before stepping aboard I joyfully flung down my miserable accoutrements, rifle, knapsack, hunting coat, that I had always worn with pride, and I slipped into my winding sheet like a girl into her wedding-dress. I lay there and waited.

Then there happened . . .

3

In the little harbour, which apart from fishing boats is normally used only by the two passenger steamers that ply the lake, there lay today a strange bark. A clumsy old craft, relatively low and very broad, as filthy as if it had been swamped with bilge water, which still seemed to be dripping down the yellowish sides; the masts incomprehensibly tall, the upper third of the mainmast snapped; wrinkled, coarse, yellowish-brown sails stretched in confusion between the yards; patchwork, too weak for the slightest gust.

I gazed in astonishment at it for a time, waited for someone to show himself on deck; no one appeared. A workman sat down beside me on the harbour wall. 'Whose ship is that?' I asked, 'this is the first time I've seen it.' 'It puts in every two or three years,' said the man, 'and belongs to the hunter Gracchus.'

4

'What is it you say, hunter Gracchus, you have been sailing for hundreds of years by now in this old boat?'

'For fifteen hundred years.'

'And always in this ship?'

'Always in this bark. Bark, I believe, is the correct expression. You aren't familiar with nautical matters?'

'No, I never gave them a thought until today, until I heard about you, until I boarded your ship.'

'Don't apologize. I come from inland too. I was no seafarer, never wanted to be, mountains and forests were my friends, and now – most ancient of mariners, hunter Gracchus, patron saint of sailors, hunter Gracchus, prayed to by the cabin-boy as he wrings his hands, cowering in the crow's-nest on a stormy night. Don't laugh.'

'Me laugh? Certainly not. With a beating heart I stood before your cabin door, with a beating heart I entered. Your friendly manner calms me a little, but I'll never forget whose guest I am.'

'You're right, of course. However it may be, I am hunter Gracchus. Won't you drink some of this wine? I don't know the brand, but it's sweet and heavy, the master looks after me well.'

'Not just now, thank you, I'm too restless. Later perhaps, if you can bear with me that long. Who is the master?'

'The owner of the bark. They are really excellent men, these masters. Except that I don't understand them. I don't mean their language, although of course I often don't understand their language either. But that is by the by. Over the centuries I've learned languages enough, and I could be an interpreter between the men of the present and their forebears of old. But I don't understand the way the masters' minds work. Perhaps you can explain it to me.'

'I'm not very hopeful. How could I explain anything to you, since I'm no more than a babbling babe by comparison?'

'Don't talk like that, I won't have it. You would oblige me if you'd be a little more manly, more self-assured. What am I to do with a mere shadow of a guest? I'll puff him through the porthole into the lake. There are several explanations that I require. You who roam around outside can give me them. But if you sit trembling here at my table, and deceive yourself into supposing that you have forgotten what little you know, then you may as well clear out at once. I believe in speaking plainly.'

'There's something in what you say. I really do have the advantage of you in some respects. So I'll try to control myself. Ask away!'

'It's far, far better for you to exaggerate in that direction and imagine that you have a certain superiority. But you must understand me properly. I'm a human being like you, but many centuries older and as many centuries more impatient. Well, we were going to speak of the masters. Pay attention. And drink some wine, to sharpen your wits. Don't be shy. Take a good swig. There's another large shipload of it.'

'Gracchus, this is an excellent wine. Here's health to the master!'

'Pity he died today. He was a good man and he departed peacefully. Fine, grown-up children stood at his deathbed, at the foot of the bed his wife fainted away, but his last thought was for me. A good man, a Hamburger.'

'Heavens above, a Hamburger, and you know down here in the south that he died today?'

'Well? Should I not know when my master dies? You really are a bit simple.'

'Are you trying to insult me?'

'No, not at all, I do it unintentionally. But you should show less amazement and drink more wine. As for the masters, it's like this: originally the bark belonged to no one.'

'Gracchus, one request. Tell me first briefly but coherently how things really stand with you. To be honest: I simply don't know. You of course take these things for granted and assume, as is your

way, that the whole world knows about them. But in this brief
human life – and life really is brief, Gracchus, try to grasp that – in
this brief life one has one's hands full enough doing the best for
oneself and one's family. And interesting as the hunter Gracchus is –
this is conviction, not flattery – there's no time to think about him,
to inquire about him, let alone worry about him. Perhaps on one's
deathbed, like your Hamburger – that I don't know. Then, perhaps,
a busy man has his first chance to stretch himself out and let the
green hunter Gracchus stroll for once through his idle thoughts. But
otherwise, it's as I've said: I knew nothing about you, business
brought me down here to the harbour, the gang-plank was in place,
I walked across – but now I'd like to hear something coherent about
you.'

'Ah, coherent. The old, old stories. All the books are full of it, in
all the schools the teachers draw it on the blackboard, the mother
dreams of it while suckling her child, and you, my friend, sit here
and ask me how it hangs together. You must have had an exceptionally dissipated youth.'

'Possibly, as is typical of anyone's youth. But as for you, I think
you would find it very useful just to look round in the world a bit. It
may seem funny to you, and sitting here it surprises even me, but
the fact is you are *not* the talk of the town; however many subjects
may be discussed, you are not among them; the world goes on its
way and you pursue your journey, but until today I have never
noticed that your paths have crossed.'

'These are your observations, my dear friend, other people have
made others. There are only two possibilities here. Either you are
concealing what you know about me, and are doing so with some
definite motive. In which case let me tell you frankly, you are on the
wrong track. Or alternatively: you really believe that you can't remember me, because you are confusing my story with someone
else's. In that case I can only tell you: I am – no, I can't, everyone
knows it, and I of all people am supposed to tell you! It's so long
ago. Ask the historians! Agape in their studies, they observe what
happened in the distant past, and they describe it continually. Go to
them, and then come back. It's so long ago. How can I be expected
to retain it in this overcrowded brain?'

'Wait, Gracchus, I'll make it easier for you, I'll ask you some questions. Where do you come from?'

'From the Black Forest, as everyone knows.'

'Of course, from the Black Forest. And so you used to hunt there in about the fourth century?'

'I say, do you know the Black Forest?'

'No.'

'You really don't know anything. The little child of the helmsman knows more, truly far more, than you do. Who wafted you in here anyway? It's a calamity. Your initial modesty was indeed only too well justified. You're a mere nothing that I'm filling up with wine. So now you don't even know the Black Forest. And I was born there. Until I was twenty-five I hunted there. If only the chamois hadn't led me on – well, now you know it – I'd have had a long and happy hunter's life, but I was lured by the chamois! I fell and was killed on the rocks below. Don't ask any more. Here I am, dead, dead, dead. Don't know why I'm here. Was loaded on to the death boat as is right and proper, a miserable corpse, the three or four ministrations were performed upon me, as on everyone – why make an exception for the hunter Gracchus? – everything was in order, I lay stretched out in the boat.'

THE PROCLAMATION

IN our house, this vast building on the outskirts of the town, a tenement-house whose fabric is interspersed with indestructible medieval ruins, there were today distributed, on this foggy ice-cold winter morning, copies of the following proclamation:

> To all my fellow tenants.
>
> I possess five toy rifles; they are hanging in my wardrobe, one on each hook. The first belongs to me, the others may be claimed by anyone who wishes; if there are more than four claimants the extra ones must bring their own rifles with them and deposit them in my wardrobe. For uniformity is essential, without uniformity we shall get nowhere. Incidentally, I have only rifles that are quite useless for any other purpose, the mechanism is broken, the corks are torn off, only the cocks still click. So it will not be difficult to obtain more such rifles if required. But in principle even people without rifles will be acceptable to begin with; at the decisive moment those of us who have rifles will rally round those who are unarmed. A tactical method that proved itself with the first American farmers against the Red Indians; why should it not prove successful here as well, since after all the conditions are similar? And so it is even possible to do without rifles permanently. And even the five rifles are not absolutely necessary, and it is only because they just happen to be there that they may as well be used. But should the four others not wish to carry them, then let them do without. In that case I alone, as the leader, will carry one. But we should have no leader, and so I too will break up my rifle or put it away.

That was the first proclamation. Nobody in our house has the time or the wish to read proclamations, let alone to think them over. Before long the little sheets of paper were floating in the current of filth that, starting from the attics and fed by all the corridors, pours down the staircase and there struggles with the opposing current that swirls up from below. But after a week there came a second proclamation:

Fellow tenants!
So far nobody has sent in his name to me. Apart from the hours when I have to earn my living I have been continuously at home, and during the periods of my absence, when the door of my room has always been left open, there has been a sheet of paper on my table where anybody who wished could enter his name. Nobody has done so.

THE GREAT WALL OF CHINA

THE Great Wall of China has been completed at its most northerly point. From the south-east and the south-west it came up in two sections that were united here. This system of piecemeal construction was also followed within each of the two great armies of labour, the eastern army and the western army. It was done by forming gangs of about a score of labourers, whose task it was to erect a section of wall about five hundred yards long, while the adjoining gang built a stretch of similar length to meet it. But after the junction had been effected the work was not then continued, as one might have expected, where the thousand yards ended; instead the labour-gangs were sent off to continue their work on the wall in some quite different region. This meant of course that many great gaps were left, which were only filled in by slow and gradual stages, and some indeed not until after the completion of the wall had actually been announced. It is even said that there are gaps which have never been filled in at all, and according to some people they are far larger than the completed sections, but this assertion may admittedly be no more than one of the many legends that have grown up round the wall, and which no single person can verify, at least not with his own eyes and his own judgement, owing to the great extent of the structure.

Now one might think at first that it would have been more advantageous in every way to build continuously, or at least continuously within each of the two main sections. After all the wall was intended, as is commonly taught and recognized, to be a protection against the peoples of the north. But how can a wall protect if it is not a continuous structure? Indeed, not only does such a wall give no protection, it is itself in constant danger. These blocks of wall, left standing in deserted regions, could easily be destroyed time and again by the nomads, especially since in those days, alarmed by the wall-building, they kept shifting from place to place with incredible rapidity like locusts, and so perhaps had an even better picture of how the wall was progressing than we who were building it. Nevertheless the work could probably not have been carried out in any other way. To understand this one must consider the following: the wall was to be a protection for centuries; accordingly, scrupulous care in the construction, use of the architectural wisdom of all known periods and peoples, and a permanent sense of personal responsibility on the part of the builders were indispensable prerequisites for the work. For the meaner tasks it was indeed possible to employ ignorant day labourers from the populace, men, women, or children, anyone who was prepared to work for good money; but even for the supervision of four labourers an intelligent man with architectural training was necessary, a man who was capable of sensing in the depths of his heart what was at stake. And of course the higher the task, the greater the requirements. And such men were actually available, if not in the multitudes which this work could have absorbed, yet still in considerable numbers.

The work had not been undertaken lightly. Fifty years before the building was begun, throughout the whole area of China that was to be walled round, architecture, and masonry in particular, had been declared the most important branch of knowledge, all others being recognized only in so far as they had some connection with it. I can still well remember the occasion when as small children, hardly steady on our legs, we were standing in our teacher's garden and had to build a sort of wall out of pebbles, how the teacher tucked up his robe, charged at the wall, knocked it all down of course, and reproved us so severely for the feebleness of our construction that we ran off howling to our parents in all directions. A trivial incident, but indicative of the spirit of the time.

It was my good fortune that the building of the wall was just beginning when, at the age of twenty, I had passed the highest examination of the lowest school. I say good fortune, because many who before that time had reached the highest grade of the training available to them could for years put their knowledge to no purpose;

they drifted around uselessly with the most grandiose architectural schemes in their heads and went to the bad in shoals. But those who were finally appointed to the great wall as overseers, even of the lowest grade, were really worthy of it. They were men who had reflected deeply on the wall and continued to reflect upon it, men who with the first stone which they sank in the ground felt themselves to some extent a part of it. But such men of course were not only eager to perform work of the greatest thoroughness, they were also fired with impatience to see the building finally erected in its full perfection. The day labourer knows nothing of this impatience, his wage is his only spur, and again the higher overseers, indeed even the overseers of middle rank, see enough of the manifold growth of the structure for it to keep them strong in spirit. But in order to encourage the men of lower rank, whose mental capacity far out-stripped their seemingly petty task, other measures had to be taken. One could not, for instance, make them spend months or even years laying stone upon stone in some uninhabited mountain region hun-dreds of miles from their homes; the hopelessness of such laborious toil, to which no end could be seen even in the longest lifetime, would have reduced them to despair, and above all diminished their fitness for the work. It was for this reason that the system of piece-meal construction was chosen; five hundred yards could be ac-complished in about five years, and indeed by that time the overseers were usually quite exhausted, they had lost faith in themselves, in the wall, in the world; but then, while they were still exalted by the festivities held to mark the uniting of the thousand-yard section, they were sent far away; on their journey they saw completed sections of the wall towering up here and there, they came past the quarters of higher commanders who presented them with decorations, they heard the cheers of new armies of labour streaming up from the depths of the provinces, they saw forests being felled to provide scaffolding for the wall, mountains being hammered into blocks of stone, in the holy places they heard the chants of the faithful praying for the wall's completion; all this soothed their impatience; the quiet life of their homeland, where they rested for a time, strengthened them; the esteem in which all builders were held, the humble credu-lity with which their accounts were listened to, the faith which the simple, peaceful citizens placed in the eventual completion of the wall, all this spanned the chords of the soul; like eternally hopeful children they bade farewell to their homeland, the desire to start work again on the great communal task became irresistible; they set off from home sooner than they need have done, half the village came out to keep them company until they were well on their way; on all the roads they were met with cheering, flags, banners; never before had they seen how vast and rich and fair and lovely their country was; each fellow-countryman was a brother, for whom one was building a protecting wall, and who returned his thanks for that throughout his life with all that he had and all that he was; unity! unity!, shoulder to shoulder, a great circle of our people, our blood no longer confined in the narrow round of the body, but sweetly rolling yet ever returning through the endless leagues of China.

Thus, then, the system of piecemeal construction becomes comprehensible; and yet there were probably other reasons for it as well. There is, by the way, nothing odd in my spending so long on this question; it is a crucial question for the entire building of the wall, however insignificant it may appear at first. If I am to convey an impression of the mental horizon and the experience of those days, and to make them intelligible, I simply cannot delve deeply enough into this particular question.

First of all one should recognize that the achievements of those days were scarcely inferior to the building of the Tower of Babel, though as far as divine approval goes they represent, at least by human reckoning, the very opposite of that structure. I mention this because in the early stages of work on the wall a scholar wrote a book in which he drew the parallels in great detail. In it he attempted to prove that it was by no means for the reasons generally advanced that the Tower of Babel had failed to reach its objective, or at least that these well-known reasons did not include the most important ones of all. His proofs did not consist merely in written documents and reports; he also claimed to have made investigations on the spot, and to have discovered that the building failed, and was bound to fail, because of the weakness of its foundations. In this respect of course our own age had a great advantage over that long-past one; almost every educated contemporary was a mason by profession and infallible in the matter of laying foundations. But that was not at all what the scholar was driving at; instead he claimed that the Great Wall alone would create, for the first time in the history of mankind, a secure foundation for a new Tower of Babel. First the Wall, therefore, and then the Tower. His book was in everybody's hands at the time, but I must confess that I do not clearly understand to this day how he conceived the construction of that tower. How was the wall, which did not even form a circle, but only a sort of quarter or half-circle, supposed to provide the foundation for a tower? That could surely only be meant in a spiritual sense. But in that case what was the need for the wall, which was definitely something concrete, the result of the labour and the lives of hundreds of thousands of people? And why were there plans for the tower, admittedly somewhat nebulous plans, sketched in the book, and detailed plans set out for mobilizing the people's energies to undertake this new project? There was a great deal of confusion in people's minds at that time – this book is only one example – perhaps just because so many were doing their utmost to combine their forces in a single aim. The nature of man, flighty in its essence, made like the swirling dust, can abide no bondage; if it fetters itself it will soon begin to tear wildly at the fetters, rip all asunder – the wall, the binding chain, and itself – and scatter them to the four quarters of heaven.

It is possible that these considerations also, which in fact militate against the whole idea of building the wall, were not left out of account by the high command when the system of piecemeal construction was decided on. It was really only in spelling out the decrees of the supreme command that we – here I can probably speak for many – came to understand ourselves, and to discover that without our commanders neither our book learning nor our common sense would have been adequate even for the small task that fell to us within the great design. In the office of the high command – where it was, and who sat there, no one whom I have ever asked could tell me, either then or now – in that office there surely revolved all human thoughts and desires, and counter to them all human goals and achievements, while through the window the reflected glory of divine worlds shone in upon the hands of the commanders as they traced their plans.

And for that reason no impartial observer can believe that the high command was not also capable of overcoming, if it had seriously wished to, the difficulties that stood in the way of building the wall continuously. One is forced to conclude, therefore, that the command deliberately chose the system of piecemeal construction. But piecemeal construction was only a makeshift and was inexpedient. So one is forced to conclude that the command willed something inexpedient. Strange conclusion, indeed; and yet from another point of view there is much justification for it. Today it is perhaps safe to speak of these things. In those days many of our people, and the best among them, had a secret principle which went as follows: Try with all your might to understand the decrees of the high command, but only up to a certain limit; then cease your reflections. A very wise principle, which moreover was further elaborated in a parable that has often been retold since: Cease from further reflection, but not because it might harm you; indeed it is by no means certain that it would harm you. It is not a question here of what is harmful or otherwise. It will happen to you as happens to the river in spring. It rises, it grows mightier, it gives richer nourishment to the land by the long reach of its banks, it retains its own character until it flows into the sea, it becomes ever more worthy of the sea and ever more welcome to it. – Thus far may you reflect on the decrees of the high command. – But then the river overflows its banks, loses outline and shape, slackens its course towards the ocean, tries to defy its destiny by forming little inland seas, damages the farmlands, yet cannot maintain itself at that width for long, but must run back again between its banks, indeed it must even dry up miserably in the hot season that follows. – Thus far do not reflect on the decrees of the high command.

Now while this parable may have been singularly pertinent during the building of the wall, it has at most only restricted application to my present account. For my own inquiry is a purely historical one; lightning no longer flashes from the thunderclouds that have long since rolled away, so I may venture to seek an explanation of the system of piecemeal construction which goes further than the one that contented people then. The limits which my powers of thought impose on me are narrow enough, but the province to be covered here is infinite.

Against whom is the Great Wall supposed to protect us? Against the peoples of the north. I come from the south-east of China. No northern tribe can threaten us there. We read about them in the books of the ancients; the cruelties which they commit in accordance with their nature make us heave deep sighs in our peaceful bowers; in the faithful representations of artists we see these faces of the damned, their gaping mouths, their jaws furnished with great pointed teeth, their screwed-up eyes that already seem to be leering at the prey which their fangs will crush and rend to pieces. When our children misbehave we show them these pictures, and at once they fling themselves sobbing into our arms. But that is all that we know of these northerners; we have never set eyes on them, and if we remain in our villages we shall never set eyes on them, even if they should spur their wild horses and keep charging straight towards us; the land is too vast and will never let them through to us, they will ride on until they vanish in the empty air.

Why then, since that is so, do we leave our native place, with its river and its bridges, our mothers and fathers, our weeping wives, our children who need our guidance, and go off for our training to the distant city, while our thoughts move on still further to the wall in the north? Why? Ask the high command. Our commanders know us. They, who are at grips with immense problems, know about us, know of our simple occupations, they can see us all gathered round in our humble dwellings, and the evening prayer that the father of the house recites in the family circle comes to their ears, to please them or to displease them. And if I may be allowed to express such ideas about the high command, I must say that in my opinion the high command was in existence earlier, and did not just assemble like some group of high mandarins, who at the prompting of a pleasant morning dream hastily summon a meeting, hastily pass resolutions, and drum the people out of their beds the same evening to carry the resolution out, even if it should be a mere matter of staging an illumination in honour of a god, who had smiled on them the previous day, perhaps only to belabour them in some dark corner the day after, almost before the lanterns are extinguished. My belief is rather that the high command has been in existence for ever, and the decision to build the wall likewise.

Already to some extent while the wall was being built, and almost exclusively ever since, I have occupied myself with the comparative history of peoples – there are certain questions whose most sensitive spot, so to speak, can only be reached by this method – and in the course of my studies I have discovered that we Chinese possess certain social and political institutions that are unique in their clarity, and again others that are unique in their obscurity. To explore the reasons for this, and particularly for the latter phenomenon, has always attracted me and still attracts me today, and these questions have a most important bearing on the building of the wall.

Now one of our most obscure institutions of all is unquestionably that of the empire itself. In Peking of course, especially in court circles, there does exist some clarity on the subject, though even that is more apparent than real; also the teachers of political law and history in the high schools claim to be exactly informed about these matters, and to be able to pass this knowledge on to their students; and the further down the ladder of the schools one goes, the more one finds, understandably enough, people's doubts of their own knowledge vanishing and a sea of semi-education rising mountain-high round a few precepts that have been rammed home for centuries – precepts which have indeed lost nothing of their eternal truth, but which also remain eternally unrecognized amid all the fog and vapour.

But on this question of the empire one should, in my opinion, turn first of all to the common people, since that is after all where the empire has its final support. Here I can admittedly only speak for my own home region. Apart from the nature gods and their ritual, which occupies the whole year in such variety and beauty, all our thoughts were turned solely to the emperor. But not to the current one; or rather they would have turned to the current one if we had known who he was, or anything definite about him. We too were of course always trying – it was the only curiosity that possessed us – to discover some information of this kind. But – strange as it may sound – it was scarcely possible to discover anything; not from the pilgrims, though they cover so much country, not from near nor from distant villages, not from the sailors, though they sail on the great sacred rivers as well as on our little stream. One certainly heard plenty, but from all that plenty nothing could be made out.

Our land is so vast, no fairy tale can give an inkling of its size, the heavens can scarcely span it. And Peking is only a dot, and the imperial palace less than a dot. But again the emperor, as such, is indeed mighty through all the many levels of the world. Yet the living emperor, a man like us, lies much as we do on a couch, which for all its generous proportions is still comparatively narrow and short. Like us he sometimes stretches his limbs, and when he is very tired, he yawns with his delicately cut mouth. How should we discover anything about that, thousands of miles away in the south, we who are almost on the borders of the Tibetan highlands? And besides, if any news should reach us it would come far too late, it would be long since out of date. Round the emperor there always presses the brilliant yet sinister throng of his courtiers, the counter-weight to the imperial power, eternally striving to topple the emperor from his balance with their poisoned arrows. The empire is immortal, but the individual emperor falls and plunges down from the heights; even whole dynasties sink in the end, and breathe their last in a single death-rattle. Of these struggles and sufferings the people will never know; like latecomers, like strangers in a city, they stand at the far end of some densely packed side-street peacefully consuming the provisions they have brought with them, while far out in front of them, in the market square in the middle of the city, the execution of their ruler is proceeding.

There is a parable which expresses this relationship well. The emperor – so it is told – has sent to you, his solitary wretch of a subject, the minute shadow that has fled from the imperial sun into the furthermost distance, expressly to you has the emperor sent a message from his death-bed. He made the messenger kneel by his bedside and whispered the message to him; so much store did he set by it that he made him repeat it in his ear. With a nod of his head he confirmed the accuracy of the words. And before all the spectators of his death – every obstructing wall has been knocked away and on the towering open stairways there stand round him in a ring all the dignitaries of the empire – before all these has he dispatched his messenger. At once the messenger set out on his way; a strong, an indefatigable man, a swimmer without equal; striking out now with one arm, now the other, he cleaves a path through the throng; if he meets with resistance he points to his breast, which bears the sign of the sun, and he forges ahead with an ease that none could match. But the throng is so vast, there is no end to their dwellings; if he could reach open country how fast would he fly, and soon you would surely hear the majestic pounding of his fists on your door. But instead of that, how vain are his efforts; he is still only forcing his way through the chambers of the innermost palace, never will he get to the end of them; and if he succeeded in that, nothing would be gained; down the stairs he would have to fight his way; and if he succeeded in that, nothing would be gained; the courtyards would have to be traversed, and after the courtyards the second, outer palace; and again stairs and courtyards; and again a palace; and so on for thousands of years; and if at last he should burst through the outermost gate – but never, never can that happen – the royal capital would still lie before him, the centre of the world, piled high with all its dregs. No one can force his way through here, least of all with a message from a dead man to a shadow. But you sit at your window and dream up that message when evening falls.

Just so, just as hopelessly and as hopefully, do our people regard the emperor. They do not know which emperor is reigning, and there are even doubts as to the name of the dynasty. Many things of that kind are learnt by rote at school, but the universal uncertainty in such matters is so great that even the best pupils are affected by it. Emperors long since departed are raised in our villages to the throne, and one who only survives in song has recently issued a proclamation which the priest reads out before the altar. Battles of our most ancient history are fought now for the first time, and with glowing cheeks one's neighbour comes rushing into one's house with the news. The ladies of the emperors, overfed and sunk in their silken cushions, estranged from noble custom by wily courtiers, swollen with their lust for power, passionate in their greed, unbounded in their debauchery, perform their dreadful deeds ever anew; the more time that has passed, the more terrible the hues in which everything glows, and one day the village hears with loud lamentation how an empress, thousands of years ago, drank in long draughts the blood of her husband.

Thus, then, do our people behave towards the past emperors, but those of the present they mingle with the dead. If once, once in a lifetime, an imperial official on a tour of the provinces happens to arrive at our village, makes certain demands in the name of the ruler, examines the tax rolls, attends the school classes, questions the priest about all our doings, and then, before stepping into his litter, calls the whole community together and sums up his findings in a long speech of admonishment – then a smile will pass over all the faces, each man will steal a glance at his neighbour, people will bend over their children so as not to be observed by the official. Why, they think, he speaks of a dead man as if he were still alive; this emperor died long ago, the dynasty is extinct; the worthy official is making his sport with us, but we will behave as if we did not notice, so as not to offend him. But our serious obedience we shall give only to our present ruler; all else would be sinful. And behind the back of the official, as he is hurried away in his litter, some ruler who has been arbitrarily resurrected from a crumbling urn asserts himself with a stamp of his foot as lord of the village.

If one were to conclude from such phenomena that basically we have no emperor at all, one would not be far from the truth. Over and over again I must repeat: There is perhaps no people more faithful to the emperor than our people in the south, but our fidelity is of no benefit to the emperor. True, the sacred dragon stands on the little column at the end of the village, and from time immemorial it has been breathing its fiery breath in homage exactly in the direction of Peking; but for the people in our village Peking itself is far stranger than the next world. Can there really be a village where the houses stand side by side, covering more fields than can be seen from the top of our hill, and can crowds of people be packed between these houses day and night? Rather than to imagine a city like that, it would be easier for us to believe that Peking and its emperor were a single entity, say a cloud, peacefully voyaging beneath the sun through the course of the ages.

Now the result of holding such views is a life that is in a certain sense free and unconstrained. By no means immoral; such moral purity as exists in my native region I have scarcely ever met with on my travels. But it is a life that is subject to no law of the present, and obeys only the instructions and warnings reaching down to us from ancient times. I must beware of generalizing, and will not assert that this holds good for all the ten thousand villages of our province, far less so for all the five hundred provinces of China. But all the same I may perhaps be permitted, on the strength of the many works that I have read on the subject, as well as on the strength of my own observations – the building of the wall in particular, with its abundance of human material, afforded any man of feeling the opportunity to explore the soul of every province – on the strength of all this, then, I may perhaps be permitted to say that the attitude which prevails in respect of the emperor has always and everywhere certain basic features in common with the attitude in my own village. However I do not at all wish to represent this attitude as a virtue; on the contrary. It is true that the basic responsibility for it lies with the government, which in this most ancient empire on earth has been unable or else too preoccupied with other things to develop imperial rule into an institution of sufficient clarity for it to be immediately and continuously effective right to the furthest frontiers of the land. On the other hand, however, this attitude also conceals a weakness of imagination or faith on the part of the people, for they fail to draw out the imperial power from the depths of Peking where it lies buried, and to clasp it in its full living presence to their obedient breasts, while at the same time they wish for nothing better than to feel its touch upon them at last, and so be consumed. So this attitude can hardly be considered a virtue. It is all the more striking that this very weakness should apparently be one of the most important unifying influences among our people ...

Such was the world into which the news of the building of the wall now penetrated. It too came belatedly, some thirty years after it had been announced. It was on a summer evening. I, then aged ten, was standing with my father on the river bank. As befits the importance of this much-discussed occasion I can recollect the smallest details. He was holding me by the hand, something he loved to do into extreme old age, and was running his other hand up and down his long, very thin pipe, as though it were a flute. His long, sparse, stiff beard was raised in the air, for as he smoked his pipe he was gazing up into the heights beyond the river. At the same time his pigtail, object of the children's veneration, sank lower, rustling faintly

on the gold-embroidered silk of his holiday robe. At that moment a
bark drew up before us, the boatman signalled to my father to come
down the embankment, while he himself climbed up towards him.
They met halfway, the boatman whispered something in my father's
ear; he put his arms round him to get really close. I could not
understand what was said, I only saw that my father seemed not to
believe the news, the boatman tried to assure him of its truth, my
father still could not believe it, then the boatman, with the vehemence
of sailor folk, almost ripped apart the clothes on his chest to prove
the truth of his words, whereupon my father fell silent and the
boatman leapt heavily into the bark and sailed away. Thoughtfully
my father turned towards me, knocked out his pipe and stuck it in
his belt, stroked me on the cheek and drew my head against his.
That was what I liked best, it filled me with good spirits, and thus
we returned home. There the rice-pap was already steaming on the
table, a number of guests were assembled, the wine was just being
poured into the goblets. My father paid no attention to any of this,
and while still on the threshold he began to recount what he had
heard. I cannot of course remember the exact words, but the sense
impressed itself on me so deeply, owing to the exceptional nature of
the circumstances that were enough to entrance even a child, that I
do feel able to give some version of what he said. I do it because it
was so very characteristic of the popular attitude. Well then, my
father said something like this:

[A strange boatman – I know all those who usually pass here, but
this one was a stranger – has just told me that a great wall is going to
be built to protect the emperor. For it seems that infidel tribes, and
demons among them, often gather in front of the imperial palace and
shoot their black arrows at the emperor.]

THE KNOCK AT THE
MANOR GATE

IT was summer, a hot day. On my way home with my sister I was passing the gate of a manor-house. I cannot tell now whether she knocked out of mischief or out of absence of mind, or whether she merely threatened the gate with her fist and did not knock at all. A hundred paces further on along the high road, where it turned to the left, a village began. It was not a village we knew, but from the very first house people emerged, making friendly but warning signs to us; these people were terrified, bowed down with terror. They pointed to the manor we had passed and reminded us of the knock at the gate. The proprietors of the manor would charge us with it, the interrogation was to begin immediately. I kept quite calm and calmed my sister down as well. Probably she had not struck the gate at all, and even if she had, nowhere in the world would one be prosecuted for that. I tried to make this clear to the people around us; they listened to me but refrained from passing an opinion. Later they told me that not only my sister, but I too, as her brother, would be charged. I nodded and smiled. We all gazed back at the manor, as one watches a distant smoke-cloud and waits for the flames to appear. And sure enough, we presently saw horsemen riding in through the wide open gate; dust rose and obscured everything, only the points of their tall spears glittered. And hardly had the troop vanished into the main courtyard when they seemed to have turned their horses again and were on their way to us. I urged my sister to get away, I myself would set everything to rights; she refused to leave me on my own; then, I told her, she should at least change her clothes, so as to appear better dressed before these gentlemen. At last she obeyed and set out on the long road to our home. Already the horsemen had reached us, and from the saddle they began asking for my sister; she wasn't here at the moment, was the apprehensive reply, but she would be coming later. This response left them almost cold; the most important thing seemed to be that I had been found. The two chief members of the party were the judge, an energetic young man, and his silent assistant, whose name was Assmann. I was ordered into the parlour of the village inn. Slowly, swaying my head from side to side and hitching up my trousers, I set off under the watchful gaze of the party. I still half believed that a word would be enough to get me, the townsman, released – perhaps even honourably released – from this group of peasants. But when I had stepped over the threshold of the inn, the judge, who had hastened in front and was already awaiting me, said: 'I am sorry for this man.' And it was beyond all possibility of doubt that he was not referring to my present situation, but to what was about to happen to me. The room looked more like a prison cell than an inn parlour. Great stone flags, a dark-grey bare wall, an iron ring embedded somewhere in the masonry, in the middle something that was half pallet, half operating table.

MY NEIGHBOUR

MY business rests entirely on my own shoulders. Two girls with typewriters and ledgers in the front office, my own room with writing-desk, safe, consulting-table, easy chair and telephone: that is my entire working apparatus. So simple to keep an eye on, so easy to manage. I am young and my affairs run along merrily; I don't complain, I don't complain.

At the new year a young man rented without further ado the small vacant apartment next door, which for so long I had foolishly hesitated to take myself. It too consists of a main room and a front room, but with a kitchen in addition. I could well have made use of the room and the front room, already there have been times when my two girls have felt overstretched – but what use would the kitchen have been to me? This minor misgiving was responsible for my letting the apartment be snatched away from me. Now this young man sits there. Harras he's called. What he actually does there I don't know. On the door it says: 'Harras, Office'. I have made some inquiries, and have been informed that it is a business similar to mine, that it would not exactly be right to warn against granting him credit, for after all he is an ambitious young man and his enterprise may have a future, but that it is not actually possible to advise granting him credit either, for by all appearances there are no assets at present. The usual information given when nothing is known.

Sometimes I meet Harras on the stairs; he must always be in an extraordinary hurry, he literally shoots past me, I've never even seen him properly yet; he holds his office key ready in his hand, in a flash he has opened the door, like the tail of a rat he has slipped inside, and there I stand again in front of the plate 'Harras, Office' which I have already read far oftener than it deserves.

These wretchedly thin walls, they betray the man engaged in honest activity but for the dishonest they provide cover. My telephone is fitted to the wall of my room that separates me from my neighbour, but I merely stress that as a particularly ironical fact, for even if it hung on the opposite wall one would be able to hear everything in the next apartment. I have trained myself not to mention the names of my customers on the telephone, but of course not much cunning is required to guess their names from characteristic but unavoidable turns of the conversation. Sometimes, goaded by anxiety, I dance round the telephone on tiptoe with the receiver at my ear, and still I can't prevent secrets being divulged. This means of course that when I'm on the telephone I become unsure in my business decisions as well, my voice begins to quaver. What is Harras doing while I'm telephoning? If I were to exaggerate greatly – but one often has to do that so as to get things clear in one's mind – I could say that Harras needs no telephone, he uses mine; he has pushed his sofa against the wall and listens; while I on the other hand must run to the telephone when it rings, take note of my customers' requirements, reach decisions of great consequence, carry out grand exercises in persuasion, and above all, during the whole operation, give an involuntary report to Harras through the wall. Perhaps he doesn't even wait for the end of the conversation, but gets up at the point where the matter under discussion has become sufficiently clear to him, flits through the town at his accustomed speed, and before I have hung up the receiver he is perhaps already at work thwarting my plans.

A CROSSBREED

I HAVE a curious animal, half kitten, half lamb. It is an heirloom that belonged to my father. But it has only developed in my own day; formerly it was far more lamb than kitten, now it is both in about equal proportions. From the cat it takes its head and claws, from the lamb its size and shape; from both its eyes, which are gentle and flickering, its coat which is soft and close-lying, its movements, which are both skipping and slinking. On the window-sill in the sunshine it curls itself up in a ball and purrs, in the meadow it rushes about like a mad thing and can scarcely be caught; it runs away from cats and has a tendency to attack lambs; on moonlit nights its favourite walk is along the tiles; it cannot mew and it has a horror of rats; by the hen-coop it can lie in ambush for hours, but it has never yet seized an opportunity for murder. I feed it on sweetened milk, which suits it perfectly; it sucks it down in long draughts through its predatory fangs. Naturally it is a great spectacle for the children. Sunday morning is the visiting hour; I sit with the little beast on my lap and the children of the whole neighbourhood stand round me. Then the strangest questions are asked, which not a soul can answer. And indeed I make no effort to do so, but confine myself without further explanation to showing off what I possess. Sometimes the children bring cats with them, once they even brought two lambs; but contrary to their expectation there was no recognition scene, the animals looked at each other calmly with their animal eyes and evidently accepted their mutual existence as a God-given fact.

On my lap the creature knows neither fear nor the urge to hunt. Pressed against me it feels happiest. It sticks by the family that brought it up. This is probably not a sign of any exceptional fidelity, merely the sure instinct of an animal which has indeed countless step-relations in the world but perhaps not a single close blood relation, and to which the protection it has found with us is therefore sacred. Sometimes I cannot help laughing when it sniffs round me and winds itself between my legs and simply will not be parted from me. Not content with being lamb and cat, it almost insists on being a dog as well. Seriously, I really do believe something of the kind. It has the restlessness of both creatures within it, that of the cat and that of the lamb, diverse as they are. That is why it feels unhappy in its own skin.

Perhaps the butcher's knife would be a release for the animal, but I have to deny it that because it is an heirloom.

A little boy once received, as his sole inheritance from his father, a cat, and through it he became Lord Mayor of London. What shall I become through my animal? Where stretches the gigantic city?

NEW LAMPS

YESTERDAY I was in the directors' offices for the first time. Our
night shift has chosen me as their spokesman, and since the construction and fuelling of our lamps is inadequate I was to go along there
and press for these defects to be remedied. The appropriate office
was pointed out to me; I knocked and went in. A delicate young
man, very pale, smiled at me from behind his large desk. He nodded
his head a great deal, a great deal too much. I did not know whether
I ought to sit down; although there was a chair available I thought
perhaps I had better not sit down straight away on my first visit, and
so I told my story standing. But obviously I caused the young man
some trouble by this very modesty of mine, for he was obliged to
turn his face round and up at me, unless he was prepared to turn his
chair round, and that he wasn't prepared to do. On the other hand,
in spite of all his willingness, he could not screw his neck round
quite far enough, and so with it halfway round he gazed up askew at
the ceiling during my story, and I could not help doing the same.
When I had finished he got up slowly, patted me on the back, said:
'Well, well – well, well', and pushed me into the adjoining room,
where a gentleman with a great wild growth of beard had evidently
been waiting for us, for on his desk there was no trace of any sort of
work to be seen, on the contrary, an open glass door led out into a
little garden full of flowers and shrubs. A short briefing, consisting
of a few words whispered to him by the young man, sufficed for the
gentleman to grasp our manifold complaints. He stood up at once
and said: 'Well now, my good –', here he paused; I thought he
wanted to know my name and so I was just opening my mouth to
introduce myself again when he caught me up short: 'Yes, yes, all
right, all right, I know all about you – well now, your request, or

that of your workmates and yourself, is certainly justifiable, I myself and the other gentlemen on the board of directors are certainly the last not to recognize that. Believe me, the welfare of our men is something that we have more at heart than the welfare of the concern. And why not? The concern can always be built up all over again, it only costs money, hang the money, but if a human being is destroyed, there you have it, a human being is destroyed and we're left with the widow, the children. Ah dear me, yes! And so that is why every suggestion for the introduction of new safeguards, new reliefs, new comforts and luxuries, is most welcome to us. Anyone who comes along with such a suggestion is the man for us. So you just leave your proposals here with us, we shall examine them closely, and if it should turn out that any kind of brilliant little novelty can be appended, we shall certainly not suppress it, and as soon as everything is finished you men will get the new lamps. But tell this to your workmates below: we will not rest here until we have turned your shaft into a drawing-room, and we'll see to it that you meet your end down there in patent-leather shoes, or not at all. And so a very good day to you!'

THE COLLECTED APHORISMS

I

The true way leads along a tight-rope, which is not stretched aloft but just above the ground. It seems designed more to trip one than to be walked along.

2

All human errors are impatience, a premature breaking-off of methodical procedure, an apparent fencing-in of what is apparently at issue.

3

There are two cardinal human sins from which all others derive: impatience and indolence. Because of impatience they were expelled from Paradise, because of indolence they do not return. But perhaps there is only one cardinal sin: impatience. Because of impatience they were expelled, because of impatience they do not return.

4

Many shades of the departed are occupied solely in licking the waves of the river of death because it comes from our direction and still has the salty taste of our seas. Then the river rears up in disgust, flows the opposite way, and washes the dead back into life. They however are happy, sing songs of thanksgiving, and stroke the indignant stream.

5

Beyond a certain point there is no return. This point has to be reached.

6

The decisive moment in the development of mankind is everlasting. That is why the revolutionary spiritual movements that declare all former things to be of no account are in the right, for nothing has yet occurred.

7

One of Evil's most effective means of seduction is the challenge to battle.

It is like the battle with women, which ends in bed.

8/9

An evil-smelling bitch, producer of countless litters and already decaying in places, though in my childhood it meant everything to me, which follows me faithfully all the time, which I cannot bring myself to beat, but instead retreat from step by step, unable even to stand its breath; and yet it will drive me, unless I determine otherwise, into the corner that I can already see looming up, where it will decompose wholly, upon me and along with me, with the purulent and wormy flesh of its tongue – is this an honour for me? – upon my hand to the very end.

10

A. is very puffed up, he thinks he is far advanced in goodness, since he – evidently as an increasingly seductive object – feels himself exposed to ever more temptations from directions that were previously quite unknown to him. But the correct explanation is this, that a great devil has entered into him, and the countless smaller devils are coming along to serve the great one.

11/12

The different views that one can have, say, of an apple: the view of the little boy, who has to crane his neck so that he can just glimpse the apple on the table-top, and the view of the master of the house, who takes the apple and freely hands it to his companion at the table.

13

A first sign of the beginning of understanding is the wish to die. This life seems unbearable, another unattainable. One is no longer ashamed of wanting to die; one begs to be moved out of the old cell, which one hates, into a new one which one must first learn to hate. One is also moved by a certain residual faith that, during transport, the master will happen to come along the corridor, look at the prisoner and say: 'This man is not to be locked up again. He comes to me.'

14

If you were walking across a plain, had every intention of advancing and still went backwards, then it would be a desperate matter; but since you are clambering up a steep slope, about as steep as you yourself are when seen from below, your backward movement can only be caused by the nature of the ground, and you need not despair.

15

Like a path in autumn: scarcely has it been swept clear when it is once more covered with dry leaves.

16

A cage went in search of a bird.

17

This is a place where I never was before: one's breath comes differently, more dazzling than the sun is the radiance of a star beside it.

18

If it had been possible to build the Tower of Babel without climbing up it, it would have been permitted.

19

Do not let evil make you believe you can keep secrets from it.

20

Leopards break into the temple and drink the sacrificial vessels dry; this is repeated over and over again; finally it can be calculated in advance and it becomes a part of the ceremony.

21

As firmly as the hand grips the stone. But it grips it firmly only to fling it away the further. But the way leads into those distances too.

22

You are the task. No pupil far and wide.

23

From the true antagonist boundless courage flows into you.

24

What it means to grasp the good fortune that the ground on which you stand cannot be greater than what is covered by your two feet.

25

How can one take delight in the world unless one flees to it for refuge?

26

There are countless hiding-places, there is only one deliverance, but possibilities of deliverance are again as many as the hiding-places.

There is a goal, but no way; what we call a way is hesitation.

27

To perform the negative is what is still required of us, the positive is already ours.

28

When one has once given Evil a lodging, it no longer demands that one believe it.

29

The ulterior motives with which you give Evil a lodging are not your own but those of Evil.

The beast wrests the whip from its master and whips itself in order to become master, not knowing that this is only a fantasy produced by a new knot in the master's whip-lash.

30

The Good is in a certain sense comfortless.

31

Self-control is something for which I do not strive. Self-control means: wanting to work effectively at some random point in the infinite radiations of my spiritual existence. But if I must draw such circles round me, then it will be better for me to do it passively, merely gaping in wonder at the immense complex, and just take home with me the strength which this spectacle, *e contrario*, provides.

32

The crows maintain that a single crow could destroy the heavens. There is no doubt of that, but it proves nothing against the heavens, for heaven simply means: the impossibility of crows.

33

Martyrs do not underrate the body, they allow it to be elevated on the cross; in this they are at one with their antagonists.

34

His exhaustion is that of a gladiator after the fight, his work was the whitewashing of one corner in a clerk's office.

35

There is no having, only a being, only a state of being that craves the last breath, craves suffocation.

36

Previously I did not understand why I got no answer to my question, today I do not understand how I could believe I was capable of asking. But I didn't really believe, I only asked.

37

His answer to the assertion that, while he might perhaps have possessions, he had no being, was only a trembling and a beating of heart.

38

There was one who was astonished how easily he moved along the road of eternity; the fact is that he was racing along it downhill.

39

One cannot pay Evil in instalments – and one tries to do so continuously.

It is conceivable that Alexander the Great, despite the military successes of his youth, despite the excellent army that he had trained, despite the powers capable of transforming the world that he felt within him, might have halted at the Hellespont and never have crossed it, and this not from fear, not from irresolution, not from weakness of will, but from force of gravity.

39a

The way is infinite, there is nothing that can be subtracted, nothing that can be added, and yet everyone holds up to it his own childish yardstick. 'Truly, this yard of the way you must go as well, it shall not be denied you.'

40

It is only our conception of time that makes us call the Last Judgement by that name; in fact it is a permanent court-martial.

41

The disproportion in the world seems, comfortingly enough, to be only an arithmetical one.

42

Letting the head that is filled with disgust and hate sink on one's breast.

43

As yet the hounds are still playing in the courtyard, but their prey will not escape, however fast it may already be charging through the forest.

44

Laughable is the way you have put yourself in harness for this world.

45

The more horses you put to the job, the faster it goes – that is to say, not the tearing of the block out of its base, which is impossible, but the tearing apart of the straps and as a result the gay empty ride.

46

The world 'sein' means two things in German: 'being' and 'belonging-to-him'.

47

They were given the choice of becoming kings or the kings' messengers. As is the way with children, they all wanted to be messengers. That is why there are only messengers, they charge through the world and, since there are no kings, call out their now meaningless messages to one another. Gladly would they put an end to their miserable life, but they dare not do so because of their oath of allegiance.

48

To believe in progress does not mean believing that any progress has yet been made. That would be no real act of belief.

49

A. is a virtuoso and heaven is his witness.

50

Man cannot live without a permanent trust in something in-destructible within himself, though both the indestructible element and also the trust may remain permanently concealed from him. One of the ways in which this lasting concealment can express itself is faith in a personal god.

51

The mediation of the snake was necessary: Evil can seduce man, but cannot become man.

52

In the struggle between yourself and the world, second the world.

53

One must defraud no one, not even the world of its victory.

54

There is nothing other than a spiritual world; what we call the world of the senses is the evil in the spiritual world, and what we call evil is only a necessity of a moment in our eternal development.

With the strongest of lights one can dissolve the world. For weak eyes it becomes solid, for weaker eyes it acquires fists, for eyes still weaker it becomes shamefaced and smashes him who dares to look upon it.

55

All is fraud: to seek the minimum of illusion, to remain at the normal level, to seek the maximum. In the first case one defrauds the Good, by trying to make it too easy for oneself to get it, and Evil by setting it too unfavourable terms of combat. In the second case one defrauds the Good by not striving for it even in earthly terms. In the third case one defrauds the Good by moving as far away from it as possible, and Evil by hoping to make it powerless through intensifying it to the utmost. What would therefore seem preferable is the second case, for the Good is defrauded in any case, while in this case, apparently at least, Evil is not.

56

There are questions we could never get over if we were not dispensed from them by our very nature.

57

For everything outside the phenomenal world language can only be used allusively, but never even approximately by way of comparison, since, corresponding as it does to the phenomenal world, it is concerned only with property and its relations.

58

One lies as little as possible only when one lies as little as possible, not when one has the least possible opportunity for doing so.

59

A stair that has not been deeply hollowed by footsteps is, from its own point of view, merely something that has been bleakly put together out of wood.

60

Whoever renounces the world must love all men, for he renounces their world too. He thus begins to have some inkling of the true nature of man, which cannot but be loved, provided that one is worthy of it.

61

Whoever in this world loves his neighbour does no greater and no lesser wrong than whoever in this world loves himself. There remains only the question whether the former is possible.

62

The fact that there is nothing else but a spiritual world deprives us of our hope and gives us our certainty.

63

Our art consists in being dazzled by the truth: The light upon the grotesque mask as it shrinks back is true, and nothing else.

64/65

The expulsion from Paradise is in its main aspect eternal: Thus it is true that expulsion from Paradise is final and life in the world unavoidable, yet despite that the eternal nature of the event not only gives us the possibility of remaining in Paradise permanently, but it means that we may in fact be permanently there, no matter whether we know it here or not.

66

He is a free and secure citizen of the earth, for he is attached to a chain that is long enough to give him the freedom of all earthly realms, and yet not long enough for anything to pull him over the earth's borders. At the same time, however, he is a free and secure citizen of heaven, for he is also attached to a similarly calculated heavenly chain. Thus if he wants to get down to earth, he is choked by the collar of heaven; if he wants to get up to heaven, by the collar of earth. And despite this he has every possibility and is aware of the fact; indeed he even refuses to attribute the whole thing to a mistake in the original chaining.

67

He runs after facts like a beginner learning to skate, who is furthermore practising somewhere where it is forbidden.

68

What is more cheerful than the belief in a household god!

69

In theory there is a possibility of perfect happiness: To believe in the indestructible element within one, and not to strive towards it.

70/71

The Indestructible is one; it is each individual human being and at the same time it is common to all, hence the unparalleled strength of the bonds that unite mankind.

72

In one and the same man there are perceptions which despite total dissimilarity have an identical object, so that one can only conclude that there are different subjects in one and the same man.

73

He devours crumbs that fall from his own table; this means that he is indeed better satisfied than anyone else for a while, but he forgets how to eat at the table itself: but this means that there are then no more crumbs either.

74

If what is supposed to have been destroyed in Paradise was destructible, then it was not decisive; but if it was indestructible, then we are living in a false belief.

75

Test yourself by mankind. It makes the doubter doubt, the believer believe.

76

This feeling: 'Here I will not anchor', and instantly to feel the billowing uplifting swell around one.

A sudden reversal. Watchful, fearful, hopeful, the answer prowls round the question, searches desperately in its impenetrable face, follows it along the most senseless paths, that is, along the paths leading as far as possible away from the answer.

77

Human intercourse tempts one to introspection.

78

The spirit becomes free only when it ceases to be a support.

79

Sensual love blinds us to heavenly love; by itself it could not do so, but since it contains the element of heavenly love unconsciously within it, it can.

80

Truth is indivisible, hence it cannot recognize itself; whoever wants to recognize it must be a lie.

81

No one can desire what is ultimately damaging to him. If in the case of a particular person it appears to be so after all – and perhaps it always does so appear – this is explained by the fact that there is somebody within the person who desires what is admittedly beneficial to that somebody, yet gravely damaging to a second somebody who has been brought in partly in order to judge the case. If the person had put himself on the side of the second somebody at the very beginning, and not only when it came to judging the case, then the first somebody would have faded away and the desire along with him.

82

Why do we complain about the Fall? It was not on its account that we were expelled from Paradise but on account of the Tree of Life, that we should not eat of it.

83

We are sinful not only because we have eaten of the Tree of Knowledge, but also because we have not yet eaten of the Tree of Life. The state in which we are is sinful, irrespective of guilt.

84

We were created to live in Paradise, and Paradise was designed to serve us. Our purpose has been changed; that this has also happened with the purpose of Paradise is nowhere stated.

85

Evil is a radiation of the human consciousness in certain transitional situations. It is not exactly the sensual world which is mere appearance, but the evil of it, which is admittedly what constitutes the sensual world in our eyes.

86

Since the Fall we have been essentially equal in our capacity to know Good and Evil; and yet it is precisely here that we seek to outdo our fellows. But it is only on the far side of this knowledge that the real differences begin. That the opposite should appear to be the case is due to the following: No one can be content with knowledge alone, but must strive to act in accordance with it. But he is not endowed with the strength to do this, hence he must destroy himself, even at the risk of not acquiring the necessary strength that way either, but nothing else remains for him save this last attempt. (This is also the meaning of the threat of death associated with the ban on eating from the Tree of Knowledge; perhaps this is also the original meaning of natural death.) Now this is an attempt he is afraid to make; he would rather annul the knowledge of Good and Evil (the term 'the Fall' has its origin in this fear); but what has once happened cannot be annulled, it can only be blurred. It is for this purpose that the justifications arise. The whole world is full of them, indeed the whole visible world is perhaps no more nor less than the self-justification of man in his wish to find a moment of peace. An attempt to distort the fact that knowledge is already given, to make knowledge a goal still to be reached.

87

A belief like a guillotine, just as heavy, just as light.

88

Death is before us, rather like a picture of Alexander's Battle hanging
on the schoolroom wall. What matters is that we should, already in
the course of this life, obscure this picture by our actions or indeed
even blot it out.

89

A man has free will, and this of three kinds: First of all he was free
when he willed this life; now, of course, he can no longer go back on
it, for he is no longer the person who once willed it, except perhaps
in so far as he puts what he once willed into practice by living.

Secondly he is free in that he can choose the mode and the route
of his progress through this life.

Thirdly he is free in that, as the person he is one day to become
again, he has the will to go through life under all conditions and thus
to find his way to himself, and what is more to go through life along
a road that is indeed a matter of choice, yet will surely be so
labyrinthine as to leave no corner of this life untouched.

Such are the three aspects of free will, but since they are present
at the same time they form a unity, and at bottom such a complete
unity that no room is left for any will, either free or unfree.

90

Two possibilities: making oneself infinitely small or being so. The
first is perfection, hence inactivity; the second is beginning, hence
action.

91

Towards the avoidance of a verbal confusion: What is to be actively destroyed must first of all have been firmly grasped; what crumbles away crumbles away, but cannot be destroyed.

92

The first worship of idols was certainly fear of things, but, connected with this, fear of the necessity of things, and, connected with this, fear of the responsibility for things. So tremendous did this responsibility appear that people did not even dare to impose it upon one single extra-human being, for the mediation of just one being would not have lightened human responsibility enough, intercourse with one sole being would still have been all too deeply tainted with responsibility, and that is why each thing was given the responsibility for itself, and what is more, these things were given a measure of responsibility for man as well.

93

Never again psychology!

94

Two tasks at the beginning of your life: To narrow your orbit increasingly, and constantly to check whether you are not hiding away somewhere outside your orbit.

95

Evil is sometimes in one's hand like a tool; recognized or unrecognized it can, if one has the will to do so, be laid aside without opposition.

96

The joys of this life are not *life's*, but *our* fear of ascending into a higher life; the torments of this life are not life's but our self-torment on account of that fear.

97

Only here is suffering suffering. Not in the sense that those who suffer here are to be raised up elsewhere on account of their suffering, but in the sense that what in this world is called suffering is in another world, unchanged and merely liberated from its opposite, bliss.

98

The notion of the infinite expanse and fullness of the cosmos is the result of the intermingling, pushed to its furthest extreme, of laborious creation and free self-contemplation.

99

How much more oppressive than the most inexorable conviction of our present sinful state is even the weakest conviction of the eventual eternal justification of our temporal existence. Only strength in the endurance of this second conviction, which in its purity entirely comprehends the first, is the measure of faith.

Many assume that, besides the great basic deception, there is in each individual case a little special deception provided additionally for their benefit, in other words that when a love-intrigue is presented on the stage, the actress has, apart from the false smile for her lover, an especially insidious smile just for the one particular spectator at the top of the gallery as well. This is going too far.

100

There can be a knowledge of the diabolical, but no belief in it, for more of the diabolical than is actually present does not exist.

101

Sin always comes openly and can at once be grasped with the senses. It walks on its roots and does not have to be extracted.

102

All the suffering around us must be suffered by us as well. We do not all have one body, but we all have one way of growing, and this leads us through all anguish, whether in this or in that form. Just as the child develops through all life's stages right up to old age and death (and basically each stage seems inaccessible to the previous one, whether longed for or feared), so also do we develop (no less deeply bound up with mankind than with ourselves) through all the sufferings of this world. There is no room for justice in this context, but neither is there any room for fear of suffering or for the interpretation of suffering as a merit.

103

You can hold yourself back from the sufferings of the world, that is something you are free to do and it accords with your nature, but perhaps this very holding back is the one suffering that you could avoid.

105

This world's means of seduction, and the token which guarantees us that this world is only a transition, are one and the same. Rightly so, for only thus can the world seduce us in a way that conforms to the truth. The worst thing, however, is that after the seduction has succeeded we forget the guarantee, and thus actually Good has lured us into Evil, the woman's look into her bed.

106

Humility provides everyone, even him who despairs in solitude, with the strongest relationship to his fellow man, though of course only in the case of complete and lasting humility. It can do this because it is the true language of prayer, at once adoration and the firmest of unions. The relationship to one's fellow man is the relationship of prayer, the relationship to oneself is the relationship of striving; from the prayer is drawn the strength for the striving.

Can you know anything else, then, but deception? If ever the deception is destroyed you must on no account look that way, or you will turn into a pillar of salt.

107

Everyone is very kind to A., rather in the way that one tries to protect an excellent billiard-table even from good players, until such time as the great player arrives, who carefully examines the surface, will tolerate no premature blemish, but then, when he begins play himself, lets himself go with ruthless fury.

108

'But then he returned to his work, just as though nothing had happened.' This is a remark we are familiar with from a vague profusion of old stories, although perhaps it does not occur in any one of them.

109

'It cannot be said that we are lacking in faith. Even the mere fact of our life is of a faith-value that cannot be exhausted.'
'Where is the faith-value here? One simply cannot not-live.'
'It is precisely in this "simply cannot" that the insane strength of faith lies; in the form of this denial it takes shape.'

It is not necessary that you leave the house. Remain at your table and listen. Do not even listen, only wait. Do not even wait, be wholly still and alone. The world will present itself to you for its unmasking, it can do no other, in ecstasy it will writhe at your feet.

AN EVERYDAY OCCURRENCE

AN everyday occurrence: the enduring of it a matter of everyday heroism. A has an important deal to conclude with B from the neighbouring village of H. He goes to H for the preliminary discussion, gets there and back in ten minutes each way, and at home boasts of this unusual rapidity. The next day he goes to H again, this time for the final settlement of the deal; since this is likely to take several hours, A sets out early in the morning; but although all the attendant circumstances, at least in A's opinion, are exactly the same as on the previous day, this time it takes him ten hours to get to H. When he arrives there weary in the evening, he is told that B, annoyed at A's failure to arrive, has gone across to A's village half an hour ago, they ought to have met each other on the way. A is advised to wait, B is sure to be back soon. But A, anxious about the deal, at once sets out again and hurries home. This time, without particularly noticing the fact, he covers the distance in no more than an instant. At home he is informed that B had actually arrived there early in the day, even before A's departure, indeed that he had met A on the doorstep and reminded him about the deal, but A had said he had no time just then, he had to go off at once on a matter of urgency. In spite of this incomprehensible behaviour on A's part, however, B had nevertheless remained here to wait for A. It was true that he had already inquired many times whether A was not back yet, but he was still upstairs in A's room. Happy at still being able to see B now and explain everything to him, A runs upstairs. He is almost at the top when he stumbles, strains a tendon, and, almost fainting with pain, incapable even of crying out, just whimpering there in the dark, he sees and hears how B – he is not sure whether a great distance off or just close to him – stamps down the stairs in a fury and disappears for good.

THE TRUTH ABOUT
SANCHO PANZA

SANCHO PANZA – who has incidentally never boasted of this – succeeded in the course of the years, by supplying numerous romances of chivalry and banditry during the evening and night hours, in diverting his devil – to which he later gave the name Don Quixote – so effectively from himself that this devil thereafter, quite out of control, performed the craziest deeds, which however for lack of their predestined object, which should have been precisely Sancho Panza, did nobody any harm. Sancho Panza, a free man, followed this Don Quixote imperturbably, perhaps from a certain sense of responsibility, on his travels, and he found great and profitable entertainment therein to the end of his days.

THE SILENCE OF THE SIRENS

PROOF that even inadequate, indeed childish measures can suffice for one's preservation:

To protect himself from the Sirens, Odysseus stopped his ears with wax and had himself chained to the mast. Of course all travellers from the very beginning could have done something of the kind (apart from those whom the Sirens lured even from the distance), but it was known to all the world that this could not possibly help. The song of the Sirens pierced everything, even wax, and the passion of those they seduced would have burst more than chains and a mast. But Odysseus did not think of that, though he had perhaps heard tell of it; he trusted completely to his handful of wax and his bundle of chains, and in innocent pleasure over his little resources he sailed towards the Sirens.

Now the Sirens have a still more terrible weapon than their song, namely their silence. Though it has never happened, it is perhaps conceivable that someone might have escaped from their singing, but from their silence certainly not. Against the feeling of having overcome them by one's own strength, and against the resultant arrogance that sweeps everything with it, no earthly resistance is possible.

And in fact, when Odysseus came, these mighty singers did not sing, whether because they believed that against this opponent only silence could achieve anything, or whether because the look of bliss on the face of Odysseus, who was thinking of nothing but wax and chains, made them forget all about their singing.

Odysseus however, if one may so express it, did not hear their silence, he believed they were singing and that only he was protected from hearing it, for a first fleeting moment he saw the movements of their necks, their deep breathing, their tearful eyes, their half-open

mouths, but he believed this went with the arias that were echoing
unheard around him. But soon all this slipped from his gaze, which
was fixed on the distance, the Sirens positively vanished from his
awareness, and at the very moment when he was nearest to them he
knew of them no longer.

But they – lovelier than ever – craned and twisted, let their
gruesome hair float free in the wind, stretched their claws wide on
the rocks; they wanted to allure no more, all they wanted was to
catch for as long as possible the reflected radiance from the great
eyes of Odysseus.

If the Sirens had possessed consciousness, they would have been
annihilated at that moment; as it was they remained, only Odysseus
escaped them.

There is moreover a supplement to this, which has also come
down to us. Odysseus, it is said, was so wily, was such a cunning fox,
that even the goddess of fate could not see into his heart; perhaps,
although this passes human comprehension, he really did notice that
the Sirens were silent, and confronted them and the gods with the
above mock episode merely as a kind of shield.

PROMETHEUS

FOUR legends tell of Prometheus:

According to the first, he was clamped to a rock in the Caucasus for betraying the secrets of the gods to men, and the gods sent eagles to feed on his liver, which perpetually renewed itself.

According to the second, Prometheus, to escape the tearing beaks, pressed himself in his agony deeper and deeper into the rock until he became one with it.

According to the third, in the course of thousands of years his treachery was forgotten, the gods forgot, the eagles forgot, he himself forgot.

According to the fourth, everyone grew weary of what had become meaningless. The gods grew weary, the eagles grew weary, the wound closed wearily.

There remained the inexplicable mountain of rock. – Legend tries to explain the inexplicable. Since it emerges from a ground of truth, it must end in the inexplicable once again.

HE

6 January. Everything he does seems to him extraordinarily new. If it lacked the freshness of life, then it would inevitably – this he knows – have as much intrinsic worth as something from the ancient pit of hell. But this freshness deceives him; it allows him to forget this fact or shrug it off, or else to recognize it painlessly. For after all, today is undeniably this very day now present, on which progress is setting out to progress further.

9 January. A superstition and a principle and an empowerment to live: Through the heaven of vices the hell of virtue is reached. Superstition is easy.

10 January. A piece like a segment has been cut out of the back of his head. The sun looks in and the whole world with it. It makes him nervous, it distracts him from his work, and moreover it irritates him that he should be the very one excluded from the spectacle.

It is no disproof of one's presentiment of a final release if the next day one's imprisonment remains unchanged, or is actually intensified, or even if it is expressly stated that it will never end. On the contrary, all this may be a necessary precondition of the final release.

On no occasion is he sufficiently prepared, but he cannot really blame himself for that, for when can one in this life, which so mercilessly requires one to be prepared every minute, find the time to prepare? And even if there were time, how could one prepare oneself before one knew the task; in other words, how can one ever be equal to any natural task whatever, any task that has not been artificially concocted? And for that reason he has long since gone under; strangely enough, but also comfortingly enough, that was what he was least of all prepared for.

He has discovered the Archimedean principle, but he has turned it to account against himself; evidently it was only on this condition that he was permitted to discover it.

13 January. Everything he does seems to him extraordinarily new, but at the same time, because of this unbelievable spate of novelty it seems extraordinarily amateurish, scarcely even tolerable, incapable of finding its place in history, breaking the chain of the generations, cutting off at its most profound source the music of the world for the first time, which before then could at least be divined. Sometimes in his arrogance he has more anxiety for the world than for himself.

He could have resigned himself to a prison. To end as a prisoner – that would have been a goal in life. But it was a barred cage that he was in. In and out through the bars flowed the din of the world, indifferently, imperiously, as if it were at home; the prisoner was actually free, he could take part in everything, nothing that went on outside escaped him, he could even have left the cage, after all the bars stood yards apart, he was not even imprisoned.

He has the feeling that merely by being alive he is blocking his own way. From this obstruction, again, he derives the proof that he is alive.

14 January. Himself he knows, the others he believes; everything is sawn apart for him by this discrepancy.

He is neither bold nor feckless. But he is not fearful either. A free life would not alarm him. Now such a life has not been vouchsafed to him, but even this does not worry him, indeed he does not worry about himself at all. But there is a certain someone, utterly unknown to him, who worries about him a great deal all the time, and about him alone. The worries of this someone about him, and especially the constant nature of these worries, give him many a racking headache in his quieter hours.

He lives in the Dispersion. His elements, a freely roaming horde, wander about the world. And only because his room also belongs to the world does he sometimes catch sight of them in the distance. How is he supposed to be responsible for them? Can that still be called responsibility?

Everything, even the most commonplace thing such as being served in a restaurant, he has to obtain by force with the help of the police. This robs life of all comfort.

17 January. His own frontal bone blocks his way (he bloodies his brow by beating against his own brow).

He feels imprisoned on this earth, he feels confined; the melancholy, the impotence, the sicknesses, the wild delusions of the captive break out in him; no consolation can console him, for the very reason that it *is* mere consolation, gentle, head-splitting consolation in the face of the brutal fact of imprisonment. But if he is asked what he actually wants he cannot reply, for – this is one of his strongest arguments – he has no conception of freedom.

Some deny the existence of misery by pointing to the sun; he denies the existence of the sun by pointing to misery.

He has two antagonists; the first presses him from behind, from his origins, the second bars his road ahead. He struggles with both. Actually the first supports him in his struggle with the second, for this one wants to push him forward, and in the same way the second supports him in his struggle with the first, for of course that one is driving him back. But that is only the case in theory; for it is not only the two antagonists that are present, but himself as well, and what his own intentions are who can really say?

He has many judges, they are like an army of birds perching in a tree. Their voices intermingle, the questions of their rank and competence are hopelessly confused, and there is also a continuous changing of places. But one can nevertheless single out individuals among them, for instance there is one who holds the view that one has only to cross over to the side of the Good and one is already saved, without reference to the past and even without reference to the future.

The self-torturing, sluggish, wave-like motion of all life, of other life and of his own, which often pauses for a long while but is at bottom unceasing, is a torture to him because it brings with it the unceasing compulsion to think. Sometimes it seems to him that this torture runs ahead of events. When he hears that a child is to be born to a friend of his, he recognizes that he has already suffered for that in his thoughts.

He can see two things: the first consists of all those calm meditations, reflections, investigations, outpourings of self, which are filled with life and impossible without a certain sense of contentment. Their number and possibilities are infinite; even a woodlouse needs a relatively large crack to lodge itself in, but for such labours no space whatsoever is needed; even where not the smallest crack is to be found they can still live in their thousands and tens of thousands, permeating one another. That is the first thing. But the second is the moment in which one is called forth to render one's account, can produce not a syllable, is flung back again upon one's meditations, etc., but now, recognizing the hopelessness of it all, finds it impossible to dabble about in them any longer, goes limp, and sinks with a curse on one's lips.

2 *February*. He remembers a picture that represented a summer Sunday on the Thames. The whole breadth of the river was filled with boats, waiting for a lock-gate to be opened. In all the boats were gay young people in light, bright-coloured clothing; they were almost reclining there, freely abandoned to the warm air and the coolness of the water. They had so much in common that their

convivial spirit was not confined to the separate boats; joking and laughter was passed on from boat to boat.

He now imagined that in a meadow on the bank – the banks were only faintly suggested in the picture, the gathering of boats over-shadowed everything – he himself was standing. He was contemplating the festival, which was not really a festival at all, but still one could call it that. He naturally had a great desire to join in, indeed he longed to do so, but he was forced to admit to himself that he was excluded from it, it was impossible for him to fit in there; to do so would have required such great preparation that in the course of it not only this Sunday, but many years, and he himself, would have passed away; and even if time here could have come to a standstill, it would still have been impossible to achieve any other result; his whole origin, upbringing, physical development would have had to be different.

So far removed, then, was he from these holiday-makers, and yet for all that he was very close to them too, and that was the more difficult thing to understand. They were, after all, human beings like himself, nothing human could be utterly alien to them, and so if one were to probe into them, one would surely find that the feeling which dominated him and excluded him from the river party was alive in them too, but of course with the difference that it was very far from dominating them and merely haunted some darker corners of their being.

The fact that there is fear, grief and desolation in the world is something he understands, but even this only in so far as these are vague, general feelings, just grazing the surface. All other feelings he denies; what we call by that name is for him merely illusion, fairy tale, mirror images of our experience and our memory. We experience them only before and after the real event, which flits by at an elemental, incomprehensible speed; they are dream-like fictions, restricted to ourselves alone. We live in the stillness of midnight, and experience sunrise and sunset by turning towards the east or the west.

15 February. It is a question of the following: One day many years

ago I was sitting, sorrowfully enough to be sure, on the slopes of the
Laurenziberg. I was examining the wishes that I had for my life.
What emerged as the most important or the most attractive was the
wish to gain a view of life (and – this was certainly a necessary part
of it – to be able to convince others of it in writing), in which life,
while still retaining its natural, full-bodied rise and fall, would simultaneously be recognized no less clearly as a nothing, as a dream, as
a hovering. A beautiful wish, perhaps, if I had wished it rightly. If it
had been, say, like the wish to hammer a table together with painfully
accurate craftsmanship, and simultaneously to do nothing, and moreover not so that people could say: 'Hammering is nothing to him',
but rather 'Hammering is to him a real hammering, and at the same
time it is nothing', whereby indeed the hammering would have
become still bolder, still more determined, still more real and, if you
will, still more insane. But he could not wish in this fashion, for his
wish was no wish, it was merely a defence, a domestication of
nothingness, a touch of animation that he wanted to give to nothingness, to that empty space in which he had by then scarcely taken his
first conscious steps, but which he already felt as his element. It was
at that time a sort of farewell that he took from the illusory world of
youth; although youth had never directly deceived him, but only
caused him to be deceived by the speeches of all the authorities
around him. Thus had the necessity of his 'wish' arisen.

He proves nothing but himself, his sole proof is himself, all his
opponents overcome him at once, but not by refuting him (he is
irrefutable), but by proving themselves.

Human associations rest on this, that someone seems by the strength
of his being to have refuted other individuals, in themselves irrefutable; which is sweet and comforting for those individuals, but it
lacks truth, and invariably therefore permanence.

He was once part of a monumental group. Round some kind of
raised centre were ranged, in carefully thought-out order, sym-
bolic figures representing the military, the arts, the sciences, the
handicrafts. Of these many figures he was one. Now the group has

long since dispersed, or at least he has left it and makes his own way through life. He no longer even has his old vocation, indeed he has actually forgotten what he once represented. Probably it is this very forgetting that gives rise to a certain melancholy, uncertainty, unrest, a certain longing for vanished ages, darkening the present. And yet this longing is an important element of man's vital strength, or perhaps that strength itself.

He does not live for the sake of his personal life, he does not think for the sake of his personal thoughts. It seems to him that he lives and thinks under the compulsion of a family, which certainly has more than enough vitality and intellectual power of its own, but for which he constitutes, in obedience to some law unknown to him, a formal necessity. Because of this unknown family and these unknown laws he cannot be released.

Original sin, the ancient wrong committed by man, consists in the complaint which man makes and never ceases making, that a wrong has been done to him, that it was upon him that original sin was committed.

Two children were hanging around in front of the window display at Casinelli's, a boy of about six, a girl of seven, expensively dressed; they were talking of God and sin. I stopped behind them. The girl, perhaps a Catholic, thought that deceiving God was the only real sin. With childish obstinacy the boy, perhaps a Protestant, asked what deceiving human beings or stealing was. 'They're a very great sin too,' said the girl, 'but not the greatest, only the sins against God are the greatest, for sins against men we have confession. When I confess, right away there's an angel standing behind me; but when I commit a sin the devil steps behind me, only you don't see him.' And tired of being half serious she spun round jokingly on her heels and said: 'Look, there's nobody behind me.' The boy spun round too and there he saw me. 'Look,' he said, without caring that I was bound to hear him, or perhaps without thinking about it, 'the devil is standing behind me.' 'I can see him too,' said the girl, 'but that's not the one I'm talking about.'

He does not want consolation, but not because he does not want it – who does not want it? – but because to seek consolation means: to devote one's whole life to this task, to live perpetually on the borders of one's existence and almost outside them, barely to remember for whom one is seeking consolation, and therefore not even being able to find effective consolation (effective, not by any means real consolation, which does not exist).

He resists being determined by the gaze of his fellow men. Had Robinson Crusoe never left the highest, or more correctly the most visible point of his island, out of desire for consolation, or out of humility, or fear, or ignorance, or longing, he would soon have perished; but since without regard for the ships and their feeble telescopes he started to explore his whole island and to take pleasure in it, he kept himself alive, and finally, as a result that was at least logically necessary, he was found.

19 February. 'You make a virtue of your necessity.'

'In the first place every one does that, and in the second, that's just what I don't do. I let my necessity remain necessity, I do not drain the swamp, but live in its feverish exhalations.'

'That's just what you make a virtue of.'

'Like every one, as I said before. In any case I only do it for your sake. So that you may remain friendly to me I take injury to my soul.'

My prison-cell – my fortress.

Everything is allowed him, with the exception of self-oblivion, wherewith in turn, however, everything is forbidden him, except the one thing that is immediately necessary for the whole.

The limitation of awareness is a social requirement. All virtues are individual, all vices social; the things that pass for social virtues, such as love, disinterestedness, justice, self-sacrifice, are only 'astonishingly' enfeebled social vices.

The difference between the 'Yes and No' that he says to his contemporaries, and the 'Yes and No' that he really ought to have said, might be likened to the difference between life and death; he can only grasp it in an equally vague sense.

The reason why posterity's judgement of individuals is juster than the contemporary one lies with the dead. One develops in one's own way only after death, only when one is alone. The state of death is to the individual like Saturday evening to the chimney-sweep; it washes the grime from his body. It becomes apparent whether his contemporaries did more harm to him, or whether he did more harm to his contemporaries; in the latter case he was a great man.

The strength to deny, that most natural expression of the human fighting organism, ever changing, renewing itself, reviving as it decays, this strength we possess always, but not the courage; and yet life itself is denial, and therefore denial affirmation.

He does not die along with his dying thoughts. Dying is merely a phenomenon within the inner world (which remains intact, even if it too should be only a thought), a natural phenomenon like any other, neither happy nor sad.

'From rising up he is prevented by a certain heaviness, a sense of being secure against any event, by the presentiment of a resting-place that is prepared for him and belongs to him alone; while from lying still he is prevented by an uneasiness that drives him from his resting-place, he is prevented by his conscience, by the ceaseless beating of his heart, the fear of death and the desire to refute it – all this will not let him lie, and he rises up again. This up-and-down, and some random, fleeting, incidental observations made on the way, make up his life.'

'Your account is dismal, but only as regards the analysis, the fundamental error of which it reveals. It is indeed so that man rises, falls back, rises again, and so forth, but at the same time it is also – and with yet far greater truth – utterly otherwise, for man is One, and hence in flight there is also repose, in repose there is flight, and both unite again in each individual being, and the union in each, and the union of the union in each, and so forth, until, well, until what is attained is real life, although this account also is just as false as yours and perhaps even more deceptive. The fact is, out of this realm there is no road leading to life, whereas there must surely have been a road from life leading into it. You see how lost we are.'

The current against which he swims races so strongly that sometimes, in a certain fit of distraction, he despairs at the desolate calm in the midst of which he is splashing, so infinitely far has he been swept backwards in a moment of inadequacy.

29 February. He is thirsty, and a mere clump of bushes separates him from the spring. But he is split in two: one part of him overlooks the whole scene, sees that he is standing here and that the spring is just beside him; but the second part notices nothing, has at most an inkling that the first part sees all. Since he notices nothing, however, he cannot drink.

THE CITY COAT OF ARMS

AT first everything was tolerably well organized for the building of the Tower of Babel; indeed the organization was perhaps excessive, too much thought was given to guides, interpreters, accommodation for the workmen and roads of communication, just as if centuries of undisturbed opportunity for work lay ahead. It was even the general opinion at the time that one simply could not build too slowly; this opinion only needed to be over-emphasized a little and people would have shrunk from laying the foundations at all. The argument ran as follows: The essence of the whole enterprise is the idea of building a tower that will reach to heaven. Beside that idea everything else is secondary. The idea, once grasped in its full magnitude, can never vanish again; so long as there are men on earth there will also be the strong desire to finish building the tower. But in this respect there need be no anxiety for the future; on the contrary, human knowledge is increasing, architecture has made progress and will make further progress, in another hundred years a piece of work that takes us a year will perhaps be done in half a year, and what is more done better, more securely. So why be in such a hurry to toil away now to the limit of one's powers? There would only be sense in that if one could hope to erect the tower in the span of one generation. But that was quite out of the question. It seemed more likely that the next generation, with their improved knowledge, would find the work of the previous generation unsatisfactory, and pull down what had been built in order to start afresh. Such thoughts caused energy to flag, and people concerned themselves less with the tower than with constructing a city for the workmen. Each nationality wanted to have the best quarter; this gave rise to disputes, which developed into bloody conflicts. These conflicts continued endlessly; to the leaders they were a new proof that, since the necessary concentration for the task was lacking, the tower should be built very slowly, or preferably postponed until a general peace had been concluded. However the time was not spent only in fighting; in the intervals embellishments were made to the city, which admittedly provoked fresh envy and fresh conflicts. Thus the period of the first generation passed, but none of the succeeding ones was any different; except that technical skill was increasing all the while, and belligerence with it. To this must be added that by the time of the second or third generation the senselessness of building a tower up to heaven was already recognized, but by that time everybody was far too closely bound up with one another to leave the city.

All the legends and songs that have originated in this city are filled with the longing for a prophesied day, on which the city will be smashed to pieces by five blows in rapid succession from a gigantic fist. That is also the reason why the city has a fist on its coat of arms.

POSEIDON

POSEIDON sat at his desk, going over the accounts. The administration of all the waters gave him endless work. He could have had as many assistants as he wanted, and indeed he had quite a number, but since he took his job very seriously he insisted on going through all the accounts again himself, and so his assistants were of little help to him. It cannot be said that he enjoyed the work; he carried it out simply because it was assigned to him; indeed he had frequently applied for what he called more cheerful work, but whenever various suggestions were put to him it turned out that nothing suited him so well as his present employment. Needless to say, it was very difficult to find him another job. After all, he could not possibly be put in charge of one particular ocean; quite apart from the fact that in this case the work involved would not be less, only more petty, the great Poseidon could hold only a superior position. And when he was offered a post unrelated to the waters, the very idea made him feel sick, his divine breath came short and his brazen chest began to heave. As a matter of fact, no one took his troubles very seriously; when a mighty man complains one must pretend to give way to him, even if he has no hope of satisfaction. No one ever really considered relieving Poseidon of his position; he had been destined to be God of the Seas since time immemorial, and that was how it had to remain.

What annoyed him most – and this was the chief cause of discontent with his job – was to learn of the rumours that were circulating about him; for instance, that he was constantly cruising through the waves with his trident. Instead of which he was sitting in the depths of the world's ocean, endlessly going over the accounts, an occasional journey to Jupiter being the only interruption of the monotony, a journey moreover from which he usually returned in a furious temper. As a result he had hardly seen the oceans, save fleetingly during his hasty ascent to Olympus, and had never really sailed upon them. He used to say that he was postponing this until the end of the world, for then there might come a quiet moment when, just before the end and having gone through his last account, he could still make a quick little tour.

FELLOWSHIP

WE are five friends, one day we came out of a house one after the
other, first one came and placed himself beside the gate, then the second came, and placed himself near the first one, then came the third,
then the fourth, then the fifth. Finally we all stood in a row. People
began to notice us, they pointed at us and said: Those five just came
out of that house. Since then we have been living together; it would
be a peaceful life if it weren't for a sixth one continually trying to
interfere. He doesn't do us any harm, but he annoys us, and that is
harm enough; why does he intrude where he is not wanted? We
don't know him and don't want him to join us. There was a time, of
course, when the five of us did not know one another, either; and it
could be said that we still don't know one another, but what is
possible and can be tolerated by the five of us is not possible
and cannot be tolerated with this sixth one. In any case, we are five
and don't want to be six. And what is the point of this continual
being together anyhow? It is also pointless for the five of us, but
here we are together and will remain together; a new combination,
however, we do not want, just because of our experiences. But how
is one to make all this clear to the sixth one? Long explanations
would also amount to accepting him in our circle, so we prefer not to
explain and not to accept him. No matter how he pouts his lips we
push him away with our elbows, but however much we push him
away, back he comes.

AT NIGHT

SUNK deep in the night. As one sometimes sinks one's head in meditation, thus utterly to be sunk in the night. All around people are asleep. It's a harmless affectation, an innocent self-deception, to suppose that they are sleeping in houses, in safe beds, under a safe roof, stretched out or curled up on mattresses, in sheets, under blankets; in reality they have gathered together as they once did of old, and again later, in a desert region, a camp in the open, a countless number of men, a host, a people, under a cold sky on cold earth, cast down where they had earlier stood, forehead pressed upon arm, face towards the ground, peacefully sleeping. And you are watching, are one of the watchmen, you find your nearest fellow by brandishing a burning stick from the brushwood pile beside you. Why are you watching? Someone must watch, it is said. Someone must be there.

THE REFUSAL

OUR little town does not lie on the frontier, nowhere near; it is so far from the frontier, in fact, that perhaps no one from our town has ever been there; desolate highlands have to be crossed as well as wide fertile plains. To imagine even part of the road makes one tired, and more than part one just cannot imagine. There are also big towns on the road, each far larger than ours. Ten little towns like ours laid side by side, and ten more forced down from above, still would not produce one of these enormous, overcrowded towns. If one does not get lost on the way one is bound to lose oneself in these towns, and to avoid them is impossible on account of their size.

But what is even further from our town than the frontier, if such distances can be compared at all – it's like saying that a man of three hundred years is older than one of two hundred – what is even further than the frontier is the capital. Whereas we do get news of the frontier wars now and again, of the capital we learn next to nothing – we civilians that is, for of course the government officials have very good connections with the capital; they can get news from there in as little as two or three months, so they claim at least.

Now it is remarkable, and it continually surprises me afresh, how we in our town humbly submit to all orders issued in the capital. For centuries no political change has been brought about by the citizens themselves. In the capital great rulers have superseded one another – indeed, even dynasties have been deposed or annihilated, and new ones have started; in the past century even the capital itself was destroyed, a new one was founded far away from it, later on this too was destroyed and the old one rebuilt, yet none of this had any influence on our little town. Our officials have always remained at their posts; the highest officials came from the capital, the less high came at least from outside, and the lowest from among ourselves – that is how it has always been and it has suited us. The highest official is the chief tax-collector, he has the rank of colonel, and is known as such. The present one is an old man; I've known him for years, because he was already a colonel when I was a child. At first he rose very fast in his career, but then he seems to have advanced no further; actually, for our little town his rank is good enough, a higher rank would be out of place. When I try to recall him I see him sitting on the veranda of his house in the market square, leaning back, pipe in mouth. Above him from the roof flutters the imperial flag; on the side of the veranda, which is so big that minor military manoeuvres are sometimes held there, washing hangs out to dry. His grandchildren, in beautiful silk clothes, play around him; they are not allowed down in the market square, the children there are considered unworthy of them, but the grandchildren are attracted by the square, so they thrust their heads between the balusters and when the children below begin to quarrel they join in the quarrel from above.

This colonel, then, commands the town. I don't think he has ever produced a document entitling him to this position; very likely he does not possess such a thing. Perhaps he really is chief tax-collector, but is that all? Does that entitle him to rule over all the other departments in the administration as well? True, his office is very important for the government, but for the citizens it is hardly the most important. One is almost under the impression that the people here say: 'Now that you've taken all we possess, please take us as well.' In reality, of course, it was not he who seized the power, nor is he a tyrant. It has just come about over the years that the chief tax-collector is automatically the top official, and the colonel accepts the tradition just as we do.

Yet while he lives among us without laying too much stress on his official position, he is something quite different from the ordinary citizen. When a delegation comes to him with a request, he stands there like the wall of the world. Behind him is nothingness, one imagines hearing voices whispering in the background, but this is probably a delusion; after all, he represents the end of all things, at least for us. At these receptions he really was worth seeing. Once as a child I was present when a delegation of citizens arrived to ask him for a government subsidy because the poorest quarter of the town had been burned to the ground. My father the blacksmith, a man well respected in the community, was a member of the delegation and had taken me along. There's nothing exceptional about this, everyone rushes to spectacles of this kind, one can hardly distinguish the actual delegation from the crowd. Since these receptions usually take place on the veranda, there are even people who climb up by ladder from the market square and take part in the goings-on from over the balustrade. On this occasion about a quarter of the veranda had been reserved for the colonel, the crowd filling the rest of it. A few soldiers kept watch, some of them standing round him in a semicircle. Actually a single soldier would have been quite enough, such is our fear of them. I don't know exactly where these soldiers came from, in any case from a long way off, they all look very much alike, they wouldn't even need a uniform. They are small, not strong but agile people, the most striking thing about them is the prominence of their teeth which almost overcrowd their mouths, and a certain restless twitching of their small, narrow eyes. This makes them the terror of the children, but also their delight, for again and again the children long to be frightened by these teeth, these eyes, so as to be able to run madly away. Even grown-ups probably never quite lose this childish terror, at least it continues to have an effect. There are, of course, other factors contributing to it. The soldiers speak a dialect utterly incomprehensible to us, and they can hardly get used to ours – all of which produces a certain shut-off, unapproachable quality corresponding, as it happens, to their character, for they are silent, serious, and rigid. They don't actually do anything evil, and yet they are almost unbearable in an evil sense. A soldier, for example, enters a shop, buys some trifling object, and stays there leaning against the counter; he listens to the conversations, probably does not understand them, and yet gives the impression of understanding; he himself does not say a word, just stares blankly at the speaker, then back at the listeners, all the while leaning his hand on the hilt of the long knife in his belt. This is revolting, one loses the desire to talk, the customers start leaving the shop, and only when it is quite empty does the soldier also leave. Thus wherever the soldiers appear, our lively people grow silent. That's what happened this time, too. As on all solemn occasions the colonel stood upright, holding in front of him two poles of bamboo in his outstretched hands. This is an ancient custom implying more or less that he supports the law, and the law supports him. Now everyone knows, of course, what to expect up on the veranda, and yet each time people take fright all over again. On this occasion, too, the man chosen to speak could not begin; he was already standing opposite the colonel when his courage failed him and, muttering a few excuses, he pushed his way back into the crowd. No other suitable person willing to speak could be found, albeit several unsuitable ones offered themselves; a great commotion ensued and messengers were sent in search of various citizens who were well-known speakers. During all this time the colonel stood there motionless, only his chest moving visibly up and down to his breathing. Not that he breathed with difficulty, it was just that he breathed so conspicuously, much as frogs breathe – except that with them it is normal, while here it was exceptional. I squeezed myself through the grown-ups and watched him through a gap between two soldiers, until one of them kicked me away with his knee. Meanwhile the man originally chosen to speak had regained his composure and, firmly held up by two fellow citizens, was delivering his address. It was touching to see him smile throughout this solemn speech describing a grievous misfortune – a most humble smile which strove in vain to elicit some slight reaction on the colonel's face. Finally he formulated the request – I think he was only asking for a year's tax exemption, but possibly also for timber from the imperial forests at a reduced price. Then he bowed low, remaining in this position for some time, as did everyone else except the colonel, the soldiers and a number of officials in the background. To a child it seemed ridiculous that the people on the ladders should climb down a few rungs so as not to be seen during this decisive pause, and now and again peer inquisitively over the floor of the veranda. After this had lasted quite a while an official, a little man, stepped up to the colonel and tried to reach the latter's height by standing on his toes. The colonel, still motionless save for his deep breathing, whispered something in his ear, whereupon the little man clapped his hands and everyone rose. 'The petition has been refused,' he announced. 'You may go.' An undeniable sense of relief passed through the crowd, everyone surged out, hardly a soul paying any special attention to the colonel who, as it were, had turned once more into a human being like the rest of us. I still caught one last glimpse of him as he wearily let go of the poles, which fell to the ground, then sank into an armchair produced by some officials, and promptly put his pipe in his mouth.

This whole occurrence is not isolated, it's in the general run of things. Indeed, it does happen now and again that minor petitions are granted, but then it invariably looks as though the colonel had done it as a powerful private person on his own responsibility, and it had to be kept all but a secret from the government – not explicitly of course, but that is what it feels like. No doubt in our little town the colonel's eyes, so far as we know, are also the eyes of the government, and yet there is a difference which it is impossible to comprehend completely.

In all important matters, however, the citizens can always count on a refusal. And now the strange fact is that without this refusal one simply cannot get along, yet at the same time these official occasions designed to receive the refusal are by no means a formality. Time after time one goes there full of expectation and in all seriousness and then one returns, if not exactly strengthened or happy, nevertheless not disappointed or tired.

As a matter of fact there is, so far as my observations go, a certain age group that is not content – these are the young people roughly between seventeen and twenty. Quite young fellows, in fact, who are utterly incapable of foreseeing the consequences of even the least significant, far less a revolutionary, idea. And it is among just them that discontent creeps in.

THE PROBLEM OF OUR LAWS

UNFORTUNATELY our laws are not generally known; they are the
secret of the small group of noblemen who govern us. We are
convinced that these ancient laws are scrupulously adhered to, but
all the same it is exceedingly distressing to be governed according to
laws that one does not know. I am not thinking here of the various
possible ways of interpreting the laws, or of the disadvantage involved
when only a few individuals and not the whole people are allowed to
take part in their interpretation. These disadvantages are perhaps not
so very great. For the laws are very ancient, centuries of work have
gone into their interpretation and by now this has probably become
law itself; there does indeed still remain a certain possible latitude of
interpretation, but it is very limited. Besides, the nobility have obviously no call to let their personal interest sway them into interpreting
the laws to our disadvantage, since these were drawn up in the
interests of the nobility from the very beginning; the nobles stand
above the law, and that seems to be the very reason why the law has
been given over exclusively into their hands. Of course, there is
wisdom in that – who doubts the wisdom of the ancient laws? – but
equally there is distress for us; probably that is unavoidable.

Moreover these apparent laws are really no more than a matter of
conjecture. There is a tradition that they exist and are entrusted as a
secret to the nobility, but this is not and cannot be more than an
ancient tradition to which age lends authority, for the character of
these laws requires that their very existence be kept secret as well.
But if we common people have been following the actions of the
nobles since the earliest times, and possess records of them made by
our forefathers which we have conscientiously continued, and if
among the myriad facts we think we can detect certain tendencies

which permit us to conclude this or that about our historical destiny, and if we then, on the basis of these most carefully sifted and sorted conclusions, try to put our lives into some kind of order for the present and the future – then all that is in the highest degree uncertain, and perhaps no more than an intellectual game, for perhaps these laws which we are trying to guess at in this way do not exist at all. There is a small party which really is of this opinion, and which seeks to prove that if any law exists, it can only run thus: What the nobility does is the law. This party sees nothing but arbitrary acts on the part of the nobility, and it rejects the popular tradition, which according to them is only beneficial in minor and incidental ways, while being for the most part seriously harmful, since it gives the people a false and deceptive sense of security and disposes them to recklessness in the face of coming events. This harmful effect cannot be denied, but it is attributed by the overwhelming majority of our people to the fact that the tradition is still far from being sufficient, that it needs to be much more fully studied, and indeed that even the material available, immense though it appears to us, is still far too meagre, and that centuries must yet pass before it will be adequate. This prospect, so gloomy as far as the present is concerned, is lightened only by the belief that one day the time will come when both the tradition and our study of it will arrive, almost with a sigh of relief, at their conclusion, when all will have become clear, when the law will at last belong to the people, and the nobility will vanish. This is not said with any hatred for the nobility; not at all, not by anyone; rather are we inclined to hate ourselves because we cannot yet be judged worthy of the law. And that is the real reason why the party which believes that there is no law – in some ways such an attractive party – has remained so small, for it too fully recognizes the nobility and its right to existence.

One can really only express the matter in a kind of paradox: Any party which would repudiate, not only belief in the laws, but the nobility as well, would instantly have the whole people behind it; but such a party cannot arise, for no one dares repudiate the nobility. It is on this razor's edge that we live. A writer once summed it up in this way: The one visible and indubitable law that is imposed upon us is the nobility, and could it really be our wish to deprive ourselves of this solitary law?

THE CONSCRIPTION OF TROOPS

THE compulsory enlistments that are so often necessary because of the never-ending frontier wars take place in the following manner:

The order goes out that on a certain day in a certain quarter of the town all the inhabitants – men, women and children without exception – have to remain in their own houses. It is usually not until about midday that the young nobleman in charge of the enlistment appears at the entrance to the quarter, where a detachment of foot soldiers and cavalry has been waiting since dawn. He is a slim young man, not very tall, frail-looking, carelessly dressed, with weary eyes; tremors of disquiet keep passing through him like the shivers of a fever. Without looking at anyone he makes a sign with the whip that forms his sole equipment; a number of soldiers join him and he enters the first house. One soldier who knows all the inhabitants of this quarter reads out the list of the occupants. As a rule they are all present, lined up there in the room with their eyes fixed on the nobleman, as if they were soldiers already. It can happen, however, that here or there someone, it's invariably a man, is missing. In this case no one will dare to produce an excuse, let alone a lie; everyone just keeps quiet, all eyes are lowered, the pressure of the command which someone in this house has disobeyed becomes almost unbearable, but the silent presence of the nobleman keeps everyone in his place. The nobleman makes a sign, it's not so much as a nod, it has to be read in his eyes, and two soldiers begin the search for the missing man. This causes no trouble at all. He is never outside the house, he never really intends to evade military service, it is only fear that has prevented him from turning up; yet it is not the fear of serving that holds him back, it is just that he is too nervous to show himself at all; the grandeur of the command is simply too much for him, it terrifies him, he has not the strength to appear of his own accord. But that does not make him run away, he merely hides, and when he hears that the nobleman is in the house he may even creep out of his hiding-place, creep up to the door of the room, there to be promptly seized by the soldiers as they come out to look for him. He is brought before the nobleman, who grasps his whip with both hands – he is so feeble that he could do nothing with one hand – and gives the man a thrashing. The pain he inflicts can hardly amount to much; then half from exhaustion, half in disgust he drops the whip, and the man who has been beaten has to pick it up and hand it to him. Only then may he join the rank with the others; incidentally, it is almost certain that he will not be recruited. But it can also happen, and this is more frequent, that the number of people present exceeds the number on the list. There may be an unknown girl there, for instance, who stares at the nobleman; she is from out of town, from the provinces perhaps, and has been lured here by the conscription; there are many women for whom a conscription in another town – conscription at home means something quite different – presents an irresistible temptation. And strangely enough it is not considered disgraceful for a woman to surrender to this temptation; on the contrary, in the opinion of many this is something that women have to go through, it is a debt which they pay to their sex. Moreover, things invariably take the same course. The girl or the woman learns that somewhere, perhaps a long way away, there is to be an enlistment at some relatives or friends of hers; she requests her family's permission for the journey; this is granted, it is not something that one can refuse; she puts on her best clothes, is gayer than usual, at the same time calm and friendly, no matter what she may be like at other times; and yet behind all the calm and friendliness she is inaccessible, like an utter stranger who is setting out for home and can now think of nothing else. In the family where the enlistment is to take place she is received quite differently from an ordinary guest; she is surrounded with attention, pressed to inspect all the rooms in the house, to lean out of all the windows, and if she lays her hand on someone's head it means more than a father's blessing. When the family is preparing for the conscription she is given the best place, which is close to the door, and where she can best see the nobleman and best be seen by him. But she only enjoys these honours until the nobleman enters; after that she positively begins to fade. He looks at her as little as at the others, and even when his eye does rest on someone, that person is not aware of being looked at. This is something that she has not expected, or rather she must certainly have expected it, for it cannot be otherwise; but neither was it the expectation of the opposite that has forced her to come here, it was just something that is now, whatever it was, definitely over. She feels shame to a degree which perhaps our women feel at no other time; only now is she fully aware that she has forced her way into a conscription where she doesn't belong; and when the soldier has read out the list and her name has not appeared on it and there comes a moment of silence, she flees cowering and trembling out of the door, and receives a blow in the back from a soldier's fist into the bargain.

If it should be a man who is not on the list, his only desire, despite the fact that he does not belong to this house, is to be conscripted along with the others. But this too is utterly out of the question; no such superfluous person has ever been conscripted and nothing of the kind will ever happen.

THE TEST

I AM a servant, but there is no work available for me. I am timid and don't push myself to the fore, indeed I don't even push myself into line with the others, but that is only one reason for my non-employment, it's even possible that it has nothing to do with my non-employment, in any case the main reason is that I am not called upon to serve; others have been called yet they have not tried harder than I, indeed perhaps they have not even felt the desire to be called, whereas I, at least sometimes, feel it very strongly.

So I lie on the pallet in the servants' hall, stare at the beams in the ceiling, fall asleep, wake up and promptly fall asleep again. Occasionally I walk over to the tavern where they sell a sour beer, occasionally I have even poured away a glass in disgust, but then I go back to it again. I like sitting there because from behind the closed little window, without the possibility of being discovered, I can see across to the windows of our house. Not that one sees very much there, to my knowledge only the windows of the corridors look out on the street, and moreover not even those of the corridors leading to the master apartments. It is possible that I may be mistaken, but someone, without my having asked him, once said so, and the general impression of this house front confirms it. Only rarely are the windows opened, and when this does occur it is done by a servant who may well then lean against the balustrade to look down for a while. It follows therefore that these are corridors where he cannot be taken by surprise. As a matter of fact I am not personally acquainted with these servants; those who are permanently employed upstairs sleep elsewhere, not in my room.

Once when I arrived at the tavern, a guest was sitting at my observation post. I did not dare look at him closely and was about to turn round in the door and leave. The guest, however, called me over, and it turned out that he too was a servant, whom I had once seen somewhere before but without having spoken to him. 'Why do you want to run away? Sit down and have a drink. I'll pay.' So I sat down. He asked me several things, but I couldn't answer, indeed I didn't even understand his questions. So I said: 'Perhaps you are sorry now that you invited me, so I'd better go,' and I was about to get up. But he stretched his hand out over the table and pressed me down. 'Stay,' he said, 'that was only a test. He who does not answer the questions has passed the test.'

THE VULTURE

A vulture was hacking at my feet. It had already torn my boots and stockings to shreds, now it was hacking at the feet themselves. Again and again it struck at them, then circled several times restlessly round me, then returned to continue its work. A gentleman passed by, looked on for a while, then asked me why I suffered the vulture. 'I'm helpless,' I said. 'When it came and began to attack me, I of course tried to drive it away, even to strangle it, but these animals are very strong, it was about to spring at my face, but I preferred to sacrifice my feet. Now they are almost torn to bits.' 'Fancy letting yourself be tortured like this!' said the gentleman. 'One shot and that's the end of the vulture.' 'Really?' I said. 'And would you do that?' 'With pleasure,' said the gentleman, 'I've only got to go home and get my gun. Could you wait another half hour?' 'I'm not sure about that,' said I, and stood for a moment rigid with pain. Then I said: 'Do try it in any case, please.' 'Very well,' said the gentleman, 'I'll be as quick as I can.' During this conversation the vulture had been calmly listening, letting its eye rove between me and the gentleman. Now I realized that it had understood everything; it took wing, leaned far back to gain impetus, and then, like a javelin thrower, thrust its beak through my mouth, deep into me. Falling back, I was relieved to feel him drowning irretrievably in my blood, which was filling every depth, flooding every shore.

THE HELMSMAN

'AM I not the helmsman here?' I called out. 'You?' asked a tall dark man and passed his hands over his eyes as though to banish a dream. I had been standing at the helm in the dark night, a feeble lantern burning over my head, and now this man had come and was trying to push me aside. And as I would not give way, he put his foot on my chest and slowly forced me to the deck while I still clung to the spokes of the wheel, wrenching it round in falling. But then the man seized the wheel and righted it, at the same time pushing me away. I soon collected myself, however, ran to the hatchway which gave on to the mess quarters, and cried out: 'Men! Comrades! Come here, quick! A stranger has driven me away from the helm!' Slowly they came up, climbing the companion ladder, tired, swaying, powerful figures. 'Am I the helmsman?' I asked. They nodded, but they had eyes only for the stranger, stood round him in a semicircle, and when, in a commanding voice, he said: 'Don't disturb me!' they gathered together, nodded at me, and withdrew down the companion ladder. What folk these are! Do they ever think, or do they only shuffle pointlessly over the earth?

THE TOP

A certain philosopher used to hang about wherever children were at play. And whenever he saw a boy with a top, he would lie in wait. As soon as the top began to spin the philosopher went in pursuit and tried to catch it. He was not perturbed when the children noisily protested and tried to keep him away from their toy; so long as he could catch the top while it was still spinning he was happy, but only for a moment; then he threw it to the ground and walked away. For he believed that the understanding of any detail, that of a spinning-top, for instance, was sufficient for the understanding of all things. For this reason he did not busy himself with great problems, it seemed to him uneconomical; once the smallest detail was properly understood, then everything was understood, which was why he busied himself only with the spinning-top. And whenever preparations were being made for the spinning of the top, he hoped that this time he would succeed; as soon as the top began to spin and he was running breathlessly after it, the hope would turn to certainty; but when he held the silly piece of wood in his hand, he felt nauseated, and the screaming of the children, which hitherto he had not heard and which now suddenly pierced his ears, chased him away; he reeled off like a top under a clumsy whip.

A LITTLE FABLE

'ALAS,' said the mouse, 'the world is growing smaller every day. At first it was so big that I was afraid, I ran on and I was glad when at last I saw walls to left and right of me in the distance, but these long walls are closing in on each other so fast that I have already reached the end room, and there in the corner stands the trap that I am heading for.' 'You only have to change direction,' said the cat, and ate it up.

HOMECOMING

I HAVE returned, I have crossed the front yard and I look round me. It is my father's old farmstead. The puddle in the middle. Old, useless implements, jumbled together, block the stairs to the store loft. The cat lurks on the banister. A torn piece of cloth, once wound round a stick in some game, lifts in the breeze. I have arrived. Who shall receive me? Who waits behind the kitchen door? Smoke is coming from the chimney, coffee is being made for supper. Do you feel you belong, do you feel at home? I don't know, I feel most uncertain. Yes, it is my father's house, but each object stands cold beside the next, as if each was preoccupied with its own affairs, which I have partly forgotten, partly never known. What use can I be to them, what do I mean to them, even though I am my father's son, the old farmer's son. And I dare not knock at the kitchen door, I only listen from a distance, I only listen standing at a distance, so as not to be surprised as an eavesdropper. And since I am listening from a distance, I can catch nothing; all I hear, or perhaps just imagine I hear, is the faint chiming of a clock that floats across to me from my childhood. Whatever else is going on in the kitchen is the secret of those sitting there, and they are keeping it from me. The longer one hesitates before the door, the more of a stranger one becomes. What would happen now if someone were to open the door and ask me something? Would not I myself be like a man who wishes to keep his secret?

THE DEPARTURE

I ORDERED my horse to be fetched from the stable. The servant did not understand me. I went into the stable myself, saddled my horse, and mounted. In the distance I heard the sound of a trumpet; I asked him what that meant. He knew nothing and had heard nothing. At the gate he stopped me and asked: 'Where are you riding to, master?' 'I don't know,' I said, 'just away from here, just away from here. On and on away from here, that's the only way I can reach my goal.' 'So you know your goal?' he asked. 'Yes,' I replied, 'I've just told you. Away-from-here – that is my goal.' 'You have no provisions with you,' he said. 'I need none,' said I, 'the journey is so long that I must die of starvation if I get nothing on the way. No provisions can save me. It is, fortunately enough, a truly immense journey.'

ADVOCATES

I WAS not at all certain whether I had any advocates, I could not find out anything definite about it, every face was unfriendly, most people who came towards me and whom I kept meeting in the corridors looked like fat old women; they had huge blue and white striped aprons covering their entire bodies, kept stroking their stomachs and turning awkwardly to and fro. I could not even find out whether we were in a lawcourt. Some facts spoke for it, others against. What reminded me of a lawcourt more than all the details was a droning noise which could be heard incessantly in the distance; one could not tell from which direction it came, it filled every room to such an extent that one could assume it came from everywhere or, what seemed more likely, that just the place where one happened to be standing was the very place where the droning originated, but this was doubtless an illusion, for it came from a distance. These corridors, narrow and austerely vaulted, turning in gradual curves with high, sparsely decorated doors, seemed in fact to have been designed for profound silence; they were the corridors of a museum or a library. Yet if it were not a lawcourt, why was I searching for an advocate here? Because I was searching for an advocate everywhere, he is needed everywhere, if anything less in court than elsewhere, for a court passes judgement according to the law; if one were to assume that this was being done unfairly or frivolously, then life would not be possible; one must have confidence that the court allows the majesty of the law its full scope, for this is its sole duty; but within the law itself all is accusation, advocacy, and verdict, and any interference by an individual here would be a crime. It is different, however, with the evidence that leads to the verdict; this rests on inquiries, on inquiries made here and there, from relatives and strangers, from friends and enemies, in the family and public life, in town and village – in short, everywhere. Here it is most urgently necessary to have advocates, advocates galore, preferably advocates in close formation, a living wall, for advocates are by nature ponderous creatures; the plaintiffs, however, those sly foxes, those nimble weasels, those invisible mice, they slip through the tiniest gaps, scuttle through the legs of the advocates. So look out! That's why I am here, I'm collecting advocates. But I have not found any as yet, only those old women keep on coming and going; if I were not on my search it would put me to sleep. I'm not in the right place – alas, I cannot rid myself of the feeling that I'm not in the right place. I ought to be in a place where all kinds of people meet, from various parts of the country, from every class, every profession, of all ages; I ought to have an opportunity of choosing carefully out of a crowd those who are suitable, those who are friendly, those who have an eye for me. Perhaps the most suitable place for this would be a huge fairground. Instead of which I am hanging about in these corridors where only these old women are to be seen, and not even many of them, and always the same ones, and even those few will not let themselves be cornered, despite their slowness; they slip away from me, float about like rain clouds, and are completely absorbed by unknown activities. Why is it then that I run headlong into a house without reading the sign over the door, promptly find myself in these corridors, and settle here with such obstinacy that I cannot even remember ever having been in front of the house, ever having run up the stairs! But back I cannot go, this waste of time, this admission of having been on the wrong track would be unbearable for me. What? Run downstairs in this brief, hurried life, accompanied as it is by that impatient droning? Impossible. The time allotted to you is so short that if you lose one second you have already lost your whole life; for your life is always just as long as the time you lose, never longer. So if you have started out on a walk, continue it whatever happens; you can only gain, you run no risk; perhaps in the end you may fall, but had you turned back after the first steps and run downstairs you would have fallen at once – and not perhaps, but for certain. So if you find nothing here in the corridors, open the doors; if you find nothing behind these doors, there are further storeys; if you find nothing up there, no matter, go leaping on up further flights; as long as you don't stop climbing, the stairs will never end, under your climbing feet they will go on growing upwards.

INVESTIGATIONS OF A DOG

HOW much my life has changed, and yet how unchanged it has remained at bottom! If I cast my mind back today and recall the time when I was still living in the midst of the dog community, taking part in all its concerns, a dog among dogs, I soon find on closer examination that something was not quite right from the very beginning; there was always a little discrepancy somewhere, a slight discomfort would overtake me in the middle of the most solemn public functions, occasionally even in a gathering of friends; no, it was not occasionally, it was very often; the mere sight of some fellow dog dear to me, this mere sight caught somehow afresh, would embarrass me, alarm me, fill me with helplessness and even despair. I tried to soothe myself as best I could; friends to whom I confessed my trouble helped me; there was a return of more peaceful times, times in which such surprises were indeed not lacking, but were accepted more calmly, were fitted into the pattern of my life more calmly; they may have induced a certain sadness and weariness, but apart from that they did not prevent me from holding my own with the others, as an admittedly somewhat cold, reserved, timid and calculating, but all things considered normal enough dog. How indeed, without these intervals for recuperation, could I have attained the age that I enjoy at present, how could I have struggled my way through to the serenity with which I view the terrors of my youth and endure the terrors of age, how could I have got to the stage of drawing the consequences from my admittedly unfortunate, or to put it more cautiously, not very fortunate disposition, and of living accordingly as far as my strength allows? Withdrawn, isolated, occupied solely with my little investigations, amateurish, hopeless investigations which are, however, indispensable to me, and so presumably they do afford some secret hope after all – such is the life I lead; but all the same I still manage to keep my people in view from the distance, news of them sometimes penetrates to me, though it is indeed becoming gradually more infrequent, and occasionally I let them hear from me as well. The others treat me with deference, they cannot understand my way of life but they do not hold it against me, and even young dogs whom I sometimes see passing in the distance, a new generation of whose childhood I have scarcely a vague memory, never refuse me their respectful greeting.

For one should not neglect the fact that despite my peculiarities, which lie open to view, I am by no means completely different from the rest of my species. Indeed, when I think about it – and I have the time and the wish and the ability to do so – the dog community as a whole has its peculiar features. Apart from us dogs there are many kinds of creatures about, poor inferior speechless beings whose utterance is restricted to a few cries; many of us dogs study them, have given them names, try to help them, to educate them, to refine them, and so on; for my part I am indifferent to them, unless for instance they try to disturb me or unless there is a chance of their supplying a tasty mouthful (in our region that rarely happens); I confuse them with one another, I ignore them; but one thing is too obvious to have escaped even me, namely how little by comparison with us dogs they stick together, how they pass one another by as strangers, silently and with a secret hostility, how only the most obvious common interest can forge a little superficial unity amongst them and how even this common interest often gives rise to hatred and conflict. We dogs on the other hand! It may well be said that we all live literally in one great crowd, all of us, however much we may otherwise differ owing to the many and profound distinctions that have arisen in the course of time. All in one great crowd! We feel the urge to draw together, and nothing can prevent us from expressing it continually; all our laws and institutions, the few that I still know and the countless number that I have forgotten or never discovered, have their roots in this longing for the greatest bliss we are capable of, the warmth of communal life. But now the other side of the picture. No kind of creature to my knowledge lives so widely dispersed as we dogs, none has such a baffling profusion of distinctions in its classes and varieties and occupations. We, who want to stick together – and again and again we manage to do so in spite of everything, even if it is only in a small way, and even this only in moments of exuberance – we are precisely the ones who live widely separated from one another, engaged in our peculiar avocations that are often incomprehensible even to our nearest dog neighbour, obeying regulations that are not those of the dog community as a whole, indeed if anything opposed to them.

What difficult matters these are, matters that one might do better to leave alone – that is a point of view I can well understand, I understand it better than my own – and yet they are matters by which I am utterly absorbed. Why do I not as the others do, live in harmony with my people and quietly accept whatever disturbs that harmony; ignore it as a small error in the great account, and keep my eyes ever fixed on what binds us happily together, not on what draws us – with a power that is admittedly so often irresistible – out of the circle of our kin?

My own sense of disquiet, a disquiet that can never be wholly assuaged, first began after a number of earlier indications with one particular incident in my youth. At that time I was in one of those blissful inexplicable states of excitement which probably everyone must experience as a child; I was still a very young dog, roughly at the end of my boyhood; everything pleased me, everything was my concern; I believed that great things were going on round me of which I was the leader and to which I must lend my voice; things that it was my duty to chase after and jump for, for else they would be left lying about wretchedly on the ground; well, these were childish fancies that fade with the years, but at that time their power was very great, I was completely under their spell, and then indeed something exceptional really did happen which seemed to justify my wild expectations. In itself it was nothing so very exceptional – I have seen many such things, and even far more remarkable ones, often enough since – but at the time it struck me strongly with the force of a first, indelible, decisive impression.

What happened was that I met a small company of dogs, or rather I did not meet them, they came up on me. At that time I had been running for a long time through the darkness with a premonition of great things to come – not a very dependable premonition, it is true, for I had it always – I had been running through the darkness for a long time, this way and that, blind and deaf to everything, led on by nothing but my vague desire; suddenly I stopped with the feeling that this was the right place, I looked up and it was the brightest daylight, with everything full of blending and intoxicating smells, I greeted the morning excitedly with confused sounds, and then – as if in response to my summons – from some dark corner seven dogs stepped forth into the light, producing a terrible clamour the like of which I had never heard before.

If I had not clearly seen that they were dogs, and that they brought this clamour with them, though I failed to understand how they produced it, I would have run away at once; but as it was I stayed. At that time I knew next to nothing of that creative musical gift with which the dog species is alone endowed; till then it had escaped my powers of observation, which were only just slowly beginning to develop; naturally music had surrounded me ever since infancy as an unquestionable and indispensable element of life, but nothing had impelled me to distinguish it from the rest of my experience; only by such hints as were suitable to a childish under-standing had my elders tried to draw my attention to it; all the more surprising to me therefore, indeed positively devastating, were these seven great musicians.

They did not speak, they did not sing, for the most part they kept almost stubbornly silent, but from the empty air they conjured music. All was music. The way they lifted and set down their feet, certain turns of the head, their running and their standing still, the positions they took up in relation to one another, the dance-like patterns they formed, as when one of them supported his front paws on another's back and they then arranged themselves so that the first dog, standing upright, took the weight of all the rest, or when they described complicated figures by slithering in and out with their bodies close to the ground, and always faultlessly; not even the last dog made a mistake, though he was a little unsure, not always finding his link with the others right away, hesitating sometimes as it were at the first note of the tune, but he was only unsure by comparison with the magnificent sureness of the others, and he could have been far more unsure, infinitely unsure, without spoiling anything, since the others – these great masters – kept such imperturbable time.

But the truth is that one hardly saw them, one hardly took any of them in. They had appeared, and one had inwardly welcomed them as dogs; the clamour that accompanied them was indeed most confusing, but after all they were dogs, dogs like you and me; one observed them in the accustomed way, like dogs one meets in the street, one wanted to go up to them and exchange greetings, for they were indeed quite close; they were much older dogs than me, certainly, and not of my own woolly long-haired kind, yet neither were they particularly strange in their size and shape, indeed they seemed quite familiar, for I had come across many of their type or something like it before; but while one was still engrossed in such reflections the music gradually took over, it positively seized one, it swept one away from these real little dogs, and quite against one's will, resisting with all one's might, howling as if in pain, one was forced to attend solely to the music, this music that came from all sides, from the heights, from the depths, from everywhere, carrying the listener along with it, overwhelming him, crushing him, and blaring still – so close that it seemed far away and barely audible – blaring its fanfares over his shattered being. And then one was given a respite, being by now too exhausted, too shattered, too weak to hear any more, one was given a respite from the noise and saw the seven little dogs performing their movements, making their leaps, one longed to call out to them despite their aloofness, to beg them for enlightenment, to ask them what they were doing – I was a child and thought I could ask anybody about anything – but hardly had I got ready to speak, hardly had I begun to feel that good, familiar, doggish sense of fellowship with the seven, when back came their music again, robbed me of my senses, whirled me round in circles, as if I myself were one of the musicians and not merely their victim, flung me to and fro, however much I begged for mercy, and finally rescued me from its own violence by driving me into a tangled thicket which grew up round that spot, though I had not noticed it before, and which now held me fast, forced my head down low, and gave me a chance to draw breath despite the music that still thundered in the open.

I must confess it was less the artistry of the seven dogs that amazed me – that was incomprehensible, but so far beyond my powers as to seem utterly remote – than their courage in exposing themselves, fully and openly, to what they were producing, and the fact that they were strong enough to endure it calmly without its breaking their very backbone. But now I noticed, as I watched them more closely from my hide-out, that it was not so much calmness as extreme tension that characterized their performance; these limbs apparently so sure in their movements trembled at every step in a perpetual anxious quivering; they gazed at one another rigidly, as if transfixed by despair, and their tongues, which they made constant efforts to control, lolled out again immediately each time. It could not be anxiety about the success of their performance that agitated them so; none who dared such things could know that kind of anxiety; of what, then, were they afraid? Who was forcing them to do what they were doing? And I could restrain myself no longer, especially since they now seemed mysteriously in need of help, and through all the clamorous din I shouted out my questions in a loud and peremptory voice. But they – incredible! incredible! – they made no reply, they behaved as if I was not there; here were dogs making no reply at all to a dog's call, an offence against the proprieties which in any dog, however great or small, is wholly unpardonable. Could it be that these were not dogs? But how should they not be dogs, when I could actually hear now, on listening more closely, the subdued calls with which they spurred one another on, pointed out hazards, warned against errors; I even saw the last and smallest dog, to whom most of these calls were directed, stealing frequent glances at me as if he would dearly like to reply, but was restraining himself because it was not permitted. But why was it not permitted, why was the very thing that our laws always unconditionally require not permitted on this occasion? My heart rebelled, I almost forgot the music. These dogs before me were violating the law. Great magicians they might be, but the law was valid for them too; although I was a child I knew that quite well. And with that in mind I made some further observations. They had indeed good cause to keep silence, assuming that they kept silence out of a sense of guilt. For what an exhibition they were making of themselves, I had not noticed it till now for sheer music, they had indeed cast off all sense of shame, the miserable creatures were doing the most ridiculous and indecent thing, they were walking upright on their hind legs. Revolting! They were exposing themselves and making a blatant show of their nakedness; they were priding themselves on it, and whenever they obeyed their better instincts for a moment and lowered their front paws to the ground, they positively took fright as if they had committed an error, as if nature herself were an error, they lifted their legs again hastily, and with their eyes seemed to beg forgiveness for having had to pause briefly in their sinfulness.

Was the world upside down? Where was I? What could have happened? For the sake of my very existence I dared hesitate now no longer, I freed myself from the thicket that enclosed me, took one leap into the open and made towards the dogs; the young pupil must now turn instructor, I had to make them grasp what they were doing, had to prevent them from continuing in sin. 'What old dogs, what old dogs!' I kept repeating to myself. But scarcely was I free and a mere two or three leaps away from the dogs, when the clamour was there again and had me in its power. Perhaps in my eagerness I might have managed to withstand even that, for I knew it by now well enough; against its fullness of sound, though terrifying, I might still have done battle; but out of this fullness there now rang out one clear, stern, unwavering tone, a tone that seemed to come literally unchanged from the remotest distance, perhaps the real melody at the centre of the din, and it forced me to my knees. Oh, what a bewitching music it was that these dogs made! I could go no further, I had no more wish to instruct them; let them go on spreading their legs, committing sin, and enticing others into the sin of silently regarding them; I was such a young dog, who could demand of me such a heavy task? I made myself even smaller than I was, I whimpered, and if those dogs had asked me just then what I thought of their behaviour I should probably have told them that I approved. Besides it was not long before the dogs vanished with all their clamour and all their radiance into the darkness from which they had come.

As I have already said, this whole episode contains nothing exceptional; in the course of a long life one encounters much that might seem far more astonishing, if taken out of context and seen through the eyes of a child. Besides one can – as the apt saying goes – 'argue the whole thing away', just like anything else, in which case it would appear that in this instance seven musicians had assembled to make music in the stillness of the morning, that a small dog had strayed into their company, a tiresome listener, whom they tried in vain to drive away by particularly terrible or lofty music. He pestered them with his questions; should they, who had been sufficiently disturbed already by the mere presence of this stranger, have paid attention to the additional nuisance of his questions and made things worse by replying to them? And even if the law does command one to reply to everybody, could such a tiny stray dog really be called a somebody worth mentioning? And perhaps they could not even understand him, for he probably barked his questions most indistinctly. Or perhaps they did understand him, and constrained themselves to answer him, but he, a youngster unaccustomed to music, was unable to distinguish the answer from the music. And as for the matter of the hind legs, perhaps they really did walk on them for once in a way; that is a sin, no doubt; but they were alone, seven friends, just among themselves, an intimate gathering, as it were within their own four walls, as it were in complete privacy, for after all friends do not constitute a public, and where there is no public present an inquisitive little street dog cannot by himself create one; so if all that is granted are we not entitled to say that on this occasion nothing whatever occurred? That is not wholly accurate, but it very nearly is, and parents ought not to let their children run around so much, but should rather teach them to hold their tongues better and respect their elders.

Having got this far, one has disposed of the matter. However, when something is disposed of for grown-ups that does not mean that it is yet disposed of for children. I ran about telling my story and interrogating people, making accusations and pursuing my inquiries, I wanted to drag everyone along to the spot where it had all happened, I wanted to show everyone where I had stood and where the seven had been and where and how they had danced and made their music; and if anyone had come with me, instead of brushing me off and laughing at me as they all did, I would probably have sacrificed my innocence and tried to get up on to my hind legs too, so as to give a clear illustration of the whole thing. Well, everything a child does meets with disapproval, but it is all forgiven him too in the end. But for my part I have preserved my childish nature and have turned in the meantime into an old dog. Just as in those days I never stopped loudly discussing that episode – which I admittedly consider far less important today – analysing it into its constituent parts, putting it to everyone present regardless of the company I was in, solely and constantly preoccupied with this question, which I found just as wearisome as all the others, but which I – here was the difference – was for that very reason determined to solve completely, so as to be free again at last to turn my eyes to the ordinary, peaceful, happy life of every day: just as I laboured then, so have I laboured in the following years – with less childish means, it is true, but the difference is not so very great – and to this day I have got no further.

But it was with that concert that it all began. I do not complain about it; it is my inborn nature that is responsible, and that would certainly have found another opportunity to break through if it had never been for that concert; it was just its happening so soon that I used to find distressing, for it deprived me of a good part of my childhood; the blissful life of a young dog, which many manage to spin out for themselves year after year, lasted in my case only a few short months. So be it! There are more important things than childhood. And perhaps age has in store for me more childish happiness, earned by a life of hard work, than any actual child would have the strength to bear, but for which I shall be strong enough then.

I began my investigations at that time with the simplest things; there was no lack of material, unfortunately; it is the very superfluity of material that makes me despair in my darker hours. I began to inquire into the question of what nourishment the dog race subsists on. Now that is, if you like, by its nature no simple question, it has occupied us since the earliest times, it is the chief object of our reflections, countless observations and essays and opinions on this subject have appeared, it has become a science of such vast dimensions that it is not only beyond the grasp of any single scholar but beyond all scholars collectively, it is a burden too weighty for all save the entire dog community, and even they groan under it and cannot bear it completely, it is constantly crumbling away into ancient pieces of wisdom, long since acquired, and has to be restored with great labour, to say nothing of the difficulties and the almost unfulfillable prerequisites of my own investigation. No one need point out these objections to me, I know them all just as well as any average dog; I would not dream of meddling in real scientific matters, I have all due respect for science, but as far as making any contribution is concerned I lack the knowledge, the application, the quiet, and – not least, especially for some years now – the appetite. I swallow my food down where I find it, but it does not seem to me to merit the slightest preliminary methodical examination from an agricultural point of view. In this respect I am content with that quintessence of all knowledge, the little rule with which mothers wean their young and send them out into life: 'Wet everything as much as you can.' And is not almost everything contained in that? What has scientific inquiry, since our ancient forebears began it, of decisive importance to add? Details, details, and how uncertain they all are; but this rule will remain for as long as we are dogs. It concerns our main diet; true, we have other resources as well, but in emergency, and given a reasonable year, we could live on this main diet; we find our main diet on the ground, but the ground needs our water, it draws its nourishment from our water, and only for that price does it give us our own sustenance, the emergence of which, however, and this should not be forgotten, can be hastened by certain recitations, songs, and movements. But in my opinion that is all; from this aspect there is nothing else that is fundamental to be said on the matter. In this opinion, moreover, I am at one with the great majority of the dog community, and must firmly dissociate myself from all heretical views on the point. I honestly have no wish to put forward out-of-the-way notions, or to be dogmatic; I am only too happy when I can agree with my fellows, as in this case I can. But my own investigations lead in another direction.

My observation tells me that when the earth is watered and turned up according to the rules of science it provides nourishment, and moreover it provides it in such quality, in such quantity, in such manner, in such places, and at such hours as the laws require, those laws which science, once again, has wholly or partly succeeded in establishing. That I accept, but my question is: 'Where does the earth get this nourishment from?' A question which people generally pretend not to understand, and to which at best they reply by saying: 'If you haven't enough to eat, we'll give you some of ours.' Notice this reply. I know well enough that the sharing out of whatever food we manage to obtain is not one of the virtues of our race. Life is hard, the earth stubborn, science rich in knowledge but poor enough in practical results; anyone who has got food, keeps it; this is not self-interest but the opposite, it is dog law, the unanimous resolution of the people, the outcome of their victory over self-seeking, for as we know the possessors are always in the minority. And that is why this answer: 'If you haven't enough to eat, we'll give you some of ours' is a mere stock phrase, a jest, a form of leg-pulling. I have not forgotten this fact. But it seemed all the more significant to me, in the days when I was trotting all over the place with my questions, that when they said it to me they left all trace of mockery aside; of course they still did not actually give me anything to eat – where could they have procured it at a moment's notice? – and even if they did just happen to have some their furious hunger naturally made them forget all other considerations; but the offer was meant seriously, and now and then I really did receive a morsel, whenever I got there quickly enough to grab hold of it. Why was it that they gave me such special treatment? Indulged me, favoured me? Because I was a skinny, feeble dog, badly fed and too little concerned about food? But there are plenty of badly fed dogs running around, and the others snatch the most miserable scraps from under their noses whenever they can, not often out of greed but usually on principle. No, they favoured me; I could hardly have given detailed evidence to prove it, but I had the firm impression that it was so. Well then, was it that they took pleasure in my questions and found them particularly clever? No, they took no pleasure in them and found them foolish without exception. And yet it could only be the questions that gained me this measure of attention. It was as if they would rather have performed the monstrous act of stuffing my mouth full of food – they did not do it, but they wanted to – than put up with my questions. But in that case they would have done better to chase me away and forbid my questions. No, that was not what they wanted; they certainly had no wish to listen to my questions, but it was precisely because I asked these questions that they had no wish to drive me away.

That was the time when despite all the ridicule, despite being treated as a foolish young puppy and pushed around, I actually enjoyed most public esteem; never again was I to enjoy anything like it; I had access everywhere, nothing was denied me, the rough treatment I received was really a pretext for pampering me. And in the end this was all simply because of my questions, because of my impatience, because of my eagerness for research. They wanted to lull me with this treatment, to divert me without violence, almost lovingly, from a false path, from a path that was not quite so indubitably false as to permit the use of violence, and anyhow a certain respect and fear restrained them from using it. Already at that time I had my suspicions of what they were up to, today I can see it quite clearly, much more clearly than those who were doing it then; the truth is that they wanted to lure me away from my own path. They did not succeed; they achieved the opposite; my vigilance was sharpened. It even became clear to me that it was I who wished to seduce the others, and that I was actually succeeding to a certain extent. Only with the help of the dog community did I begin to understand my own questions. For instance when I asked: 'Where does the earth get this nourishment from?', was I – as one might have the impression – concerned about the earth, was I concerned about the earth's troubles? Not in the least; that, as I soon recognized, was utterly remote from my mind; I was concerned only about us dogs, and about nothing else whatever. For what else is there apart from dogs? Who else can one appeal to in the wide, empty world? All knowledge, the totality of all questions and all answers, is contained in the canine race. If one could only make this knowledge effective, if one could only bring it into the light of day, if only dogs did not know infinitely more than they will admit, more than they will admit to themselves! Even the most talkative dog guards his tongue more closely than the best feeding places usually guard their food. Stealthily one circles round one's fellow dog, frothing with desire, whipping oneself with one's own tail; one asks, one begs, one howls, one bites, and achieves – one achieves what could have been achieved just as well without any effort: affectionate attention, friendly touchings, honourable sniffings, loving embraces; two howls of longing unite in one, all energies are turned to finding oblivion in ecstasy; but the one thing that one hoped above everything to achieve, the admission of knowledge, that is not forthcoming; to that request, whether it be silent or spoken, the most that one receives by way of answer after deploying one's greatest powers of seduction are vacant expressions, shifty looks, veiled and troubled eyes. It is much the same as it was on that occasion in the past, when as a puppy I appealed to the dog musicians and they remained silent.

Now one might say: 'You complain about your fellow dogs, about their silence on the really important matters, you claim that they know more than they admit, more than they are prepared to acknowledge in their lives, and that this suppression on their part, the source of which they naturally suppress as well, poisons your life and makes it unendurable, so that you must either change it or have done with it; that may be, but after all you are a dog yourself, you have this dog knowledge too; well then, declare it, not just in the form of questions but as an answer. If you speak out, who will be able to resist you? The great chorus of dogs will join in as if it had been waiting for that moment. Then you will have all the truth, all the clarity, all the admission that you desire. The roof of this lowly life that you speak so ill of will be raised, and all of us, flank to flank, will ascend to freedom on high. And even if we should not achieve that final goal, if things should become worse than before, if the whole truth should be more unendurable than the half, if it should be confirmed that the silent ones, as the preservers of life, are in the right, if the faint hope that we still possess should turn to utter hopelessness, yet speaking out is still worth the attempt, since the permitted way of life is no life you wish to lead. So why, then, do you reproach others with their silence, and keep silent yourself?' Easy to answer: because I am a dog. At bottom just as stubbornly reticent as the others, resisting my own questions, encrusted with the hard crust of fear. For have the questions I have been putting to my fellow dogs, at least since I was grown up, really been put so as to get answers out of them? Have I such foolish hopes? When I see the foundations of our life and guess how deep they go, when I see the builders at work, at their dark labour, do I still expect all this to be abandoned, destroyed, forsaken because of my questions? No, that I truly expect no longer.

With my questions I now harry myself alone, I wish to spur myself on with the silence that is now the sole response I get from all around. How long will you be able to bear the fact that the dog race keeps silent and always will keep silent, as your researches make you increasingly aware? How long can you bear it? – that is the really decisive question of my life, over and above all questions of detail; it is a question for me alone and need trouble no one else. Unfortunately I can answer it more easily than the questions of detail: I shall probably be able to hold out until my natural end; for the calm of age is an ever more effective antidote to disturbing questions. I shall probably die peacefully in silence, surrounded by silence, and I look forward to that almost with composure. An admirably strong heart, lungs that cannot be worn out before their time, have been given to us dogs as if in malice; we survive all questions, even our own, bulwarks of silence that we are.

Recently I have been occupied more and more in reviewing my life, searching for the decisive error that I may perhaps have made and that has been the cause of all the trouble, but I cannot find it. And yet I must have made it, for if I had not made it, and had still failed to achieve what I wanted after a long life of honest effort, that would prove that what I wanted was impossible, and complete hopelessness would follow. Consider your lifetime's work! First of all those investigations into the question: where does the earth get our nourishment from? A young dog, naturally greedy and full of animal spirits, I renounced all enjoyments, gave all manner of amusement a wide berth, buried my head between my legs in the face of temptation, and addressed myself to my task. It was no scholarly task, either as far as the degree of learning, or as far as the method, or as far as the aim was concerned. That was probably a defect, but it could not have been a decisive one. I have had little schooling, for I left my mother's care at an early age, soon grew accustomed to standing on my own feet, led an independent life; and premature independence is inimical to systematic learning. But I have seen a great deal, heard a great deal, spoken with a great many dogs of the

most diverse kinds and conditions, and I think I can say that I have
grasped everything pretty well and correlated my particular observations pretty well; that has made up to some extent for my lack of
scholarship; and moreover independence has certain advantages when
one is pursuing one's own investigations, even if it may be a handicap
to learning. In my case it was all the more necessary since I was not
in a position to proceed in the proper scientific manner, that is, to
use the work of my predecessors and establish contact with contemporary researchers. I was thrown entirely on my own resources, I
had to begin at the very beginning and in the full awareness – which
is blissful for the young but extremely depressing for the old – that
whatever conclusion I happened to arrive at must also be the de-
finitive one. Have I really been so alone in my investigations, from
that day to this? Yes and no. It is inconceivable that there must not
always have been some individual dogs in the same position as
myself, and that there are not some today. I cannot be in quite such
dire case as that. I do not depart by a hair's breadth from the general
nature of dogs. Every dog feels as I do the urge to ask questions, and
I feel, like every dog, the urge to keep silent. Every one feels the
urge to ask questions. How else could my own questions have
provoked even such minor tremors as to my delight – an exaggerated
delight, I must confess – they often did? And to show that I feel the
urge to keep silent no special proof, alas, is necessary. Essentially,
then, I do not differ from all other dogs, and that is why at bottom
every one of them is prepared to acknowledge me, despite all differences of opinion and all personal dislikes, and why I am prepared to
do the same to them. It is only the mixture of the elements that
varies, a variety that is very important for the individual but insignificant for the race as a whole. And can it really be supposed that the
mixing of this permanent stock of elements has never, past or present,
produced a mixture like mine, and indeed an even unhappier mixture,
if one likes to call mine an unhappy one? That would run contrary to
all other experience. We dogs are engaged in the strangest occupations, occupations in which one would refuse to believe if one did
not possess the most reliable information about them.

My favourite example in this connection is that of the aerial dogs.
The first time I heard of one I laughed, I simply refused to be

persuaded. What? There was supposed to be a diminutive type of dog, not much bigger than my head, even at an advanced age no bigger than that, and this dog, being of course feeble and to all appearances an artificial, immature sort of product with an excessively well-tended coat, incapable of making an honest jump, this dog was supposed, so the story went, to move about for the most part high in the air, performing no visible work up there, but simply resting? No, to try to convince me of that sort of thing was to exploit the open-mindedness of a young dog altogether too much, I thought. But shortly after that I heard an account of another aerial dog from a different source. Was there a conspiracy to make a fool of me? But then I saw the dog musicians, and from that day on I considered all things possible, no prejudices restricted my mental capacity; I investigated the most absurd rumours and followed them up as far as I could; in this absurd world the absurdest things seemed to me more probable than the reasonable ones, and a particularly rich field for my researches. So it was with the aerial dogs. I discovered a great many things about them; I must admit that to this day I have not succeeded in seeing one, but of their existence I have long been firmly convinced, and they occupy an important place in my picture of the world. It is, of course, not the artistic accomplishment that sets me thinking in this case, any more than it usually is. It is wonderful – who can deny it? – that these dogs are capable of floating in the air; in my astonishment at that I am at one with my fellow dogs. But far more wonderful to my mind is the absurdity, the silent absurdity of these curious individuals. Generally speaking no reason for it is offered; they float in the air, and that is as far as it goes; life continues on its way, now and then there is some talk of art and artists, but that is all. But why, O most benevolent race of dogs, why do these dogs float? What sense is there in their occupation? Why can one get no word of explanation out of them? Why do they float about up there, letting their legs, the pride of dogs, grow stunted, why are they cut off from the nourishing earth, why do they sow not, and yet they reap, indeed are exceptionally well provided for, according to all accounts, and at the expense of the dog community too?

I can flatter myself that my questions have brought a little life into these matters. People are beginning to put forward reasons, to weave some kind of rational explanation together; they have made a beginning, even though they will get no further. But that is something after all. And in the process we do glimpse, if not the truth – for never will we get that far – at least something of the profound labyrinth of falsehood. For the fact is that all the absurd phenomena of our life, and the most absurd ones in particular, are susceptible of a rational explanation. Not wholly of course – that is the diabolical joke – but sufficiently for one to be able to ward off embarrassing questions. Take the aerial dogs as an example once again. They are not haughty, as one might imagine at first, but rather exceptionally dependent on their fellow dogs; if one tries to put oneself in their position one can understand that. For they must do what they can, even if they cannot do it openly – since that would be an infringement of their duty to remain silent – they must do what they can by other means to seek forgiveness for their way of life, or at least to distract attention from it, to make people forget about it – and they do this, so I am told, by an almost unbearable amount of chatter. They have forever some tale to tell, whether it is about their philosophical reflections, with which, since they have quite renounced all physical exertion, they can occupy themselves continually, or whether it is about the observations that they make from their exalted station. And despite the fact that they are not very remarkable for their intellectual power, which is quite understandable in view of their dissolute mode of life, despite the fact that their philosophy is as worthless as their observations, and that science can make hardly any use of what they have to offer, and is in any case not dependent on such miserable material, in spite of all this one is always being assured, when one asks what the point of the aerial dogs can be, that they contribute a great deal to science. 'That is correct,' one then says, 'but their contributions are worthless and wearisome.' The reply to that is a shrug, or a diversion, or annoyance, or laughter, and a little later, when you ask again, you learn once more that they contribute to science, and finally, when you are next asked the question yourself, unless you are very careful you give the same answer. And perhaps it is anyhow best not to be too obstinate and to submit, at least to tolerate such aerial dogs as already exist, though not to recognize their existence as justified, for that would be impossible. But more than that cannot be asked of one; that would be going too far; and yet it is asked of one for all that. One is asked to put up with a stream of new aerial dogs who are constantly appearing. It is not at all clear where they come from. Do they multiply by reproduction? Have they enough strength left for that? – they consist, after all, of not much more than a handsome coat, so what is there here to reproduce itself? But even supposing the improbable were possible, when could it take place? For one invariably sees them alone, sufficient to themselves up in the air, and if for once in a while they lower themselves to take a run it lasts only a moment or two, a few mincing steps and back they are again in strict solitude, supposedly absorbed in their thoughts, from which they cannot tear themselves away even with an effort, or so at least they say. But if they do not reproduce themselves, is it conceivable that there should be dogs who voluntarily renounce life at ground level, voluntarily become aerial dogs, and for the sake of comfort and a certain technical accomplishment actually choose that dreary, cushioned life up there? That is inconceivable; neither reproduction nor voluntary affiliation is conceivable. And yet the facts show that there are always new aerial dogs about; from which one must conclude that, despite what seem to our mind insurmountable obstacles, no species of dog, once extant, and however curious it may be, ever dies out, or at least not easily, at least not without there being something in every species which puts up a long and successful resistance.

If this holds good for such an out-of-the-way and senseless species as the aerial dogs, so very strange in external appearance and so ill-fitted for life, must I not accept it as true for my own type as well? Besides, outwardly I am not strange in the least, just an ordinary middle-class dog such as is quite common, anyway in this neighbourhood; in no way especially outstanding, in no way especially despicable; I was even a distinctly handsome dog in my youth, and to some extent still in maturity, so long as I attended to my appearance and took plenty of exercise; my front view was particularly admired, my slim legs and the fine way I carried my head, but also much approved was my grey, white and yellow coat that just curled at the tips; nothing of this is at all strange, the only thing that is strange is my nature, and even this, as I must never allow myself to forget, has its foundation in the general nature of dogs. Now if not even the aerial dog is wholly isolated, if here and there in the great world of dogs there is always another one of his type to be found, and if they can even conjure new generations out of nothingness, then I too can live in the confidence that I am not quite forlorn. The lot of those who belong to my own type must certainly be unusual, and their existence can never be of visible help to me, if for no other reason than that I can scarcely ever hope to recognize them. We are the dogs to whom silence is oppressive, who want to break the barrier of silence because we are positively gasping for air; the others seem content with silence, though that is only what it seems, just as in the case of the musical dogs, who seemed to make their music so calmly but were really intensely agitated; yet the illusion is strong, one tries to grapple with it and it mocks every attempt.

Then how do the dogs of my own type manage? What form do their efforts to go on living despite everything take? They may take various forms. My own efforts, so long as I was young, took the form of asking questions. So I might perhaps stick to those who ask a lot of questions, and there I would have my comrades. And indeed that is what, with great self-control, I tried for a time to do; great self-control, because of course I am primarily concerned with those who are supposed to answer; the ones who are constantly butting in with questions, to which I usually have no answer myself, I find repellent. Moreover, who is not fond of asking questions when he is young, so how am I going to pick out the genuine questioners from among so many? One question sounds like another; it is the intention that counts, but that is often hidden even from the questioner. And besides, asking questions is a characteristic of the dog race, they all ask them together in a confused babble; it is as if by doing so they were trying to obliterate all trace of the genuine questioners. No, my real comrades are not to be found among the questioners, among the young, any more than they are to be found among the old and silent to whom I now belong. But what good are all these questions anyhow, for I have failed with them completely; probably my comrades are far wiser than me, and employ excellent means of a quite different sort to endure this life, means which, however, as I feel bound to add, though they may perhaps at a pinch help them, soothe them, lull them, and effect some change in their character, remain on the whole just as impotent as my own, for no matter where I look I see no sign of their success. I am afraid that the last thing by which I shall be able to recognize my comrades is success.

But where, then, are these comrades of mine to be found? Yes, that is my complaint, that is precisely my trouble. Where are they? Everywhere and nowhere. Perhaps my next-door neighbour, only three jumps away, is one of them; we often call over to each other and he comes across to visit me too, though I do not go to him. Is he my comrade? I do not know, I certainly see no sign of it in him, but it is possible. It is possible, but all the same nothing is more improbable; when he is away I can, for my own amusement, by using my imagination to the full, discover much about him that is suspiciously familiar, but when he stands before me all my inventions become ridiculous. An old dog, a little smaller even than myself – and I am hardly medium size – brown, short-haired, with a wearily drooping head and a shuffling gait, aggravated by the fact that he trails his left hind leg after him a little, as a result of some illness. For a long time now I have kept closer company with him than with anyone else; I am glad that I can still put up with him tolerably well, and when he goes off I shout the friendliest things after him, but it is not out of affection, it is in anger at myself, because when I observe him I merely find him quite repulsive again, as he goes slinking off with his foot dragging behind and his much too low hindquarters. Sometimes it seems to me as if I was trying to deride myself by privately calling him my comrade. Nor does he show signs of comradeship when we talk together; certainly he is clever, and well enough educated as things go in these parts, I could learn a lot from him; but is it cleverness and education that I am looking for? We converse usually about local questions, and it astonishes me – my isolation has made me more clear-sighted in this respect – how much intelligence is needed even by an ordinary dog, even in circumstances that are generally not too unfavourable, just to stay alive and to protect oneself from the worst of the usual dangers. Science, it is true, provides the rules to follow, but to understand them even remotely and in rough outline is not easy, and once one has understood them the real difficulty begins, namely to apply them to the local conditions – here almost nobody can help, almost every hour brings new tasks, and each new patch of earth its own special ones; for anyone to assert that he has settled down somewhere for good, and that his life can more or less take care of itself, is quite impossible; it is even impossible for me, though my needs shrink literally from day to day. And all this endless labour – to what end? To none save to bury oneself ever deeper in silence, so deep that no one will ever be able to drag one out of it again.

People often extol the universal progress made by the dog race throughout the ages, and one presumes that what they have chiefly in mind is the progress of science. Certainly science progresses, its advance is irresistible, it even progresses at an accelerating speed, ever faster, but what is there praiseworthy about that? It is as if one were to praise someone for growing older with increasing years and for approaching death ever more rapidly in consequence. That is a natural and moreover an ugly process in which I can find nothing to praise. I can see nothing but decline everywhere, though by that I do not mean that earlier generations were essentially better than ours, they were merely younger, that was their great advantage, their memory was not yet so overburdened as ours is today, it was easier to get them to speak out; and even if no one actually succeeded in doing so the possibility of it was greater, and it is just this greater sense of possibility that stirs us so deeply when we listen to those old, yet really so childishly simple stories. Here and there we catch a strangely suggestive phrase and we would almost like to leap to our feet, if we did not feel the weight of the centuries upon us. No, whatever objections I may have to my own age, earlier generations were no better than the recent ones, indeed in a sense they were far worse and far weaker. It is true that even in those days wonders did not walk the streets openly for anyone to lay hands on, but – how else can I put it? – dogs were not yet as doggish as they are today, the fabric of the dog community was still loose, the true word could still at that time have intervened, have determined or re-determined the whole structure, altering it at will, transforming it into its opposite, and that word was there, or at least was near, it was on the tip of every tongue, everyone might discover it; and today, what has become of it? – today one may tear one's insides out and still not find it. Our generation is perhaps lost, but it is more innocent than that generation of old. The hesitation of my generation I can well understand, indeed it is no longer a hesitation at all, it is the forgetting of a dream dreamed a thousand nights ago and a thousand times forgotten; who will wax angry with us on account of this thousandth forgetting? But I think I can also understand the hesitation of our forefathers; probably we should not have acted otherwise, indeed I almost feel inclined to say: it is well for us that we were not the ones who had to take the guilt upon us, that instead we were permitted to hasten towards death in almost guiltless silence, in a world that others have already darkened. When our forefathers erred, they probably had no thought of an endless aberration, they could literally still see the crossroads, it was easy to turn back whenever they pleased, and if they hesitated to turn back it was merely because they wanted to enjoy their dog's life for a little while longer; it was not yet even a genuine dog's life, but it already seemed to them intoxicatingly beautiful, so what would it be like a little later, just a little bit later? – and so they went on straying further. They did not know what we can now sense as we contemplate the course of history: that change begins in the soul before it shows in our lives, and that by the time they began to enjoy their dog's life they must already have had a real old dog's soul, and were by no means still so near their starting-point as they thought, or as their eyes tried to persuade them while they revelled in all the doggish pleasures. Who can still speak of youth today? They were the genuinely youthful dogs, but their sole ambition was unfortunately directed towards becoming old dogs, something which they could indeed not fail to achieve, as all succeeding generations have proved, and our own – the last one – most clearly of all.

Naturally I do not talk to my neighbour of all these matters, but I am often forced to think of them when I am sitting opposite him, typical old dog that he is, or burying my nose in his coat which already has something of the whiff of old hides. It would be pointless to talk about these things anyway, either with him or with anyone else. I know what course the conversation would take. He would have a few small objections to raise here and there, but finally he would agree –

agreement is the best weapon – and the matter would be buried; so why bother to exhume it at all in the first place? And yet all the same I do perhaps have a deeper understanding with my neighbour, one that goes beyond mere words. I feel bound to go on asserting this, even though I have no evidence for it and am perhaps merely the victim of a simple delusion, because he has been my only companion for so long and I must therefore cling to him. 'Are you perhaps my comrade after all? In your own way? And are ashamed because you have failed in everything? But look, it has been the same with me. When I am alone I howl about it; come, it is sweeter to howl together' – thus do my thoughts often run, and I gaze at him fixedly meanwhile. On these occasions he does not lower his glance, but he remains inscrutable; he looks at me dully, wondering why I am silent and have broken off our conversation. But perhaps that very look is his way of questioning me, and I disappoint him just as he disappoints me. In my youth, if other questions had not been more important to me then, and I had not been amply sufficient to myself, I might perhaps have asked him straight out and received some lame word of agreement, that is to say less than I get today from his silence. But are we not all just as silent? What is there to prevent me from believing that everyone is my comrade, that I do not merely have here and there some companion in my researches, who is sunk and forgotten along with his infinitesimal achievements, and whom I have no means of reaching through the darkness of the ages or the throng of the present; why should I not rather believe that all dogs from the beginning of time are my comrades, all of them striving in their own way, all unsuccessful in their own way, all silent or tiresomely prattling in their own way, just as this hopeless quest entails? But in that case I need not have isolated myself at all, I could have stayed quietly among the others, I had no need to push my way out like a naughty child through the ranks of the grown-ups; for they want to find a way out just as much as I do, and all that disturbs me about them is their common sense, which tells them that no one succeeds in getting out and that all thrusting is foolish.

Such thoughts, however, are plainly due to the influence of my neighbour; he confuses me, he makes me feel quite melancholy; and yet for himself he is cheerful enough, at least when he is in his own domain I can hear him shouting and singing away until it becomes most disagreeable. It would be a good thing for me to renounce this last contact also, to stop giving way to the vague dreams which all contact with the dog world must provoke, however hardened one imagines oneself to be, and to employ the short time that remains to me exclusively for my own researches. The next time he comes I shall creep off and pretend to be asleep, and then repeat the procedure for as long as necessary until he stops coming.

Also my researches have become disorganized, I am slackening off, I am growing weary, now I merely trot mechanically where once I ran with a good spirit. I remember the time when I began to investigate the question: 'Where does the earth get our nourishment from?' Then indeed I really lived among the people, I pushed my way through to where the crowd was thickest, I wanted to make everyone a witness to the work I was doing; indeed to have witnesses was more important to me than the work itself, for I was still expecting to make some kind of universal impression. Naturally that fired me with a great enthusiasm, which now that I am on my own I have no longer. But in those days I felt so strong that I did something unheard-of, something that runs counter to all our principles, and I am sure that everyone who was then an eyewitness can still remember it as a strangely disturbing episode.

I had observed that science, which normally seeks to make endless distinctions, was content in one respect with a remarkable simplification. It teaches that, in the main, it is the earth which produces our nourishment, and having made this assumption it then enumerates the methods by which the different foods may be obtained in best quality and greatest abundance. Now it is of course true that the earth produces our nourishment, of that there can be no doubt, but it is by no means as simple as it is generally made out to be, by no means so simple as to make all further inquiry superfluous. Suppose one just takes the most primitive sort of occurrences that are repeated every day. If we were to be wholly inactive, as with me is by now almost the case, and after a perfunctory preparation of the soil we were just to curl up and wait for things to happen, then we should indeed find, assuming that anything happened at all, our nourishment upon the ground. Nevertheless that is not the regular pattern. Anyone

who has preserved even a little open-mindedness in scientific matters
– and there are certainly not many of them, for the circles of science
are ever widening – any such person can easily recognize, even if he
does not set out to make any specific observations, that the greater
part of the nourishment which is then found lying on the ground
comes down from above; indeed we even catch most of it, according
to the measure of our dexterity and greed, before it touches the
ground at all. By saying that I do not mean to say anything against
science; the earth does of course produce this nourishment also,
naturally; whether it draws one kind of nourishment out of itself, or
calls another kind down from on high, may indeed make no essential
difference, and since science has established that preparation of the
ground is necessary in both cases, it has perhaps no need to concern
itself with such distinctions, for is it not said: 'If you have food in
your jaws, you have for the present solved all problems.' But it
seems to me that science does take a veiled interest in these matters
none the less, at least to some extent, inasmuch as it recognizes two
main methods of procuring nourishment: namely, the actual preparation of the ground, and then the supplementary improvement-process
in the form of incantation, dance, and song. Here I find a division,
not a total division but one that is obvious enough, and which
corresponds to the distinction that I myself draw in the matter. In
my opinion the preparation of the ground serves to obtain both
kinds of nourishment, and remains always indispensable; incantation,
dance, and song, on the other hand, do not so much affect the
ground nourishment in the narrower sense, they serve principally to
draw down the nourishment from above. Tradition fortifies me in
this interpretation. Here the ordinary people seem to rectify science,
without their being aware of it and without science daring to resist
them. If, as science claims, these ceremonies serve the earth only, in
order perhaps to give it the strength to summon the nourishment
from above, then logically they should be performed exclusively
close against the earth; it is to the earth that all the whispering, all
the singing, and all the dancing should be addressed. And to the best
of my knowledge nothing other than this is required by science. But
now comes the remarkable thing: the people address all their ceremonies towards the heights. This is no offence against science, for

science does not forbid it; it allows the husbandman complete freedom in this respect; in its teaching it has only the earth in mind, and if the husbandman gives effect to the specific teachings about the earth, then science is content; but in my opinion the train of scientific thought ought really to require something more. And for myself, though I have never been deeply initiated into science, I just cannot conceive how it is that the learned scientists are willing to permit our people, in the passionate way that they have, to chant their spells into the air, to wail the ancient folk-songs at the sky, to perform their high-leaping dances as if they wished to forget the ground and soar aloft for ever. I made the emphasis on these contradictions my starting-point; whenever the time was approaching, according to scientific doctrine, for harvest time, I restricted my attention solely to the ground; I scrabbled it in the dance, I twisted my neck to get down as close to it as possible, later I dug a hole in it for my nose, and thus I sang and declaimed, so that only the earth could hear me and no one else around or above me.

My experimental results were meagre. Sometimes the food did not appear, and I was on the point of rejoicing at this discovery, but then the food appeared again after all; it was as if my strange behaviour had caused some initial confusion, but that the advantages it brought were now recognized, and my calls and leaps could be gladly dispensed with; often the food even came in greater abundance than before, but then again it failed to appear altogether. With a diligence hitherto unknown in young dogs I drew up an exact account of all my experiments, I fancied now and again that I had hit on a track which might lead me further, but then everything dissolved once more in uncertainty. I was undoubtedly handicapped here by my insufficient grounding in science. What assurance had I, for example, that the non-appearance of the food was caused by my experiments rather than by my unscientific preparation of the ground; and if that was so, then all my conclusions were invalid. I might under certain conditions have achieved an almost scrupulously exact experiment, that is to say, if I had succeeded just once in achieving the descent of food by upwards-directed ceremony, without any preparation of the ground, and then the non-appearance of food by exclusively ground-directed ceremony. Indeed I attempted that sort of thing, but without any firm belief in it and not in perfect experimental conditions; for it is my unshakeable conviction that at least some measure of ground preparation is always necessary; and even if the heretics who deny this should be right their theory could never be proved, since the watering of the ground occurs under compulsion and within certain limits simply cannot be avoided. Another experiment of mine, admittedly a somewhat eccentric one, met with greater success and caused a certain amount of stir. Prompted by the customary method by which food is caught in mid-air, I resolved to adopt the scheme of encouraging the food to drop but not catching it. To this end I always made a small leap in the air when the food came, but I judged it carefully so as to miss; usually it fell to the ground then just the same, in a dull and indifferent manner, and I flung myself on it furiously, not only furious with hunger but furious with disappointment as well. But in isolated cases something else happened, something really wonderful; the food did not fall, but followed me through the air; the food pursued the hungry. That did not last for long, just for a brief stretch, and then it fell after all, or vanished completely, or – this was most often the case – my greed put a premature end to the experiment and I swallowed the stuff down.

All the same I was happy at that moment, a murmur of interest ran through my neighbourhood, the public began to pay uneasy attention, I found my acquaintances more accessible to my questions, I could see in their eyes some kind of imploring gleam; and even if it was only the reflection of my own glance I asked for nothing more, I was content. But then I soon discovered – and the others discovered it with me – that this experiment of mine had long since been described in the scientific literature, others had made a far more impressive success of it than I had, and though it had not been attempted for a long time on account of the extreme self-control it required, there was in any case no need to repeat it, for it was allegedly quite without scientific value. It only proved what was already known, that the ground not only attracts nourishment vertically from above, but also slant-wise, indeed even in spirals. So there I stood, but I was not discouraged, I was still too young for that; on the contrary it inspired me to what has been perhaps the greatest achievement of my life.

I did not believe that science had disvalued the experiment, but belief was of no avail here, only proof, so I resolved to offer that proof, and by doing so to bring what had been initially a somewhat out-of-the-way experiment into the full light of day, and to place it at the very centre of research. I wished to prove that when I retreated before the food it was not the ground that attracted it at a slant, but I who enticed it to follow me. Admittedly I was unable to develop this particular experiment further; to see the provender before one and meanwhile to experiment in a scientific manner, that was not something one could keep up in the long run. But I decided to do something else; I decided to fast completely for as long as I could stand it, while at the same time avoiding all sight of food, all temptation. If I were to withdraw myself in this manner, if I stayed lying down day and night with my eyes closed, making no effort either to pick up nourishment from the ground or to intercept it in the air, and if, as I dared not assume but faintly hoped, without my taking any further measures, and merely in response to the unavoidable irrational watering of the ground and the quiet repetition of the spells and songs (the dancing I wished to omit, so as not to weaken my powers) the food were then to descend of itself from above, and without paying attention to the ground were to come knocking at my teeth for admittance – if that were to happen, then it would indeed be no confutation of science, for science has enough elasticity to admit exceptions and special cases, but what would be the reaction of the ordinary folk, whose elasticity of mind is fortunately not so great? For this would not be the kind of exceptional case that history records, as for instance when an individual refuses because of bodily illness or melancholia to prepare for, seek out, and absorb his nourishment, whereupon the whole dog community unites in its incantations, and succeeds in making the food deviate from its customary path straight into the jaws of the invalid. I, on the contrary, had all my health and strength; my appetite was so magnificent that it prevented me for days on end from thinking of anything else; believe it or not, I subjected myself to fasting of my own free will; I was quite capable of effecting the descent of food myself, and that was exactly what I wished to do, so I required no assistance at all from the dog community and indeed most firmly forbade it.

I sought out a suitable place in a remote clump of bushes, where I should hear no talk of food, no smacking of chops or crunching of bones; I ate my fill for the last time and then I lay down. I wanted as far as possible to pass the whole time with my eyes shut; so long as no food came it was to be constant night for me, even if it should last for days and weeks. But what made things much more difficult was the fact that I could permit myself hardly any sleep, preferably no sleep at all, for not only did I have to call down the food, I had also to take good care not to sleep through its arrival; on the other hand, however, sleep was very welcome, for I would be able to fast much longer asleep than awake. For these reasons I resolved to divide up my time carefully, and to sleep a lot, but always for short periods only. I achieved this by always sleeping with my head supported on some frail twig, which soon snapped and so awoke me. Thus I lay, sleeping or waking, dreaming or singing quietly to myself. To begin with, the time passed uneventfully; perhaps, in the place whence nourishment comes, it had still remained somehow unobserved that I was setting myself up here in opposition to the normal course of things; and so all remained quiet. My efforts were a little disturbed by the fear that the other dogs would miss me, would soon track me down and take some kind of steps against me. My second fear was that the ground, even though this was declared by science to be an unfruitful area, might in response to mere watering produce what is known as random nourishment, and that the smell of this might seduce me. But for the time being nothing of that kind happened, and I could go on fasting. Apart from such fears, I was at the outset calmer than I could ever remember before. Although my work was really an attempt to undermine science, I felt a deep contentment and something like the proverbial calm of the scientific worker. In my reveries I obtained the forgiveness of science, room was to be found within it for my researches too; a consoling voice seemed to sound in my ears, assuring me that even if my researches met with great success, and indeed especially if so, I was by no means lost to doggish life; science was well-disposed to me, it would itself undertake the interpretation of my findings, and that promise already meant fulfilment; whereas hitherto I had felt an outcast to the depths of my being and had run my head against the walls of my people like a savage, now I was to be received with full honours, the longed-for stream of warmth from the assembled pack of bodies would lap round me, amid resounding praise I would be borne swaying on my people's shoulders.

Remarkable effect of my initial fasting. My achievement appeared to me so great that from emotion and self-pity I began to weep there among the still bushes, which I must confess was not entirely comprehensible, for if I was anticipating my well-earned reward why then did I weep? Probably it was just from contentment. My weeping has never met with approval. I have always only wept when I was content, and that has been seldom enough. But on that occasion my contentment soon passed. My beautiful dreams fled one by one before the increasing urgency of my hunger; it was not long before I had paid an abrupt farewell to all my fantasies and all my sentiment, and found myself all alone with the hunger that burned in my entrails. 'That is hunger,' I said to myself countless times, as if I wanted to convince myself that hunger and I were two separate entities, and I could shake it off like a wearisome lover; but in reality we were most painfully one, and when I told myself: 'That is hunger' it was really the hunger that was speaking, and mocking me as it did so.

A bad, bad time! I still shudder when I think of it, and that is not only because of the suffering which I then endured but above all because at that time I had failed to bring it to a conclusion, because I shall have to go through this suffering once again if I am to achieve anything; for today I still regard fasting as the ultimate and most powerful means of my research. It is through hungering that the way lies; the highest things can only be achieved, if they can be achieved at all, by the highest effort, and in our case that highest effort is voluntary hungering. So when I think about those times – and I take the greatest pleasure in raking them over – I also think about the threatening times ahead. It would seem that one must let almost a lifetime pass before one recovers from such an experiment; all my manhood years lie between me and that bout of fasting, but I am still not recovered. When I next begin fasting I shall perhaps have more determination than before, but my physical powers are now weaker, they are still impaired by that first attempt, and I shall surely begin to flag at the mere approach of those familiar terrors. My feebler appetite will not help me, it will only reduce the value of the attempt a little and probably also compel me to fast for longer than I should have had to the first time. About these and other conditions I think I am clear in my mind; during the long intervening period there has been no lack of preparatory attempts, often enough I have literally got my teeth into hungering, but without yet feeling strong enough to go on to the end, and of course the naïve attacking spirit of youth is gone for ever. It vanished already in the course of that original fast. Many different kinds of reflections tormented me. Our forefathers appeared threateningly before me. I must confess that I regard them, even if I dare not say so openly, as being responsible for everything; it is they who bear the guilt for our dog's life, so I could easily respond to their threats with counter-threats, but before their knowledge I bow, it came from sources that are known to us no longer, and for that reason, much as I feel the urge to contend with them, I would never actually transgress their laws, I merely slip out through the loopholes in the law for which I have a particularly good nose.

In respect of fasting, I take my stand on that well-known dialogue in the course of which one of our sages expressed his intention of prohibiting fasts, whereupon a second advised against it by asking: 'But who will ever think of fasting?' and the first sage allowed himself to be persuaded and withheld the prohibition. But now the old question arises: 'Is not fasting forbidden after all?' The great majority of commentators deny this and regard fasting as freely permitted; they also agree with the second sage, and thus they fear no ill-effects even if this interpretation should be false. I had naturally assured myself on this point before I began my fast. But now that I was twisted with the pangs of hunger, and already in some confusion of spirit sought relief in my own hind legs, desperately licking them, gnawing them and sucking at them up to my haunches, the generally accepted interpretation of that dialogue seemed to me utterly false; I cursed the commentators' science, I cursed myself for having been led astray by it; for the dialogue contained, as any hungering child could recognize, obviously more than just the one prohibition of fasting; the first sage wished to forbid fasting, and what a sage wishes is already done, so fasting was forbidden; the second sage not only agreed with the first, but actually held fasting to be impossible, that is, he piled on the first prohibition a second one imposed by the very nature of dogs; the first sage accepted this and withheld his explicit prohibition, in other words he commanded all dogs, in the light of what had been made clear, to use their own discernment and prohibit fasting for themselves. So here was a threefold prohibition instead of the normal single one, and I had violated it.

Now at this point I might at least have belatedly obeyed and stopped my fast, but through all the pain I felt the temptation to go on hungering, and I followed it greedily as I would follow a strange dog. I could not stop, and anyhow I was perhaps too weak by then to rise and seek my safety in inhabited places. I tossed about on the strewn leaves, I could no longer sleep, I heard noises on every side; the world, which had been asleep during the previous course of my life, seemed to have been awakened by my hungering; I began to imagine that I would never be able to eat again, for by doing so I must reduce the uninhibited clamour of the world to silence once more, and that I should never be capable of doing; but the greatest noise of all I heard from my own belly; I often laid my ear against it and I must have looked horrified, for I could hardly believe what I heard. And now that things were becoming too much to bear, my very nature seemed to be caught up in the frenzy and made the maddest attempts to preserve itself; I began to smell food, choice dishes that I had long since forgotten, the delights of my childhood; yes, I even smelt the scent of my mother's teats; I forgot my resolve to resist all smells, or rather I did not forget it; when I dragged myself off in all directions, never more than a yard or two away, to do some sniffing, I kept this resolve in mind as if it accorded with what I was doing, as if I were merely seeking the food so as to be on my guard against it. The fact that I found nothing did not disappoint me; the food must be there, only it was always a few steps away, my legs failed me before I could reach it. And yet at the same time I knew that nothing at all was there, and that I made these little excursions simply because I was afraid of total collapse in a place which I should never be able to leave again. My last hopes faded, the last allurements vanished; a miserable end awaited me here; of what use were my researches, those childish attempts of childish happy days? – what faced me here and now was earnest, this was where research could have proved its worth, but where had it gone? Here was only a dog snapping helplessly at the empty air, a dog who indeed still kept watering the ground in convulsive haste without being aware of it, yet who could not recall to mind a single fragment from the whole jumble of magic spells, not even the little rhyme which the new-born puppy recites as it ducks down under its mother. I felt here as if I was not just cut off by the space of a short run from my brothers, but infinitely far removed from everybody, and as if I would die, not really of hunger at all, but because I was so forsaken. For it was evident that no one cared about me, no one beneath the earth, no one upon it, no one above; I was being destroyed by their indifference; their indifference said: 'He is dying', and so it would be. And did I not give my assent? Did I not say the same thing? Had I not wished to be thus forsaken? Yes, my brothers, but not so as to perish here like this; it was in order to pass over into the truth, out of this world of falsehood where there is no one from whom truth can be learned, not even myself, for I too am a native citizen of falsehood. Perhaps the truth was no longer so very far off, and I was therefore not so forsaken as I thought; perhaps I was not so much forsaken by the others as by myself, by my own failure and my dying.

But one does not die so easily as a nervous dog imagines. I merely fainted, and when I came to and raised my eyes a strange hound was standing before me. I felt no hunger, I was full of strength, my limbs were in my opinion quite springy, although I made no attempt to test this by getting to my feet. I was not really capable of seeing more than usual; I could see that a handsome but not very extraordinary dog stood before me, that was all I saw, and yet I seemed to perceive something more in him. Beneath me lay some blood, which for a moment I thought was food, but then I recognized it at once as blood that I had brought up. I turned away from it and looked at the strange hound. He was lean, long-legged, brown with a patch of white here and there, and had a fine, strong, piercing glance. 'What are you doing here?' he asked. 'You must go away from here.' 'I can't go away now,' I said without further explanation, for how could I explain it all to him, and he seemed to be in a hurry anyway. 'Please, go away,' he said, lifting one leg after the other in a restless manner. 'Leave me alone,' I said, 'go off and don't worry about me, the others don't worry about me either.' 'I am asking you for your own sake,' he said. 'Ask me for any reason you like,' I said, 'I can't go even if I wanted to.' 'There's no fear of that,' he said with a smile, 'you can go all right. It is just because you seem to be weak that I beg you to go off slowly now; if you linger now, a bit later you will have to run.' 'That's my affair,' I said. 'It's mine too,' said he, saddened by my stubbornness, and now it was obvious that he was prepared to let me be for the time being but that he wanted to take the opportunity of making friendly approaches. At any other time I would have accepted this from such a handsome hound, but at that moment, I know not why, the idea filled me with terror; 'be off!' I screamed, all the louder since I had no other means of protection. 'All right, I'll leave you,' he said, slowly retreating. 'You're a strange dog. Don't you like me then?' 'I shall like you if you go away and leave me in peace,' I said, but I was no longer so sure of myself as I wanted to make him think. There was something about him that my senses, sharpened by fasting, seemed to see or hear; it was just beginning, it grew, it came closer, and then I knew: this hound really does have the power to drive you away, even if you cannot imagine how you will ever be able to get to your feet.

And I gazed at him – he had merely shaken his head gently at my rough answer – with ever-mounting desire. 'Who are you?' I asked. 'I'm a hunter,' he said. 'And why won't you let me stay here?' I asked. 'You disturb me,' he said, 'I can't hunt while you're here.' 'Try,' I said, 'perhaps you'll still be able to hunt.' 'No,' he said, 'I'm sorry, but you must go.' 'Leave your hunting just for today,' I begged. 'No,' he said, 'I must hunt.' 'I must go off, you must hunt,' I said, 'nothing but musts. Do you understand why we must?' 'No,' he said, 'but there is nothing to understand about it, these are self-evident, natural things.' 'But no,' I said, 'you are sorry that you must drive me away, and yet you do it.' 'That's so,' he said. 'That's so,' I repeated crossly, 'that is no answer. Which would you find easier to renounce, to renounce hunting or to renounce driving me away?' 'To renounce hunting,' he said unhesitatingly. 'Well then,' I said, 'there's a contradiction here.' 'What sort of contradiction is that?' he said. 'My dear little dog, do you really not understand that I must? Don't you understand what is self-evident?' I made no more reply, for I observed – and new life pulsed through me, the sort of life terror generates – I observed from indefinable details, which perhaps no one but me could have noticed, that the hound was about to strike up a deep-throated song. 'You are going to sing,' I said. 'Yes,' said he gravely, 'I'm going to sing; soon, but not yet.' 'You're beginning it already, although you deny it,' I said trembling. He said no more. And it was then that I thought I detected something such as no dog before me has ever encountered, at least there is not the slightest hint of it in our tradition, and in infinite fear and shame I hastily bowed my head in the pool of blood before me. What I seemed to detect was that the hound was already singing without being aware of it, nay more, that the melody, separated from him, was floating through the air in obedience to its own laws, and, as though he had no part in it, was aiming at me, at me alone.

Today, of course, I deny all such perceptions, and ascribe them to my overwrought state at that time, but even if the whole thing was an error it was not without a certain grandeur; it remains the sole reality, if only an apparent reality, that I have carried over into this world from my time of fasting, and shows at least how far we can go when we are in a state of being wholly beside ourselves. For I really was wholly beside myself. In ordinary circumstances I would have been very ill, incapable of moving, but the melody, which now the hound soon seemed to take over as his own, was quite irresistible. It grew ever stronger; its waxing power seemed to have no limits, and already it almost burst my eardrums. But the worst was that it seemed to exist solely for my sake, this voice before whose sublimity the woods fell silent, for my sake alone; who was I, that I dared still remain here, spreading myself out in my own blood and filth? With shaking limbs I rose and looked down at me; this body will never run, I was just thinking, when all at once I went bounding off in the mightiest of leaps with the melody at my heels. To my friends I said nothing; on my first arrival among them I should probably have told all, but I was too weak to do so, and then later it seemed impossible to communicate it. Certain hints which I could not restrain myself from dropping were lost without trace in the general talk. Physically, by the way, I recovered in a few hours; spiritually the effects are still with me today.

But I now extended my researches into the field of dog music. Science had of course not been idle in this field either; if I am correctly informed, the science of music is possibly even more comprehensive than the science of nourishment and certainly more firmly based. This may be explained by the fact that it is possible to work more dispassionately in the former field than in the latter, and that while in the field of music it is simply a matter of observation and systematization, in the field of nourishment the main object is to reach practical conclusions. Related to that is the fact that the science of music enjoys greater respect than the science of nourishment, but has never been able to penetrate so deeply into the life of the people. And I, too, found the science of music more foreign to me than any other branch of science, until the time that I heard that voice in the woods. It is true that my experience with the dog musicians had drawn my attention to it, but I was still too young then; nor is it by any means easy even to approach that field of study; it is regarded as especially difficult and with a superior air it holds itself aloof from the crowd. Besides, although it was initially the music that had seemed the most striking thing about those dogs, I found their music less significant than their taciturn nature; I could find, I suppose, no counterpart whatever to their terrible music and so felt justified in neglecting it, but from that time on I kept discovering their taciturn nature in all dogs everywhere. However, in order to penetrate into the true nature of dogs nourishment research seemed to me the most suitable, and likely to lead by a direct path to the goal. Possibly I was wrong there. Certainly there was a border region between the two sciences which already at that time aroused my suspicions. I refer to the doctrine of song calling down nourishment from above. Here again I am at the great disadvantage of never having seriously come to grips with musical science, so in this respect I am far from being able to consider myself even one of those semi-educated persons whom scientists always particularly despise. This must ever be very much in my mind. Faced by a learned scientist I should fare very badly even in the simplest academic test, as I have regrettable evidence to show. The reasons for that, apart from the above-mentioned circumstances of my life, lie of course primarily in my scientific incapacity, my limited powers of thought, my bad memory, and above all in my inability to keep the scientific aim continuously in view. All this I am prepared to admit to myself, even with a certain pleasure. Because the deeper reason for my scientific incapacity seems to me to be an instinct, and indeed by no means a bad instinct. If I wanted to brag I might say that it was precisely this instinct that had destroyed my scientific capacities, for it would certainly be a very peculiar thing if I, as a person who shows a tolerable degree of intelligence in the ordinary matters of life, which are unquestionably not all that simple, and above all as a person who has – as my results can testify – at least a very good understanding of scientists, if not of science, should have been incapable from the outset of raising his paw even to the first rung of scientific knowledge. The instinct I speak of was the instinct that impelled me – perhaps for the very sake of science, though of another science than the one practised today, for the sake of a most ultimate science – to prize freedom higher than anything else. Freedom! Such freedom as is possible today, I freely admit it, is a poor and stunted growth. But it is freedom none the less, it is a possession none the less.

THE MARRIED COUPLE

BUSINESS in general is so bad that sometimes when I have time to spare in the office I pick up the case of samples myself and call on my customers personally. Among other things I had long since intended to pay a visit to K.; we used to have a regular business relationship, but for some unknown reason it has almost completely lapsed during the past year. There need in fact be no genuine reasons for this kind of breakdown; in the present unstable conditions a mere nothing, a change of mood, can be decisive, and equally a mere nothing, a word, can put the whole thing right again. But it is a little complicated to get access to K.; he is an old man, in very poor health of late, and though he still keeps the reins of his business in his own hands he hardly ever goes to the office nowadays; if you want to speak to him you have to go to his house, and one is only too glad to postpone a business call of that kind.

Nevertheless, yesterday evening after six o'clock I did set out; it was certainly too late for paying calls, but after all it was not a matter of social considerations, but a matter of business. I was in luck, K. was in; he had just come back from a walk with his wife, so I was told in the hall, and was now in his son's bedroom, who was unwell and confined to bed. I was invited to join them; at first I hesitated, but then my desire to get this disagreeable visit over as quickly as possible got the upper hand, and just as I was, in my overcoat and with my hat and case of samples in my hand, I allowed myself to be conducted through a dark room into a faintly lit one, where a small company was assembled.

My first glance fell, probably by instinct, on a commercial agent only too well known to me, who is to some extent my competitor. So he had managed to sneak up in front of me. He was sitting at his ease, close by the invalid's bed, as if he were the doctor; with his fine overcoat unbuttoned and ballooning out round him, he sat there powerfully enthroned; his effrontery is unequalled; the invalid may have been thinking something of the same kind too, as he lay there, cheeks faintly flushed with fever, and gave him an occasional glance. He is no longer young either, K.'s son, a man of my own age with a short beard, somewhat unkempt on account of his illness. Old K., a tall, broad-shouldered man, but to my astonishment now quite wasted, bent and shaky as a result of his lingering disease, was still standing there in his fur coat just as he had come, mumbling something to his son. His wife, small and frail, but exceedingly lively, if only as far as her husband was concerned – us others she hardly noticed – was busy helping him off with his coat, which was a matter of some difficulty owing to their great difference in height, but she succeeded at last. Perhaps, indeed, the real difficulty was caused by K.'s impatience, for with restless hands he kept groping for the easy chair, which his wife, once the overcoat was off, quickly pushed forward for him. She herself took up the fur coat, beneath which she almost vanished, and carried it out.

Now, it seemed to me, my moment had come at last, or rather it had not come and in these circumstances it probably never would come, but if I was to attempt anything further at all it must be done at once, for I felt that the conditions for a business interview here could only become increasingly unfavourable; and to take root on this spot for all eternity, as the agent apparently intended to do, was not my way; besides I was not going to pay him the slightest consideration. So without further ceremony, even though I noticed that K. was just inclined to have a little chat with his son, I started to state my business. Unfortunately I have the habit, when I have talked myself into a state of some excitement – which happens very quickly, and in this sick-room it happened even more quickly than usual – of getting up and walking about as I talk. Though a good enough arrangement in one's own office, in a strange house it may be somewhat burdensome. But I could not restrain myself, particularly as I was feeling the lack of my usual cigarette. Well, every man has his bad habits, and I can even congratulate myself on mine when I think of the agent's. What should one say to this, for instance:

he holds his hat on his knee, shoving it slowly to and fro there, and every now and then he suddenly, quite unexpectedly, claps it on his head; admittedly he takes it off again at once, as if it had been a mistake, but all the same he has had it on his head for a second or two, and he keeps repeating this performance from time to time. Surely such conduct must be called unpardonable. I am not disturbed by it, however; I walk up and down, completely absorbed in my proposals, and ignore him; but there are people whom that trick with the hat might put off completely. However when I am thoroughly worked up I disregard not only such annoyances as these, but absolutely everybody; I see, it is true, all that goes on, but do not admit it, so to speak, to my consciousness until I have finished, or until I actually hear some objection raised. Thus I noticed quite well, for instance, that K. was by no means in a receptive state; holding on to the arms of his chair, he twisted about uncomfortably, never even glanced up at me, but gazed blankly, as if searching for something, into space, and his face seemed so impassive that one might have thought that no syllable of what I was saying, indeed no awareness of my presence, had penetrated to him. All this pathological behaviour, rather unpromising from my point of view, I took in perfectly well, but I talked on just the same, as if by my words, by my advantageous offers – I was myself alarmed at the concessions I was granting, concessions that nobody asked for – I still had some prospect of getting everything back on to an even keel again. It also gave me a certain satisfaction that the agent, as I casually observed, had at last left his hat in peace and folded his arms across his chest; my discourse, which I must confess was partly designed for him, seemed to have dealt a severe blow to his plans. And in the elation which this gave me I might perhaps have talked on for a long time yet, if the son, whom I had hitherto regarded as a negligible figure for my purposes, had not raised himself in his bed and brought me to a full stop by shaking his fist. Obviously he wanted to say something, to point something out, but he had not the strength for it. At first I put it all down to delirium, but when I then glanced involuntarily at old K. I understood better.

K. sat there, his eyes wide open, glassy, bulging, only momentarily serviceable; he was bent forward and quivering, as if someone were seizing or striking the back of his neck; his lower lip, indeed the whole lower jaw with the gums fully exposed, hung down helplessly; his whole face had gone to pieces; he still breathed, though with difficulty; but then, as if delivered, he collapsed against the back of his chair and closed his eyes, an expression of some severe strain passed over his face, and all was over. Quickly I sprang to his side and grasped the hand that hung there, lifeless, cold and chilling; no pulse beat there now. So it was all over. Ah well, an old man. Let us hope we all have such a peaceful end. But now how much was to be done! And what was the most urgent? I looked round for help; but the son had drawn the bedclothes over his head, one could hear his interminable sobbing; the agent, cold as a fish, sat tight in his chair, two paces away from K., and was plainly resolved to do nothing save await developments; so that left me, and me only, to do something, and the first thing was the hardest of all, namely to break the news somehow, in some bearable form, that is in some form that did not exist, to his wife. And already I could hear the approach of her eager, shuffling steps from the next room.

Still wearing her outdoor clothes – she had not had time to change – she brought in a nightshirt that she had been warming on the stove and now wanted to put on her husband. 'He's fallen asleep,' she said, smiling and shaking her head, when she found us sitting so still. And with the infinite trustfulness of the innocent she took up the same hand that I had just held in mine with such repugnance and awe, kissed it with a touch of wifely playfulness, and – imagine the faces of us three others! – K. moved, yawned loudly, allowed his nightshirt to be put on, suffered with a half-annoyed, half-ironical expression the tender reproaches of his wife for having over-exerted himself with such a long walk, and said in reply, no doubt to give a different explanation for his having fallen asleep, strangely enough something about boredom. Then, so as not to catch cold on the way to another room, he lay down for the time being in his son's bed; with two cushions hastily brought by his wife, a pillow was made for him alongside the feet of his son. After all that had gone before I no longer found that odd. Then he asked for the evening paper, opened it without regard for his visitors, did not settle down to read it however, but merely looked into it here and there, making several very unpleasant observations on our offers as he did so, observations that showed astonishing shrewdness, while all the time he made disparaging gestures with his free hand and indicated by clicking his tongue that our business methods had left a bad taste in his mouth. The agent could not restrain himself from making one or two untimely remarks; no doubt he felt, even in his own insensitive way, that some kind of amends was needed for what had occurred, but of course he was the last person to know how to set about it. I now took my leave rapidly, I was almost grateful to the agent; if he had not been there I should not have had the resolution to leave so soon.

In the hall I met Frau K. again. At the sight of that pathetic figure I said impulsively that she reminded me a little of my mother. And as she remained silent I added: 'Whatever one may say, she could do wonders. Anything we destroyed she could make whole again. I lost her when I was still a child.' I had deliberately spoken with exaggerated slowness and distinctness, for I suspected that the old lady was hard of hearing. But she must have been deaf, for she asked without transition: 'And how does my husband look?' From a few parting words I noticed moreover that she confused me with the agent; I should like to think that otherwise she would have been more forthcoming.

Then I went down the stairs. The descent was more wearisome than the ascent had been in the first place, and not even that had been easy. Oh, how many business calls come to nothing, and one has to struggle on somehow under the load.

A COMMENT

IT was very early in the morning, the streets clean and deserted, I was going to the station. As I compared my watch with the clock on a tower I saw that it was much later than I had thought, I had to make great haste; in my alarm at this discovery I became unsure of the way, I was still something of a stranger in this town; luckily there was a policeman at hand, I ran up to him and breathlessly asked him the way. He smiled and said: 'Do you expect to discover the way from me?' 'Yes,' I said, 'since I cannot find it myself.' 'Give it up, give it up,' said he, and he turned away with a great flourish, like a man who wants to be alone with his laughter.

ON PARABLES

THERE were many who complained that the words of the wise are always mere parables, and of no use in daily life, which is the only life that we have. When the wise man says: 'Go across', he does not mean that one should cross over to the other side of the street, which is at least something that one could manage if the result were worth the effort; he means some fabulous yonder, something that is unknown to us and that even he cannot designate more precisely, and therefore something that cannot help us down here in the very least. All these parables mean really no more than that the inconceivable is inconceivable, and that we knew already. But the cares that we actually have to struggle with each day are a different matter.

One man then said: 'Why do you resist? If you followed the parables, then you would become parables yourselves, and thus free of your daily cares.'

Another said: 'I bet that is also a parable.'

The first said: 'You have won.'

The second said: 'But unfortunately only in parable.'

The first said: 'No, in reality; in parable you have lost.'

THE BURROW

I HAVE laid out the burrow and it appears to be successful. All that can really be seen from the outside is a big hole, but in fact this does not lead anywhere; after just a few steps you come up against natural firm rock. I can make no boast of having contrived this ruse intentionally; it is simply the remains of one of my many abortive building attempts, but finally it seemed to me advisable to leave this one hole without filling it in. True, some ruses are so subtle that they defeat themselves, I know that better than anyone, and it is certainly bold to let this hole draw attention to the fact that there may be something in the vicinity worth investigating. But you do not know me if you suppose that I am a coward or that it is out of mere cowardice that I build my burrow. At a distance of some thousand paces from this hole, covered by a detachable layer of moss, lies the real entrance to the burrow; it is as well secured as anything in this world can be secured, admittedly someone could tread on the moss or poke through it, and then my burrow would lie open, and anybody who had the wish to do so – let it be noted, however, that certain none too common abilities would be needed as well – could force his way in and destroy everything for good. I know that very well, and even now at the summit of my career I can scarcely pass an hour in complete tranquillity; at that one point in the dark moss I am vulnerable, and in my dreams a greedy muzzle often goes sniffing round it persistently. It will be objected that I could have filled in this real entrance too, with a thin layer of hard earth on top and with loose soil further down, so that it would not have cost me much trouble to dig myself out again as often as I wished. But that is just not possible, prudence itself demands that I should have the opportunity of immediate flight, prudence itself demands, as alas! so

often, that one should risk one's life; these are all most wearisome
calculations, and it is often only the delight in one's own sharp-
wittedness that makes one keep on calculating. I must have the
opportunity of immediate flight, for despite all my vigilance may I
not be attacked from the most unexpected quarter? I live in peace in
the heart of my burrow, and meanwhile from somewhere or other
the enemy is boring his way slowly towards me. I do not say that he
has a better scent than I, perhaps he knows as little of me as I of
him, but there are some insatiable robbers who plough their way
blindly through the ground, and in view of the vast extent of my
burrow even they have some hope of hitting eventually on one of my
passages. I certainly have the advantage of being in my own house,
and knowing exactly where all the routes are and how they run; a
robber may very easily become my victim, and a succulent one too;
but I am growing old, there are many who are stronger than I, and
my enemies are countless; it could well happen that in fleeing from
one enemy I might run into the jaws of another. Alas! so many
things might happen, but in any case I must have the reassurance of
knowing that there is an exit somewhere that is easy to reach and
quite unobstructed, where I can get out without any further labour
at all, so that there is no fear that while I am burrowing away there
desperately, even if it is only in loose soil, I might suddenly feel –
Heaven protect me! – the teeth of the pursuer in my flanks. And it is
not only by external enemies that I am threatened, there are also
some in the bowels of the earth; I have never yet seen them, but
legend tells of them and I believe in them firmly. They are creatures
of the inner earth, not even legend can describe them, even those
who have become their victims have scarcely seen them; they come,
you hear the scratching of their claws just beneath you in the earth,
which is their element, and already you are lost. Here it can no
longer be said that you are in your own house, you are rather in
theirs. From such enemies not even that exit of mine can save me,
indeed it will probably not save me in any case, but more likely
destroy me; yet it is a hope, and I cannot live without it.

Apart from this main exit I am connected with the outside world
by quite narrow, reasonably safe passages which provide me with
good fresh air; they are the work of the field mice, and I have

managed to incorporate them successfully into my burrow; they also permit me to get wind of things from the distance, thus affording me protection, and all sorts of small fry come running through them as well which I can devour, so that I get a certain amount of hunting, enough for a modest subsistence, without leaving my burrow at all; that is naturally a great advantage.

But the most beautiful thing about my burrow is its stillness; admittedly this is deceptive, at any moment it may be shattered and all will be over, but for the present it is still there; I can steal for hours along my passages and hear nothing but the occasional rustling of some little creature, which I then immediately reduce to silence between my jaws, or the pattering of soil which indicates to me the need for some repair; otherwise all is still. The air from the woods floats in, I have at the same time warmth and a cooling breeze, sometimes I stretch out and roll over in the passage for sheer contentment. It is a fine thing to have a burrow like mine as old age approaches, to have brought oneself under cover as autumn sets in.

Every hundred yards or so I have widened the passages into little circular chambers; there I can curl myself up comfortably in the warmth of my own body and rest. There I sleep the sweet sleep of peace, of satisfied desire, of achieved ambition, the sweet sleep of the householder. I do not know whether it is a habit that persists from former days, or whether even in this house the perils are great enough to awaken me, but regularly from time to time I start up out of a deep sleep and listen, listen into the stillness which reigns here unchanged by day and night, smile with relief and sink back, my limbs relaxed, into still deeper sleep. Poor wanderers without a home, on the roads, in the woods, huddled at best in a heap of leaves or in a herd of their comrades, exposed to all the perils of heaven and earth! I lie here in a chamber that is secured on every side – there are more than fifty such chambers in my burrow – and pass whatever time I choose between dozing and unconscious sleep.

Not quite in the middle of the burrow, carefully planned to withstand the worst danger short of direct pursuit, namely siege, lies the central stronghold. While all the rest of the burrow is probably more the product of intense intellectual work than of physical exertion, this castle keep was fashioned by the most arduous labour of my whole body in every limb. Several times, in the despair of physical exhaustion, I was on the point of abandoning everything; I rolled about on my back and cursed the burrow, I dragged myself outside and left it exposed to all the world; I could afford to do that, for I had no more wish to return; until at last, after some hours or days, I came repentantly back, could almost have raised a hymn of praise at finding the burrow unharmed, and in the best of spirits started on the work again. My work on the castle keep was made unnecessarily more difficult (unnecessarily in the sense that the burrow derived no real benefit from the additional work) by the fact that precisely at the spot where the keep was planned to be the earth was very loose and sandy; it had to be literally hammered firm in order to make the great rounded and beautifully vaulted chamber. But for such a task I have nothing but my brow. So with my brow I battered against the earth, thousands and thousands of times, for days and nights on end; I was glad when my brow ran with blood, for that was a proof that the wall was beginning to harden; and in this way, as may perhaps be granted, I richly earned my castle keep.

In this castle keep I assemble my provisions; everything that I hunt down within the burrow over and above my immediate needs, and everything that I bring back with me from my hunting expeditions outside, I pile up here. The keep is so large that provisions for half a year cannot fill it. Consequently I can spread them well out, move about among them, play with them, enjoy their plenty and their various smells, and always see at a glance exactly what is available. I can then always undertake rearrangements, and make the necessary advance calculations and hunting plans, taking into account the season of the year. There are times when I am so well provided for that in my indifference to food I never even touch the smaller fry that go scurrying about, though that is perhaps imprudent of me from another point of view. My constant preoccupation with defensive measures means that my views on how the burrow can best be exploited for this purpose are always changing and developing, at least within certain limits. Thus it often seems to me dangerous to base my defence solely on the castle keep; after all, the ramifications of the burrow allow me a wide range of possibilities, and it seems more in accordance with prudence to divide up my stores somewhat,

and put a supply in several of the smaller chambers; so I then
allocate, let us say, every third chamber as a reserve storeroom, or
every fourth chamber as a main and every second as an auxiliary
storeroom, and so forth. Or I exclude certain passageways altogether
as far as piling up provisions is concerned, so as to throw the enemy
off the scent, or I choose just a few chambers at random, being
guided solely by their distance from the main exit. Each of these new
plans involves of course heavy transport work; I have to make my
calculations and carry the loads to and fro. True, I can do that at my
leisure and without any hurry, and it is not at all unpleasant to carry
these tasty things in one's jaws, to lie down and rest wherever one
likes, and to have a nibble at whatever happens to take one's fancy.
But it is not so pleasant when it sometimes strikes me, usually when
I have just started up out of my sleep, that my present distribution
of stores is totally misguided, liable to bring great dangers in its
train, and must be set right immediately with all speed, no matter
how tired or sleepy I may be; then I rush, then I fly, then I have no
time for calculation; although my intention is to put a new and most
exact plan into operation, I find myself wildly seizing the first thing
I happen to get my teeth into, dragging and heaving, panting and
groaning, stumbling about, and any change of any sort in the present
state of affairs, that now seems so excessively dangerous, is enough
to satisfy me. Until gradually, as I become fully awake, soberness
returns and I can hardly understand my panic haste; I breathe in
deeply the tranquillity of my house which I have myself disturbed,
return to my resting-place, fall asleep at once in new-won exhaustion,
and wake again to find, as it might be, a rat still dangling from my
jaws, as incontrovertible evidence of the night's labours which seem
by now almost like a dream. Then again there are times when it
seems to me the very best plan to gather all my stores together in
one place. What use can the stores in the smaller chambers be to me,
and how little can be accommodated there in any case; besides,
whatever I put there blocks the passageway and is more likely to be a
hindrance to me one day, when I have to defend myself, when I
have to run. And furthermore it may be foolish, but is none the less
true, that one suffers a loss of self-confidence if one cannot see all
one's stores assembled together, and so know at a single glance how

much one possesses. And may one not lose a good deal in the course of all these redistributions? I can't be always galloping up and down my criss-cross passageways to make sure that everything is in good order. The basic idea of distributing my stores is indeed a sound one, but really only if one had several chambers similar to my castle keep. Several such chambers! Yes indeed! But who is to achieve that? In any case they cannot be worked into the general plan of my burrow at this late stage. But I will admit that that is a fault of my burrow; it is always a mistake to have only a single specimen of anything. And I confess too that during the entire building operations I felt a vague awareness – yet it was clear enough if I had been willing to respond to it – that a number of castle keeps were required; I did not yield to it, I felt too weak for the enormous labour involved, I even felt too weak to face up to the necessity of that labour; somehow or other I managed to console myself with an equally vague feeling, which suggested to me that what would be inadequate in all other cases would suffice just this once in my own, by way of exception, as a gift of grace, probably because providence had a special interest in the preservation of that stamp-hammer, my brow. So now I have only one castle keep, but the vague feeling that in this case the one would suffice has gone. However that may be, I must content myself with just the one, the smaller chambers are no possible use as a substitute, and so, when this conviction has grown on me, I begin once again to drag everything out of the small chambers and back to the castle keep. For some time after that it is a great comfort to me to have all the chambers and passageways clear, to see the quantities of meat piling up in the central chamber, and sending the rich mixture of their various smells, each one of which I find delightful in its own way and can distinguish accurately from the distance, out into the furthest corridors. Then there usually follow times of particular tranquillity, in which I slowly and gradually transfer my sleeping-places from the outer circles towards the centre, steeping myself ever more profoundly in the smells, until I can stand it no longer and one night charge into the castle keep, taking a mighty toll of the provisions and filling myself to the point of complete stupor with the best things I have. Happy, but dangerous hours; if someone knew how to take advantage of them, he could destroy me

easily and without risk to himself. Here too the absence of a second
or third main chamber has a damaging effect; it is the single great
accumulation of food that seduces me. I try to guard myself against
this in various ways, indeed the distribution of food among the
smaller chambers is also a measure of this kind, but unfortunately,
like other similar measures, it leads through privation to still greater
greed, which then overturns all reason and changes my defence plans
arbitrarily to suit its own ends.

To regain my composure after such periods I make a practice of
inspecting the burrow, and then, after carrying out the necessary
repairs, I frequently leave it, though always for a short spell only.
Even on such occasions it seems to me too harsh a punishment to do
without the burrow for any length of time, but I recognize that brief
excursions are necessary. There is always a certain solemnity about it
when I approach the exit. During my periods of home life I steer
clear of it, I even avoid entering the last ramifications of the passage
that leads to it; it is in any case no easy matter to wander about
there, for I have contrived in that area a little mad maze of passages;
it was there that my burrow began, and at that time I dared not hope
that I would ever be able to complete it in accordance with my plan;
I started almost playfully at this corner, and here my first enthusiasm
for work ran riot in the construction of a little labyrinth; at the time
it seemed to me the crown of all buildings, but today I consider it,
probably with more justice, as altogether too trivial a piece of handi-
work, not really worthy of the burrow as a whole; it may perhaps be
delightful in theory – here is the entrance to my house, I declared in
those days ironically to my invisible enemies, and saw them all
smother in the labyrinth to a man – but in practice it is a far too
flimsy piece of fiddle-faddle that would hardly withstand a serious
assault or an enemy fighting desperately for his life. Should I therefore reconstruct this part of my burrow? I keep on postponing the
decision, and it will probably remain as it is. Apart from the great
labour that I should confront myself with, the task would be the
most dangerous imaginable; in those days when I was starting the
burrow I could work there in comparative peace, the risks were not
much greater than on any other occasion, but today it would mean
attracting the whole world's attention almost wilfully to my burrow,

today it is no longer possible. I am almost glad of that; a certain sentimental attachment to this first work of mine cannot be denied. And suppose a serious attack should come, what kind of entrance design could save me? An entrance can deceive, can lead astray, can torment the attacker, and so can my present one at a pinch. But any really serious attack I should have to try and meet immediately with all the resources of the entire burrow, and with all the powers of my body and soul – that is indeed obvious. So this entrance may as well remain as it is. The burrow has so many faults that are imposed on it by nature, it may as well also retain this one fault that my own hands have created and that I now clearly, if belatedly, recognize. All this does not mean to say, however, that this defect does not worry me from time to time, or perhaps always. If on my customary walks I avoid this part of the burrow, that is primarily because I find the sight of it unpleasing, because I don't wish to be constantly inspecting a defect in my burrow, however much this defect may go on rumbling at the back of my mind. If that fault up by the entrance must remain there ineradicably, at least I wish to be spared the sight of it for as much of the time as possible. I need only walk in the direction of the entrance and already, even though I am still separated from it by passageways and chambers, I seem to sense an atmosphere of great danger; I sometimes feel as if my coat were growing thin, as if I might soon be left with my bare flesh exposed, and be greeted at that moment by the howls of my enemies. Certainly, such unhealthy feelings are provoked in any case by my departure from the burrow, by my leaving the protection of home behind, and yet it is this entrance labyrinth that torments me most of all. Sometimes I dream that I have reconstructed it, that I have transformed it completely, rapidly, with Herculean strength, in a single night, unobserved by anyone, and that now it is impregnable; the sleep which brings me that dream is the sweetest of all, tears of joy and deliverance still glisten on the hairs of my beard when I awaken.

So whenever I leave the burrow I must surmount the torments of this labyrinth in their physical form as well, and I find it at once irritating and touching when, as sometimes happens, I lose my way for a moment in my own construction; it then seems to me as if this work of mine were still making an effort to prove to me that its existence is justified, despite the fact that my judgement of it has long since been fixed. But then I find myself beneath the moss covering, which I sometimes allow time enough – so rare are the intervals at which I stir from the house – to grow together with the other ground cover of the wood; and now I only need to give a little push with my head and I have ventured abroad. For a long time I do not dare to make that little movement, and if it were not that I should have to master the labyrinth once again I would certainly give up on this occasion and wander back. Just consider. Your house is well protected, self-sufficient. You live in peace, in warmth, you are well-nourished, you are master, sole master of an abundance of passages and chambers; and all this you are prepared, not quite to sacrifice, one hopes, yet in some sense to abandon; you are indeed confident that you will regain it, but still you are letting yourself in for a game that is played for high, for over-high stakes. Can there be any sensible reasons for doing so? No, for that sort of thing there can be no sensible reasons. But all the same I then cautiously raise the trapdoor, and I am outside; cautiously lower it, and race off as fast as I can away from the treacherous spot.

Yet I am not really at liberty; true, I no longer squeeze my way through the passages but instead go chasing through the open woods, I feel new powers in my body for which there was no room, so to speak, in the burrow, not even in the castle keep, had it been ten times bigger; the food also is better outside, the hunting may be more difficult, success more rare, but the results must be rated higher in every respect; I do not deny all this, I can appreciate it and enjoy it at least as much as anyone else, and probably much better; for I do not hunt like some prowler out of thoughtlessness or desperation, but methodically and calmly. Also I am not committed and delivered over to this free life, for I know that my term is measured, that I do not have to hunt here for ever; instead, more or less whenever I wish it and am weary of life here, someone will call me to him whose invitation I shall not be able to withstand. And so I can make the most of my time up here and pass it without any cares; or rather, that is what I could do and yet cannot. My thoughts dwell too much on the burrow. I run off from the entrance fast enough, but now I soon come back again. I seek out a good hiding-place and spy upon the entrance to my house – this time from the outside – for days and nights on end. One may call it foolish, but it gives me inexpressible pleasure; what is more, it reassures me. At such times it is as if I were not so much standing before my house, as before myself while sleeping, and knew the joy of being in a deep slumber and keeping a sharp watch on myself simultaneously. It is in a certain sense my distinction, not only to be able to meet the spectres of the night in the helplessness and blind trust of sleep, but at the same time to confront them in reality as well, with the full powers and the calm judgement of my waking state. And strangely enough I find that my situation is not so bad as I had often thought, and as I will no doubt think again when I descend into my house. In this respect – perhaps in others too, but in this one especially – these excursions of mine are truly indispensable. Despite the care that I took to choose an out-of-the-way spot for the entrance to my burrow – admittedly the overall plan imposed certain restrictions on me here – the amount of traffic that goes by is certainly very considerable, if one adds together the observations made in the course of a week or so; but perhaps that is the case in all inhabited regions, and probably it is actually better to expose oneself to a great weight of traffic, which carries itself past with its own impetus, than to be in total solitude and thus at the mercy of the first slowly exploring intruder who comes along. Here there are plenty of enemies, and even more of their accomplices, but they fight against one another, and while thus employed they go rushing past my burrow on their way. In all this time I have not seen anyone actually investigating the entrance, which is fortunate both for me and for him, for I would certainly have flung myself blindly at his throat in my anxiety for the burrow. It is true that certain folk have come along in whose proximity I dared not stay, and from whom I had to run at the mere hint of their approach in the distance; on their behaviour towards the burrow I am not really in a position to pronounce with certainty, but it is at least reassuring to note that I soon came back, found none of them still present, and the entrance undamaged. There were happy periods when I could almost persuade myself that the world's hostility towards me might have ceased, or have calmed down, or that the power of the burrow had raised me above the life-and-death struggle in which I had been engaged hitherto. Perhaps the burrow was more of a safeguard to me than I had ever thought or ever dared to think when I was inside it. Things went so far that I sometimes conceived the childish wish never to go back into the burrow at all, to settle down here in the neighbourhood of the entrance, to spend my life observing the entrance, and to find my happiness in ceaselessly reminding myself just how securely my burrow could protect me if I were inside. Well, there soon comes a rough awakening from childish dreams. What exactly does this security which I can observe from here amount to? Can I possibly judge the dangers which beset me in the burrow from the evidence that I collect outside? Can my enemies even get proper scent of me when I am not in my burrow? Some scent of me they must certainly get, but not the full scent. And is it not often the case that the full scent must be available before one can speak of a normal state of danger? So the experiments I am making here are but half-measures, fractional measures, calculated only to reassure me, and by falsely reassuring me to put me in the greatest peril. No, I do not watch over my own sleep, as I imagined; rather it is I who sleep, while the destroyer wakes. Perhaps he is one of those who saunter casually past the entrance, always making sure, just as I do, that the door is still unharmed and awaiting their attack, and who only pass by because they know that the owner is not at home, or perhaps even because they know that he is lurking innocently in the bushes close by. And I abandon my observation post, I have had enough of this life in the open; it seems to me that I have nothing further to learn here, neither now nor later. And I feel the desire to bid farewell to everything up here, to go down into the burrow and never return again, to let things take their course instead of trying to delay them by useless observations. But now that I have grown so accustomed to seeing everything that happens above ground near the entrance, I find it a great torment to undertake the positively sensational procedure of the descent, without knowing what may be going on all round me behind my back, and then behind the trapdoor after it has been replaced. I first begin the attempt by quickly flinging in the spoils of my hunting, under the cover of stormy nights; that appears to be successful, but whether it has really been successful will only be known after I have climbed down myself; it will be known, but no longer to me, or if it is known to me as well, it will be known too late. So I give up the attempt and do not climb down. I dig an experimental tunnel, far enough away, of course, from the real entrance, a tunnel that is no longer than I am and that is also sealed with a covering of moss. I creep into the tunnel, close it after me, wait there for carefully calculated long or short spells at the different times of the day, then fling off the moss, come out again, and register my observations. I have the most varied experiences, both good and bad, but no general law or infallible method of descent can I discover. I am consequently relieved that I have not yet made my descent down the real entrance, and desperate at the prospect of soon having to do so. I almost reach the point of deciding that I must go right away from here, and resume my desolate life of old, a mode of life which had no security whatever, but which, being one indiscriminate mass of dangers, prevented me from recognizing and fearing each particular danger clearly, as I am constantly being reminded when I compare my secure burrow with the life elsewhere. Certainly such a decision would be an arrant piece of folly, brought on simply by living too long in senseless freedom; the burrow is still mine, I have only to take one step and I am in safety. And I tear myself free from all my doubts and in broad daylight run straight for the door, this time quite determined to open it up; yet I cannot, I rush past it, and fling myself deliberately into a thorn bush, as a punishment, a punishment for I know not what transgression. And at this point I am indeed forced to admit that I was right after all, and that it is really impossible to make the descent without leaving my most precious possession, for a short while at least, freely exposed to all those who surround me, on the ground, in the trees, in the air. And this is no imaginary danger, but a very real one. It need not be exactly an enemy that I provoke into following me, it may just as well be some little innocent or other, some disgusting little female beast that pursues me out of curiosity, and so becomes, without knowing it, the leader of all the world against me; it need not even be that, it may perhaps be – and this is no less bad, in some respects it is the worst of all – it may perhaps be someone of my own kind, a connoisseur and admirer of earthworks, a hermit of the woods, a lover of peace, but all the same a vile scoundrel who wants to lodge where he has not built. If only he were to come along now, if only in his filthy lust he were to discover the entrance, if only he were to set to work raising the moss, if only he were to succeed, if only he were to squeeze nimbly through and were already so far down that I could barely catch a last glimpse of his hindquarters; if only all that were to happen, then at last, freed from all my scruples, I could charge furiously after him and leap upon him, then I could bite him and claw him to pieces, tear him apart and drink his blood, and stuff his carcass straight down to join the rest of my spoils, but above all – this would be the main thing – I should then finally be back in my burrow once more, willing even to admire the labyrinth this time, but first determined to draw the moss covering over me and stretch out, for a rest that might well last for the whole remainder of my life. But nobody does come and I am left to my own resources. Continuously occupied thus with the difficulty of the task, I lose much of my timidity, I no longer even make a pretence of avoiding the entrance, it becomes my favourite pastime to prowl around it in circles; by now it is almost as if I were the enemy and were spying out a suitable opportunity to break in successfully. If only I had someone I could trust, someone whom I could place at my observation post, then I could climb down without any qualms. I would arrange with this trusty confederate that he was to keep a careful watch on the situation during my descent, and for quite a long time afterwards, and to knock on the moss cover if – but only if – he saw any signs of danger. That would make a clean sweep of my difficulties up here; no problem would remain, except possibly that confederate of mine. For is he not likely to demand some service from me in return, will he not at least want to see the burrow? That in itself, letting someone voluntarily into my burrow, would be extremely painful to me; I built it for myself, not for visitors, and I think I would refuse to admit him; even for the sake of being helped back into my burrow, I would not let him in. But I could not let him in anyway, for I should either have to let him go down alone, which is simply unimaginable, or we should both have to descend at the same time, in which case the very advantage he is supposed to bring me, that of keeping a lookout in the rear, would be lost. And what sort of trust can I really put in him? Can someone whom I trust face to face still be trusted just as much when I can't see him, when we have the moss covering between us? It is comparatively easy to trust someone if one is keeping, or at least can keep, an eye on him at the same time; it is perhaps even possible to trust someone from a distance; but to have, from the inside of the burrow, that is from the inside of another world, complete trust in someone outside, that I believe to be impossible. But it is not even necessary to consider such doubts, it is enough merely to reflect that during or after my descent any one of the countless accidents of existence might prevent my trusted representative from fulfilling his duty, and what incalculable results might it not have for me if he were to encounter even the slightest obstacle? No, if one takes it by and large, I have no cause to complain that I am alone and have nobody that I can trust. I certainly lose no advantage by it and probably spare myself trouble. My only trust can be placed in myself and the burrow. I should have thought of that before, and taken measures to meet the difficulty that so preoccupies me now. When I first began the burrow, that would have been at least partly possible. I should have had so to construct the first passage that it had two entrances, adequately spaced, so that after going through all the unavoidable complications of descent by the one entrance I might have rushed along this front passage to the second entrance, slightly raised the moss covering, which would have had to be suitably arranged for the purpose, and tried to keep watch on the position for some days and nights from there. That would have been the only right way of doing it; two entrances do of course double the risk, but I should have had to ignore that objection, especially since the entrance that was intended merely as an observation post could have been quite narrow. And with that I lose myself in a maze of technical speculations, I begin once more to dream my dream of a completely perfect burrow, and that calms me a little; with delight I contemplate behind my closed lids clear or less clear structural devices for enabling me to slip in and out unobserved. As I lie there thinking about it I set great store by these devices, but only as technical achievements, not as real advantages; for this freedom to slip in and out at will, what does it amount to? It is the mark of a restless frame of mind, of inner uncertainty, of disreputable desires, bad qualities that seem still worse alongside the burrow, which stands so firm in its place and can flood one with peace if one is only willing to open oneself to it fully. For the present, however, I am outside it and seeking a possibility of return, and for that the necessary technical devices would be most desirable. Yet perhaps not so desirable as all that. Is one not seriously underrating the burrow if one regards it, in moments of nervous anxiety, as merely the safest possible cavity to creep into for refuge? Certainly it is a safe cavity among other things, or it should be, and when I picture myself in the midst of danger then I wish with all my power, clenching my teeth, that the burrow were nothing but the hole designed for my preservation, and that it should perform this clearly defined task as completely as possible, and I am ready to absolve it from every other duty. But the truth is that in reality – and in times of great emergency one has no eye for reality, and even in threatening times one has first to develop an eye for it – in reality the burrow does provide considerable security, yet by no means enough – for is one ever free from anxieties inside it? These anxieties are different from ordinary ones, prouder, richer in content, often long repressed, but in their ravaging effects they are perhaps much the same as the anxieties that life outside gives rise to. Had I constructed the burrow exclusively to assure my safety I would not exactly have been deceived in the result, but the relation between the enormous amount of labour and the actual security provided, at least in so far as I can be aware of it and in so far as I can profit from it, would not have been a favourable one for me. It is most painful to have to admit that to oneself, but one is forced to do so when one is confronted by that entrance over there, which now positively shuts itself off and clenches itself against me, its own builder and possessor. But the fact is that my burrow is not merely a bolt-hole. When I stand in the castle keep, surrounded by the great piles of my meat supplies, and survey in turn the ten passageways that begin there, each one raised or sunken, straight or curving, growing wider or narrower, as the general plan dictates, and all of them equally still and empty, and ready by their various ways to conduct me to my many chambers, which are also all of them still and empty – then the thought of safety is far from my mind, then I know very well that here is my castle, which I have wrested from the refractory earth with tooth and claw, with pounding and hammering blows, my own castle, which can never by any means belong to another, and is so essentially mine that within it, in the end, I shall even be able to receive the mortal thrust of my enemy undismayed, for my blood will ebb away here in my own soil and will not be lost. And what else but this is the meaning of those blissful hours that I so often spend in my passages, now peacefully sleeping, now cheerfully awake, in these passages which are so exactly designed for me, for comfortable stretchings and childish rollings, for dreamy repose and blessed slumber. And those smaller chambers, each so familiar to me, each of which, though exactly like the next, I can clearly distinguish with my eyes shut by the mere sweep of the wall: they enclose me more peacefully and warmly than any bird is enclosed in its nest. And everything, everything, still and empty.

But if that is the case, why do I hesitate, why do I dread the thought of the intruder more than the possibility that I may never see my burrow again? Well, luckily this is an impossibility; there is really no need for me to persuade myself by my reflections of what the burrow means to me; I and the burrow belong so indissolubly together that I could calmly settle down here, calmly despite all my anxiety; I do not need to try and force myself to open the entrance in the teeth of my scruples; it would be quite enough if I waited passively, for in the long run nothing can keep us apart, and somehow I shall quite certainly get down inside again. But on the other hand how much time may pass before then, and how much may happen in that time, up here no less than down below? And it lies with me alone to cut short that interval and do what is necessary at once.

And so, by now too tired to be capable of thought, with hanging head, trembling legs, half asleep, more groping than walking, I approach the entrance, slowly raise the moss, slowly climb down, leaving, in my abstracted state, the opening uncovered for a needlessly long time; then I remember what I have failed to do, climb out again to repair the omission – but what, pray, am I climbing out for? I am just supposed to be closing the moss cover, very well, so I climb down once again, and this time I do at last draw the moss cover across. It is only in this state, exclusively in this state, that I can carry out this operation. So then I lie there beneath the moss, on top of my collected spoils, encompassed by blood and flesh juices, and could begin to sleep my longed-for sleep. Nothing disturbs me, no one has followed me, above the moss everything seems, so far at least, to be quiet, and even if all were not quiet I do not think I could stop now for further observations; I have changed my place, I have come out of the upper world into my burrow, and I feel its effect at once. It is a new world, giving new strength, and what was fatigue up above has here a different quality. I have come back from a journey, dog-tired from my exertions, but the sight of my old home again, the task of settling in that awaits me, the necessity of taking at least a superficial look at all my rooms immediately, but above all of making my way at full speed through to the castle keep; all this transforms my fatigue into restlessness and energy; it is as though I had taken a long and profound sleep during the first moment of my entering the burrow. My first task is a very laborious one and occupies all my attention: that is, to get my spoils through the narrow and thin-walled passages of the labyrinth. I shove them ahead with all my might, and the work progresses, but far too slowly for me; to speed things up I drag part of the mass of flesh back again and push my way over the top of it, through the middle of it; now I have only a portion of my spoil before me, now it is easier to propel it onwards, but I am so deeply embedded in the profusion of flesh, here in these narrow passages which I don't always find easy to negotiate even on my own, that I could well be stifled by my own supplies; sometimes their pressure is such that I can only preserve myself by eating and drinking. But the work of transport is successful, I complete it before so very long, the labyrinth is behind me, with a sigh of relief I find myself in one of the regular passageways, push my spoils through a communicating passage into a main passage, which is expressly designed for the purpose and leads down at a steep slope to the castle keep. Now it is no labour any more, now it all rolls and flows down practically by itself. The castle keep at last! At last I shall be able to rest. Everything is unchanged, no major disaster seems to have occurred, the small defects that I note at a first glance will soon be repaired. First, however, comes my long round of the passages, but that is no hardship, it is a sort of chat with friends, like the chats I used to have in the old days, or rather — I am not yet so very old, but my memory of many things is already quite confused – like the chats that I actually had or that I just heard were customary. I begin now with the second passage, deliberately taking my time; having seen the castle keep I have an endless amount of time, always within the burrow I have endless time, for everything I do there is good and important and in a way satisfying. I begin with the second passage, then break off my inspection in the middle and go over to the third passage, and let that lead me back to the castle keep, and now of course I must take up the second passage again, and so I play with my work and increase it and chuckle to myself and take delight in everything and grow quite confused with all the quantity of work, yet I still keep at it. It is for your sake, you passages and chambers, and you above all, castle keep, that I have come, that I have counted my life as nothing, after having spent so long foolishly trembling for it and delaying my return amongst you. What do I care for danger now that I am with you? You belong to me, I to you; we are bound together, what harm can come to us? Even if the crowds should already be gathering up above, and the enemy's muzzle should be ready to burst through the moss? And thereupon the burrow welcomes me with its silence and emptiness, and confirms the truth of my words.

But now a certain lassitude does overcome me after all, and I curl myself up a little in one of my favourite chambers; I have not yet inspected everything by a long way, and I have every intention of continuing my inspection to the end; I do not want to sleep here, I have merely succumbed to the temptation of settling myself down here as if I did want to sleep; I should like to see if I can still manage that as well as I used to. I do manage it, but I don't manage to tear myself away again, and I remain here in deep slumber. I must have slept for a long time, I am only aroused from the last light sleep that dissolves of its own accord; my sleep must have been really very light, for it is an almost inaudible whistling noise that wakes me. I understand it at once: the smaller fry, whom I have watched over far too little and spared far too much, have bored a new channel somewhere in my absence, this channel has run into an old one, the air is being sucked in there, and that is what is producing the whistling noise. What an indefatigably busy lot they are, and what a nuisance their industry causes. I shall first have to locate the disturbance by listening carefully at the walls of my passage and making test borings, and only then will I be able to get rid of the noise. However, the new channel may be quite welcome as additional ventilation, provided it fits in at all with the general plan of the burrow. But from now on I shall keep a much sharper eye on the small folk than I used to; none of them shall be spared.

Since I have a good deal of experience in investigations of this kind it should not take long, and I can begin at once; there are other jobs waiting to be done, it is true, but this is the most urgent; I must have quiet in my passages. This noise is in any case a comparatively harmless one; I did not hear it at all when I arrived, though it must certainly have already been there; I had to feel completely at home again before I could hear it; it is, so to speak, only audible to the householder who is really in his house and carrying out his function. And it is not even constant, as such noises usually are; it makes long pauses; these must obviously be caused by blockages in the flow of air. I start on the investigation, but I fail to find the spot where intervention is necessary; I do make some diggings, but they are only random ones; naturally they do not achieve anything, and the great labour of digging and the even greater labour of filling in and smoothing out is all in vain. I get no closer at all to the source of the noise; it just goes on unchanged on the same thin note, with regular pauses, now like a whistling, now more like a piping. Well, I could simply leave it alone for the time being; it is very disturbing, certainly, but there can hardly be any doubt about what I take to be the origin of the noise; so it will scarcely get louder, on the contrary it can well happen – though up till now I have admittedly never waited long enough – for such noises to vanish of themselves in the course of time, through the further activities of the little burrowers; and apart from that some chance can often put one on the track of the disturbance quite easily, while systematic searching may fail for a long time. Thus I try to comfort myself, and I should greatly prefer to go on roaming through the passages, visiting the chambers, many of which I have not even seen since my return, and always romping about a little in the castle keep between times; but I can't get away from it, I must continue my search. The small fry cost me a lot of time, a lot of time that could be better employed. In such cases as the present it is usually the technical problem that attracts me; for example, from the noise, which my ear is well trained to distinguish in its finest shades and which I am capable of recording exactly, I visualize its cause, and then at once I feel impelled to check whether my picture corresponds with the facts. And with good reason, for until something has been firmly diagnosed here, I cannot feel secure, even if it were merely a matter of knowing where a single grain of sand that falls from a wall will roll to. And from this point of view a noise of the present kind is by no means a trifling matter. But trifling or not, however much I search I find nothing, or rather I find too much. This had to happen in my favourite chamber of all places, I think to myself, and I move well away from there, almost halfway along the passage to the next chamber; I really do it as a joke, as if I wanted to prove that it was not just my favourite chamber that had caused me this disturbance, but that there were disturbances to be found elsewhere as well, and with a smile I begin to listen; but I soon stop smiling, for, yes indeed, I find the same whistling here. It isn't really anything, sometimes I think no one except me would hear it; but at this point I can, in fact, hear it more clearly than ever, now that my ear has become attuned with practice, though it is really exactly the same noise everywhere, as I can easily prove to myself by comparing my impressions. Nor is it growing any louder, as I discover when instead of holding my ear close to the wall I listen in the middle of the gangway. Then it is only by straining my ears, by listening with utter absorption, that I can more divine than hear the faintest breath of a sound now and again. But it is precisely this uniformity of the noise in all places that disturbs me most, for that cannot be made to square with my original assumption. If I had guessed the cause of the noise correctly it should be emanating at maximum intensity from one particular spot, which would just need finding, and as one moved away from there it should grow fainter and fainter. But if my explanation did not hold water, what could the answer be? There still remained the possibility that there were two separate centres of noise, that up to now I had been listening at some distance from these centres, and that as I drew closer to one of them the noise from that centre increased, while owing to the decreasing volume of sound from the other centre the net result for the ear remained approximately constant. And already by listening closely I almost thought I could detect, if very indistinctly, differences of tone which supported the new assumption. At all events I must extend the area of my investigations much further than I have done hitherto. So down the passage I go to the castle keep and begin to listen there. Strange, the same noise here too. Well, then it is a noise produced by the burrowings of some insignificant creatures or other who have infamously exploited the period of my absence; in any case they can have no kind of hostile intention towards me, they are occupied solely with their own work and so long as they meet with no obstacle they will keep on in the direction they have taken; I know all that, yet what I find incomprehensible and agitating, what fills my mind with confusion when I need so badly to have it clear for my work, is that they should have dared to come right up as far as the castle keep. I will not attempt here to distinguish between the various possible reasons, but whether it was the depth at which the castle keep lies – which is after all not inconsiderable – or whether it was its vast extent and its correspondingly powerful currents of air that had previously scared off burrowers, or whether the mere fact that it was the castle keep, the solemnity of the place, had penetrated to their dull minds by some channel of information or other, at all events I had never until now noticed any sign of burrowings in the walls of the castle keep. Certainly, quantities of little creatures had come along here, attracted by the powerful exhalations, this was my best hunting-ground, but these had bored their way somehow into my upper passages and then, full of trepidation yet irresistibly drawn on, they had come running down the passages to the keep. But now they were evidently burrowing in the walls as well. If only I had carried out the most important schemes of my youth and early manhood, or rather, if only I had had the strength to carry them out, for the will to do so was not lacking. One of these favourite plans of mine was to isolate the castle keep from the earth surrounding it, that is to say, to limit the thickness of its walls to about my own height, and to create a hollow space of the same width right round the exterior, apart from a small foundation for the keep to rest on, which would unfortunately have to remain attached to the ground. I had always imagined this surrounding space, probably not without justification, as the most beautiful haunt I could wish for. To be able to cling on to the dome, to pull oneself up and slide down, to tumble off and find ground beneath one's feet again, and to play these games literally on the back of the castle keep and yet not within its actual chamber; to be able to avoid the castle keep, to be able to give one's eyes a rest from it, to postpone the joy of seeing it until later, and yet not to have to do without it, but instead literally to hold it firm between one's claws, a thing that is impossible if one has only the one, ordinary, open access to it; but above all to be able to watch over it, and thus to have such rich compensation for being denied the sight of it from within, that if one had to choose between staying in the keep or staying in the surrounding space one would surely choose the surround for the rest of one's days, just so as to be able to wander up and down there for ever, protecting the castle keep. Then there would be no noises in the walls, no insolent burrowings up to the very keep itself; then peace would be assured there, and I should be its guardian; then I should not have to listen with loathing to the small folk's burrowings but with delight to something that I am now wholly denied: the whispering silence of the castle keep.

But none of these beautiful dreams has materialized, and I must set to work; I ought almost to be glad that my work has now a direct connection with the castle keep, since that spurs me on. Certainly it becomes more and more obvious that I need all my energies for this task, which at first seemed quite a trifling one. I now set about sounding the surface of the castle keep, and wherever I listen, high or low, at the walls or on the floor, at the entrances or in the centre of the chamber, everywhere, everywhere I hear the same noise. And how much time, how much effort is required for this protracted listening to the steady coming and going of the noise. One can, if one wishes, provide oneself with a little illusory consolation by observing that here in the castle keep, as opposed to the passageways, one hears nothing at all if one removes one's ear far enough from the surface, owing to the sheer size of the chamber. Simply for a rest, simply to regain my composure, I make this experiment quite frequently; I listen intently, and am delighted not to hear anything. But the question remains: what on earth can have happened? Confronted with this phenomenon my original explanations fall to the ground

completely. But other explanations which suggest themselves I soon
have to reject as well. One might conceive, for instance, that what I
hear is simply the noise of the small fry themselves at their work.
But that would fly in the face of all experience: I cannot suddenly
begin to hear something that has always been going on but that I
have never heard before. During the years I may perhaps have
grown more sensitive to disturbances in the burrow, but my hearing
has certainly not grown any keener. It is of the very nature of small
fry not to be heard. Would I have ever tolerated them otherwise?
Even at the risk of starvation I would have rooted them out. But
perhaps – this thought also insinuates itself into my mind – what I
am concerned with here is some beast as yet unknown to me. It is
not impossible. True, I have observed the life down here long and
carefully enough, but the world is full of variety and there is never a
lack of unpleasant surprises. But of course it could not be a single
animal, it would have to be a whole horde that has suddenly invaded
my territory, a whole horde of little creatures, which being audible
must be superior to the small fry, but only slightly superior, for the
sound of their workings is really quite faint. So what it may be is a
troop of unknown creatures on their wanderings, who are just passing
this way, who disturb me, but whose procession will soon be over.
So I could really just wait, and refrain from doing work that will
prove in the end to be superfluous. But if these strange creatures are
responsible, why is it that I never see any of them? By now I have
made a number of diggings in the hope of catching one of them, but
not one do I find. It occurs to me that they might be quite diminutive
creatures, much smaller than any I am acquainted with, and that it is
only the noise which they make that is greater. Accordingly I examine
the earth I have dug out, I throw the lumps in the air so that they
break up into the tiniest pieces, but the noise-makers are not among
them. I slowly come to recognize that I can achieve nothing by small
random diggings of this kind; in the process I am merely ploughing
up the walls of my burrow; I scrabble here and there in haste, have
no time to fill in the holes again, at a number of points there are by
now heaps of earth which obstruct my way and my view; but all that
is merely an incidental worry, for I can now no longer wander about,
nor take stock, nor rest; already I have often fallen asleep for a while

at my work, in some hole or other, one paw stuck fast in the patch of earth above me, from which I was still trying to claw a piece down when I dropped off. From now on I shall change my method. I shall dig a regular full-size tunnel in the direction of the noise and I shall not stop digging until, independently of all theories, I find the true cause of the noise. Then I shall eradicate it, if that lies within my power, or if not I shall at least have certainty about it. This certainty will bring me either comfort or despair, but whichever it may be, the one or the other, it will be justified and unquestionable. This decision gives me new strength. All that I have done so far seems to me far too hasty; in the excitement of my return, not yet free of the cares of the upper world, not yet fully wrapped in the peace of the burrow, rendered hypersensitive by having had to do without it for so long, I allowed what is admittedly a curious phenomenon to deprive me of my senses completely. What is it after all? A faint whistling, audible only at long intervals, a mere nothing, that I won't say one could actually get used to – no, one could not get used to it – but that one could just observe for a while without taking any positive steps about it for the time being, that is, listen out occasionally every few hours and patiently register the results, instead of crawling about with one's ear to the wall as I had been doing, and tearing up the earth practically every time the noise became audible, not so much in the hope of finding anything as to be doing something to satisfy one's inner disquiet. All that will now be changed, I hope. And yet again I hope it will not – as in fury at myself, with my eyes tight shut, I have to admit – for my disquiet is still quivering within me exactly as it has been doing for hours, and if my reason did not restrain me I would probably like nothing better than to start digging away somewhere or other, irrespective of whether I could hear anything there or not, stolidly and defiantly, simply for the sake of digging, almost like the small fry who burrow either without any object at all or simply because they eat the soil. I find this new, rational plan of mine both attractive and unattractive. There is no objection to it, at least I know of no objection; it is bound, so far as I can see, to achieve my aim. And yet at bottom I do not believe in it, I believe in it so little that I don't even fear the terrors that its results may bring, I don't even believe that there will be any terrible result; indeed it seems to me that I have had this idea of digging a methodical tunnel in mind ever since the noise first appeared, and have only refrained from starting on it yet because I had no faith in it. None the less I shall of course start the tunnel; I have no other alternative; but I shall not start it at once, I shall postpone the work for a little; if reason is to be reinstated it must be reinstated fully; I shall not rush into the task. At all events I shall first repair the damage that I have done to the burrow by my wild ploughing-up of the surfaces; that will take a good long time, but it is essential; if the new tunnel is really to reach its goal it will probably have to be a long one, and if it should fail to reach its goal it will be endless; in any case this task will mean a protracted period of absence from the burrow, not indeed so painful an absence as that in the upper world, for I shall be able to break off my work when I like and return home, and even if I don't do that the air from the castle keep will be wafted along to me and surround me at my labour – but it does mean that I shall be departing from the burrow all the same, and surrendering myself to an uncertain fate, so for that reason I want to leave the burrow in good order behind me; it shall not be said that I, who am fighting for its peace, disturbed that peace myself without restoring it immediately. So I begin by shovelling the earth back into the holes, a job of work that I am quite familiar with, that I have done countless times almost without regarding it as work, and that particularly as regards the final pressing and smoothing down – this is no empty boast, but the simple truth – I can perform with unequalled skill. But this time I find it difficult, I am too distracted; every now and then, in the middle of my work, I press my ear to the wall and listen, without even caring that the earth which I have just lifted is trickling back into the passage again beneath me. The final embellishments, which demand a stricter attention, I can hardly carry out at all. Hideous protuberances, disturbing cracks remain, quite apart from the general fact that it is impossible to restore the original flourish to a wall that has been patched up in this way. I try to comfort myself with the reflection that my present work is only temporary. When I return, when peace has been established once more, I shall repair everything finally; all will go smoothly then. Oh yes, in fairy tales all goes smoothly, and this comfort of mine belongs to the realm of fairy tale too. It would be better to complete the work thoroughly now, right away; that would be far more to the point than constantly interrupting it and wandering off down the passageways to discover new sources of noise, which is easy enough in all conscience, for all that is required is to stop at any point one likes and listen. And that is not the end of my useless discoveries. Sometimes I fancy that the noise has stopped: it does make long pauses, and one can miss the occasional whistling because of one's own blood pounding all too loudly in one's ears, so then two pauses run together and for a while one thinks that the whistling has stopped for ever. One listens no longer, one leaps up, one's whole life is transformed; it is as if the source from which the silence of the burrow flows were opened. One refrains from verifying this discovery at once, one wants first to find someone to pass it on to while it is still unquestioned, so one gallops to the castle keep; there one is reminded that one has awakened to new life with all one's being and that it is a long time since one has eaten anything, one tugs out something from among the supplies that are half-buried in soil, and before one has finished swallowing it down one is running back to the site of the incredible discovery, one would just like to reassure oneself fleetingly about it during the meal, one listens, but the most fleeting attention shows at once that one has been ignominiously mistaken: away there in the distance the whistling continues unperturbed. And one spits out the food and would like to trample it into the ground, one goes back to one's job, no longer knowing which it is; at some spot where it seems necessary, and there is no shortage of such spots, one mechanically starts on something or other, just as if the overseer had arrived and one had to put on a show for his benefit. But hardly has one been working for a while like that when it can happen that one makes a fresh discovery. The noise seems to have become louder, not much louder of course – here it is always only a matter of the finest distinctions – but a little bit louder all the same, enough for the ear to detect quite clearly. And this growing-louder seems to be a coming-nearer; still more distinctly than one hears the increase of sound, one can positively see the steps with which it is approaching. One leaps back from the wall, one tries to grasp at once all the possible consequences that this discovery will entail. One has the feeling that one had never really organized the burrow for defence against an assault; one had intended to do so, but despite all one's experience of life the danger of an assault, and consequently the need to make arrangements for defence, had seemed remote – or rather not remote (how could that be!) but of far less importance than the arrangements for a peaceful life, which had therefore been accorded priority in the burrow throughout. Many things in this direction might have been done without affecting the basic plan; in a really most incomprehensible manner they have been neglected. I have had a great deal of good fortune during all these years, good fortune has spoilt me; I have had my anxieties, but anxiety can lead nowhere when things are going well.

The first thing to do now would really be to carry out a careful inspection of the burrow from the point of view of defence, taking every conceivable eventuality into account, to work out a plan of defence and a corresponding building plan, and then with youthful vigour to start on the work at once. That would be the essential job to do, for which, incidentally, it is now far too late, but that is what it would be, and not the digging of some grand exploratory tunnel, the real effect of which would simply be to divert me with all my energies, defenceless as I am, into seeking out the danger that threatens me, all because of a foolish notion that it might not arrive quickly enough of its own accord. Suddenly I cannot comprehend my former plan; in what had seemed so reasonable I can find no slightest trace of reason; once again I abandon my work, and abandon my listening too, I have no wish to discover any further increase of noise, I have had enough of discoveries, I abandon everything, I should be content if I could merely quieten the turbulence within me. Once more I let my passages lead me off where they will, I come into ever more outlying ones that I have not yet seen since my return, that are still untouched by my scratching paws, and whose stillness is stirred up by my approach and descends to enclose me. I do not surrender to it, I hurry on, I do not even know what I am looking for, probably I just want to gain time, and I stray so far that I find myself at the labyrinth: I am tempted by the idea of listening at the moss covering; such remote things, at present so remote, claim my interest. I push my way up there and listen. Deep stillness; how lovely it is here, nobody outside troubles about my burrow, everybody is engaged in his own affairs which have no connection with me; how have I managed to achieve that? Here at the moss covering is perhaps the only place in my burrow where I can now listen for hours and hear nothing. A complete reversal of the situation in the burrow; the former place of danger has become a place of tranquillity, while the castle keep has been caught up in the clamour and the perils of the world. Still worse, even here there is no real state of peace, here nothing has changed; whether silently or noisily, danger still lurks as before above the moss, but I have grown insensitive to it, I am far too preoccupied with the whistling in my walls. Am I really preoccupied with it? It grows louder, it comes nearer, but I wriggle my way through the labyrinth and choose my resting-place up here beneath the moss; it is almost as if I were abandoning the house to the whistler, content if I can only have a little peace up here. To the whistler? Have I then some new considered opinion about the origin of the noise? But surely the noise is caused by the channels bored by the small fry? Is not that my considered opinion? I do not appear to have departed from it so far. And if the noise is not caused by the channels directly, then in some indirect way. And if it should have no connection with them whatsoever, then it is probably impossible to frame any kind of hypothesis and one must just wait until one eventually finds the cause, or until it reveals itself. One could of course play with hypotheses even at this late stage; one might hold, for example, that somewhere in the distance water had flooded in, in which case what seems to me like a whistling or a piping would really be a rushing. But apart from the fact that I have no experience at all in this respect – the groundwater that I found at first I diverted immediately, and in this sandy soil it has never returned – apart from that, it just is a whistling, and cannot be reinterpreted as a rushing. But what is the use of all the exhortations to remain calm; my imagination will not rest, and I have actually reached the stage of believing – it is pointless not to admit this to myself – that the whistling is made by some creature, and what is more not by a number of small ones, but by a single great one. There is much to be said against this: that the noise can be heard everywhere and always at the same strength, and moreover regularly both by day and night. Certainly, one would first of all rather incline to the hypothesis of a number of small beasts, but since I would have been bound to find these in the course of my diggings, and I found nothing, the assumption of one great beast is all that remains to me; especially since all the things that seem to contradict this assumption are not things that make the beast impossible, they merely mean that it is quite inconceivably dangerous. That is the only reason why I have resisted this hypothesis. I shall cease from such self-deception. For some time now I have played with the idea that the beast can be heard at such a great distance because it works so furiously; it burrows through the ground as fast as a walker stepping out freely; the earth surrounding its tunnel trembles even after it has passed; this reverberation and the noise of its actual burrowing fuse in the far distance, and it is just the final dispersed ebbing of that combined sound that I hear, so that it comes to me at the same strength everywhere. A contributory factor is that the beast is not heading towards me; that is why the noise does not change; there is rather a plan in operation, whose purpose I cannot fathom: I merely assume that the beast, though I have no wish to assert that it knows of my existence, is encircling me; it has probably described several circles round my burrow already since I have been observing it. And now the noise is becoming louder after all, which means that the circles are narrowing. The nature of the noise, its whistling or piping, gives me much food for thought. When I scratch and scrape at the earth in my own fashion the sound is quite different. The only explanation I can find for the whistling is that the beast's chief tool for digging is not its claws, which it probably just uses in support, but its muzzle or snout, which must of course, apart from its obviously enormous strength, have some kind of sharpness to it. It probably bores its snout into the earth with a single mighty thrust and tears out a great lump; during that time I hear nothing, that is the pause; but then it draws breath again for a new thrust, and this drawing-in of breath, which must be an earth-shaking noise, not only because of the beast's strength but also because of its haste, its appetite for work, this noise reaches me then as a faint whistling. But what is totally incomprehensible to me is its ability to work without ceasing; perhaps during the short pauses there is just time for it to snatch a moment's rest, but never yet does it appear to have taken really proper rest; day and night it digs away, always with the same freshness and vigour, fixedly pursuing its plan, which is so very urgent and which it has all the requisite abilities to put into practice. Well, I could not have anticipated an opponent like that. But apart from the peculiarities of the beast, what is happening now is no more than what I should really have feared all along, what I should have been constantly preparing against: somebody is on the advance. However did it happen that for so long everything went on so quietly and happily? Who can have guided the ways of my enemies, so that they gave a wide berth to my domain? Why have I been protected for so long, only to be terror-stricken now? What were all the many petty dangers, that I spent my time reflecting on, compared with this present single one? Was it my hope that I, as owner of the burrow, would have the upper hand of anyone who came? But it is obvious that precisely as the owner of this vast, vulnerable work I am defenceless against any serious attack; the joys of ownership have spoilt me, the vulnerability of the burrow has made me vulnerable; the injuries done to it hurt me as if they were mine. This is just what I should have foreseen; instead of thinking only of my own defence – and how perfunctorily and vainly I have done even that – I should have thought of the defence of the burrow. Above all, provision should have been made, in case of attack, for cutting off individual sections of the burrow – and as many individual sections as possible – from the sections in less immediate danger, by means of landslides that could be engineered at a moment's notice, and moreover by such massive landslides, forming such effective barriers, that the attacker would not even guess that the real burrow only began on the other side. Furthermore, these landslides should have been so devised that they not only concealed the burrow but buried the attacker as well. Not the slightest attempt have I made to achieve anything of the sort; nothing, nothing at all has been done in this direction; I have been as careless as a child, the years of my manhood have been spent in childish games, I have done no more than play even with the thoughts of danger, and I have failed really to think about the dangers that really threaten. And there has been no lack of warnings.

Nothing has ever happened before to approach the gravity of the present situation, but all the same there was an incident not unlike it in the earliest days of the burrow. The main difference lies simply in the fact that those were the burrow's earliest days. At that time, as really no more than a young apprentice, I was still working on the first passageway; the labyrinth was only sketched out in rough outline; I had already hollowed out one small chamber, but in its proportions and in the treatment of the walls it was a total failure; in short, everything was so rudimentary that it could only be regarded as an experiment, as something which one could still abandon without much regret if one were to lose patience with it. Then one day it happened, as I lay among my heaps of earth during a pause from my work – throughout my life I have taken too many pauses from my work – that I suddenly heard a noise in the distance. Being young at the time I was more curious than frightened. I let my work lie and began to listen; at that time I did at least listen, instead of running up to my hiding-place beneath the moss, to stretch out there and avoid having to listen. I did at least listen. I could clearly recognize that it was the noise of some sort of digging like my own; it sounded rather fainter, but how far that was attributable to the distance it was impossible to say. I was tense, but otherwise calm and cool. Perhaps I am in someone else's burrow, I thought, and now the owner is digging his way towards me. If that assumption had proved to be correct I would have moved off to build somewhere else, for I have never had any desire for aggression or conquest. But of course I was still young then, I had as yet no burrow, so I could afford to be calm and cool. The further development of this incident did not cause me any real disturbance either, although it was not to easy to interpret. If whoever was digging there was really making for me because he had heard me digging, then it was not clear why he should change direction, as now in fact happened; was it that my pause from work had deprived him of his bearings, or was it rather that he had changed his own plans? But perhaps I had been deceived altogether, and he had never been actually heading in my direction; at all events the noise went on growing louder for a while, as if he were approaching, and being young at that time I might not have been at all displeased to see the burrower suddenly emerging out of the earth; but nothing like that happened, from a certain point on the sound of digging began to fade, it grew fainter and fainter, as if the burrower were gradually moving away from his original course, and all at once it broke off completely, as if he had now decided on a diametrically opposite course and were moving directly away from me into the distance. For a long time I went on listening for him in the silence, before I returned once more to my work. Well, that warning was clear enough, but I soon forgot about it, and it has had scarcely any influence on my building plans.

Between that day and this lie the years of my manhood; but is it not as if nothing at all lay between them? Here I am still taking a long break from my work, and listening at the wall, and the burrower has recently changed his intention, he has turned about, he is returning from his journey, he thinks that in the meantime he has allowed me long enough to prepare his reception. But on my side everything is worse prepared than it was then; the great burrow stands here defenceless; and I am no longer a young apprentice, but an old master-builder, and such powers as I still have desert me when it comes to the decision. Yet, old as I am, it seems to me that I would gladly be still older, so old that I could no longer raise myself from my resting-place beneath the moss. For the fact is that I cannot bear to remain up here after all, I raise myself to my feet and charge down into the house again, as if this place had filled me, not with peace, but with fresh anxieties. How had things stood when I was last below? The whistling had grown fainter? No, it had grown louder. I listen at ten points at random, and my error is clearly discernible: the whistling has remained constant, nothing has changed. Over there on the other side no changes occur, there one is at peace and beyond the reach of time, while here every instant grips the listener by the throat. And back I go again down the long road to the castle keep; all round me the burrow seems to be agitated, seems to look at me, then to look away again at once so as not to disturb me, then again to search my expression eagerly for signs of the decisions that will save us. I shake my head, I have still not reached any. Nor am I going to the castle keep in order to carry out any particular plan. I pass the spot where I had intended to build my exploratory tunnel, I examine it once more, the place would have been a good one; the tunnel would have led in the direction where most of the little ventilation channels lie, which would have eased my work considerably; perhaps I should not have had to dig very far after all, perhaps it would never have been necessary to dig right up to the source of the noise, perhaps listening at the ventilation holes would have sufficed. But no consideration is strong enough to inspire me to undertake this laborious excavation. This tunnel is supposed to bring me certainty? I have reached the stage where I no longer have any wish for certainty. In the castle keep I select a good piece of skinned red meat and creep with it into one of the heaps of earth; there at least I shall have silence, in so far as silence is still to be had here at all. I lick and nibble at the meat, thinking now of the strange beast pursuing its way in the distance, and then again that I ought to enjoy my supplies to the full while I still have the chance. This last is probably the only practicable plan that I have. For the rest I try to unriddle the plan of the beast. Is it on its travels or is it working in its own burrow? If it is on its own travels then perhaps some understanding with it might be possible. If it really does break through to me I shall give it some of my supplies and it will continue on its way. Continue on its way, indeed! In my heap of earth I can of course dream of anything, even of an understanding, though I know well enough that there can be no such thing, and that the instant we see each other, indeed the instant we sense each other's presence, we shall both immediately, blindly, show each other our claws and our teeth, neither of us a second sooner, neither a second later, both filled with a new and different sort of hunger, however gorged we may otherwise be. And with entire justice, as always, for who, even if he were on a journey, would not change his itinerary and his future plans on catching sight of the burrow? But perhaps the beast is digging in its own burrow, and in that case I cannot even dream of an understanding. Even if it should be such a strange beast that its burrow could tolerate a neighbour, my burrow cannot; at least it cannot tolerate an audible neighbour. But it is true that the beast does seem to be a long way off; if it were only to withdraw a little bit further, then probably the noise would disappear too, then perhaps everything might come right again as in the old days; all this would then be just a painful but salutary experience, spurring me on to make all sorts of improvements; if I have peace, and no immediate danger threatens, I am still quite capable of doing various kinds of respectable work. Perhaps the beast, in view of the enormous possibilities that its capacity for work seems to give it, may renounce the idea of extending its burrow in the direction of mine and seek compensation for that in some other quarter. That, of course, cannot be achieved by negotiation either, but only by the good sense of the beast itself, or by some compulsion exercised from my side. In both cases the decisive factor will be whether the beast knows about me, and if so how much. The more I think about it, the less likely it seems that the beast has heard me at all; it is possible, though I cannot myself conceive it, that it has received some news of me by other means, but it is most improbable that it has heard me. So long as I was unaware of it, it simply cannot have heard me, for at that time I was keeping quiet, nothing could be more quiet than my returning to the burrow; afterwards, when I was making my test borings, it could perhaps have heard me, although my style of digging makes very little noise; but if it had heard me, then I too would have observed some sign of it, for at least it would have had to interrupt its work frequently in order to listen; but everything remained unchanged ...

READ MORE IN PENGUIN

In every corner of the world, on every subject under the sun, Penguin represents quality and variety – the very best in publishing today.

For complete information about books available from Penguin – including Puffins, Penguin Classics and Arkana – and how to order them, write to us at the appropriate address below. Please note that for copyright reasons the selection of books varies from country to country.

In the United Kingdom: Please write to *Dept. EP, Penguin Books Ltd, Bath Road, Harmondsworth, West Drayton, Middlesex UB7 0DA*

In the United States: Please write to *Consumer Services, Penguin Putnam Inc., 405 Murray Hill Parkway, East Rutherford, New Jersey 07073-2136.* VISA and MasterCard holders call 1-800-631-8571 to order Penguin titles

In Canada: Please write to *Penguin Books Canada Ltd, 10 Alcorn Avenue, Suite 300, Toronto, Ontario M4V 3B2*

In Australia: Please write to *Penguin Books Australia Ltd, 487 Maroondah Highway, Ringwood, Victoria 3134*

In New Zealand: Please write to *Penguin Books (NZ) Ltd, Private Bag 102902, North Shore Mail Centre, Auckland 10*

In India: Please write to *Penguin Books India Pvt Ltd, 11 Community Centre, Panchsheel Park, New Delhi 110017*

In the Netherlands: Please write to *Penguin Books Netherlands bv, Postbus 3507, NL-1001 AH Amsterdam*

In Germany: Please write to *Penguin Books Deutschland GmbH, Metzlerstrasse 26, 60594 Frankfurt am Main*

In Spain: Please write to *Penguin Books S. A., Bravo Murillo 19, 1°B, 28015 Madrid*

In Italy: Please write to *Penguin Italia s.r.l., Via Vittorio Emanuele 45/a, 20094 Corsico, Milano*

In France: Please write to *Penguin France, 12, Rue Prosper Ferradou, 31700 Blagnac*

In Japan: Please write to *Penguin Books Japan Ltd, Iidabashi KM-Bldg, 2-23-9 Koraku, Bunkyo-Ku, Tokyo 112-0004*

In South Africa: Please write to *Penguin Books South Africa (Pty) Ltd, P.O. Box 751093, Gardenview, 2047 Johannesburg*

BY THE SAME AUTHOR

Metamorphosis and Other Stories

A companion volume to *The Great Wall of China and Other Short Works*, these translations bring together the small proportion of Kafka's works that he thought worthy of publication.

This volumes contains his most famous story, 'Metamorphosis'. Other works include 'Meditation', a collection of his earlier studies; 'The Judgement', written in a single night of frenzied creativity; and 'The Stoker', the first chapter of a novel set in America. There is also a fascinating occasional piece, 'The Aeroplanes at Brescia', Kafka's eye-witness account of an air display in 1909. Taken together, these stories reveal the breadth of Kafka's literary vision and the extraordinary imaginative depth of his thought.

'One of the few great and perfect works of poetic imagination written during the twentieth century' Elias Canetti on 'Metamorphosis'

Metamorphosis, read by Steven Berkoff, is also available as a Penguin Audiobook

The Trial

'It is the fate and perhaps the greatness of that work that it offers everything and confirms nothing' Albert Camus

'Somebody must have laid false information against Josef K., for he was arrested one morning without having done anything wrong.' From this first sentence onwards, Josef K. is on trial for his right to exist in a novel which, more than any other, is infinitely perceptive about the nature of terror. Idris Parry introduces his remarkable translation with an essay in which he points to the autobiographical elements in *The Trial*, in particular Kafka's broken engagement to Felice Bauer.

'This compelling, prophetic novel anticipates the insanity of modern bureaucracy and the coming of totalitarianism' Mordecai Richler, *Daily Telegraph*

Also published:

The Castle